FLAME
OF
EROS

CHRIS TURNER

This is a work of fiction. All the characters and events portrayed in these stories are either fictitious or are used fictitiously.

Cover Art: Dreamstime
Map: Trevor Porter

Published by Innersky Books
www.innersky.ca

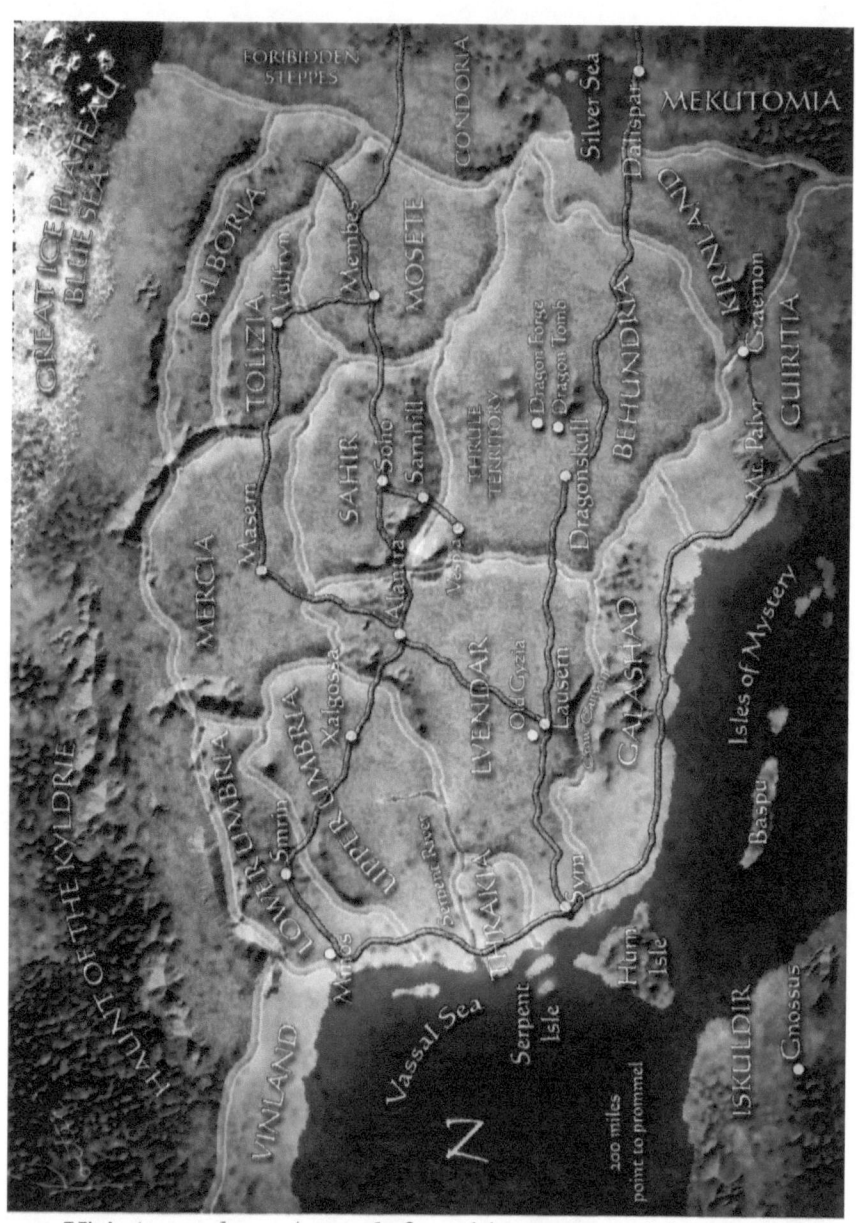

Visit *innersky.ca/swords* for a hi-res map of the world

Chapter 1

Below the Hall of the Mages dwelled a warren of catacombs and ancient halls rich in murk and mystery. Who built them or for what purpose none knew. Legend says by the hands of some bygone race. It might have been the slave-wards of the mad king Marizon or the race of beings who lived far below the earth which had tunneled up. Skirl the apprentice thought not. Just myths to prevent adventurous thieves like himself from looting the place when it became abandoned after the reign of the sorcerer priest Hunak or some such figurehead. He only knew that if he were caught here, slinking and creeping about the tomblike darkness with his spitting, fast-dwindling candle, he would face a harsh punishment, if not death. The end thus of his masquerading as a 'wizard's apprentice'.

With the love jewel of Eros clamped in his other fist, much was at stake. Indeed, kingdoms could fall or be born. Such was the power of the charm he held in his fingers. He alone knew the far-reaching implications of it in the wrong hands, be it monarch, wizard or thief, let alone stealing it out of the wizards' circle. That the talisman was much coveted by the head Archmagrix Taranis herself was another matter.

Taranis. What a piece of evil hatchery she was, and the most splendid specimen of vixenish flesh imaginable. The ultimate desire of every man.

A wily smirk spread across Skirl's chiseled features, roughly handsome in good light. In the prime of his youth, a young schemer, he was just past his twenty-first year and reveled in the fact that he was likely the youngest of the apprentices to have ever reached this far in the catacombs.

He stole forward down yet another set of wide, broken steps. Far beyond his years in cunning and lore, yet still green in many phases of life, in his brain existed a fledgling logic which had barely saved him from being skewered on a spit or roasted over a royal fire. That, or being stretched thin on a rack in the king's dungeons.

The pads of his fingers walked along the smooth curve of a dolomite colonnade that formed part of the ancient passageway's walls.

It was risky skulking around these subterranean ruins but the husky murmur of the Archmagrix, dallying with one of her apprentices in the upper tapestried chambers, had unnerved him. He could not be caught anywhere near her inner sanctum, and so had taken the easiest escape route possible: the open door leading to the crypts.

The steep staircase that cascaded down into untold depths had not been an easy one to navigate. Indeed, the molder was intense, and stifling murk and stale air smote his nostrils like an ogre's club. He had ducked his head under cobwebs thick as yokkle stalks to come to a surface level with the Hall far above. It formed the beginnings of this wide passageway and led into a sepulchral underground hall. He had counted the steps—99 to be exact.

Skirl crept by an area in the wall where blocks of stones had been stacked in a crisscross fashion, some removed, revealing dark spaces beyond. They formed a kind of grate to an inner chamber where the stench was overwhelming. Rotten meat? Worse?

Such was the lightness of Skirl's movements and stealth of his passage that he had slipped unnoticed by whatever might be living beyond that dank stone. He sensed no movement. Yet he felt a living presence there. This foul reek of unwashed hide signified something far worse. But he dismissed the idea as fanciful imagination as he hurried on.

The dust ran thick in this wide, eerie hall. More thick webs pocketed the upper grouting and tiers of stone and it looked as if not a soul had ventured into this mausoleum for a century.

The passageway that his light-footed boots trod now opened up and led to an even more immense hall. He raised his candle high. In three directions ran the ruins of ages.

Along a footworn, flagstoned path he threaded his way. Among loose bricks, chipped flagstones, fallen statues of kings and overlords: one which looked like some horned statue and still leaned on a drunken angle. A horrid thing, pocked with age, bearing a face most disturbing. A sprawl of desiccated bones, what might have been half elk, lay at its feet. The statue's face, a grim, two-fanged visage, half bestial, humanoid with dog ears stared at him. He could not repress a shudder. Was this a giant shrine, or cryptic fane, or some bestial homage to a long lost god or devil? The sight of such statuary brought another round of shivers prickling his back. He escalated his pace. Trepidation and wonderment chased him in a circle as his young mind imagined all manner of rites, rituals and sacrifices that had been practiced here in years far past.

Expelling a slow breath, he could feel the blood pulsing in his ears.

A soft crunch of brittle stone sounded under his boot heel. He winced. As catlike as his tread had been, echoes as these carried far and he wished to alert no creature of his presence. Creature? Why would he even think that? He stifled a nervous cough. These haunts hadn't seen the light of day for years, so how could any life form exist?

A drip-drop echo sounded from faraway down the hall. An ominous plink into a still pool. The sound conjured up nightmarish things in his mind's eye.

Into the gloom he squinted. Pocked columns piked drunkenly to either side. Another crooked stair of broad steps beckoned at the far end which rose to dusky heights somewhere above. But the main passageway continued on, or seemed to go on in its buckled, crooked way to a lower level. Places that harbored yet stranger mysteries and dooms: a square-cut shaft like an old mine.

Skirl paused, prickled by indecision. Lofty heights of arched darkness reached above him which the small candle would not illuminate. Somewhere above, the elegant marble halls of the mages dwelled where he had recently run errands for Keren and Voydred, resident mages bearing titles of beastmaster and spellcaster.

The ghost of a smile quirked his thin lips, spread across his sharp features as he recalled the circumstances that led up to his journey to this eerie, disquieting place. A rare moment had presented itself. The Archmagrix, not in her chambers, had left on some business. Five quick strides and he had seized her famous necklace draped over the tall chair before the gothic mirror. He had stripped the Eros jewel from its twine of leather hide, replaced it with a clever imitation he'd had wrought by a gemsmith earlier. Now he meant to steal off with the jewel, and be rid of this band of arrogant spellcasters who called themselves mages. The ones who thought they ruled Umbria, or at least the capital, Xalgossa.

But no, a sound had unnerved him. He'd fled beyond the iron-bound door to the side that had been left slightly ajar, admitting the faintest, coolest breath of dank air into her tapestried quarters lest he be discovered by the Hall's guards.

Why had the sorceress been so careless? Perhaps she'd been caught in a moment of distraction? What dwelled down here that might interest her?

He licked his lips. Dissatisfaction bit at his heart. For the second time he swallowed the sour taste in the back of his throat. More unanswered questions. They only added to the pile that escalated his unease and the pace of his thudding heart.

The jewel's reflection stung his eyes. He turned it over in his palm, bringing the candle ever closer to the sapphire-like surface. A gem of great worth and beauty, the size of a fallen chestnut. A living flame wavered within the red glow, scarlet as a rose, but at odd times it turned ultramarine in a queer way. Even he could sense the gemstone's emanation of power. It oozed of mesmerism, an eldritch, eerie love feeling, warming and melting the heart, bringing with it rapture alternating with an odd feeling of dizziness, if such were possible from an inanimate object. It was a mystery that both frightened and thrilled him. Indeed, it left such a discord in his mind that he tripped and barely caught himself in time before he smashed his teeth into a jutting wedge of loose brick.

With a cursing grunt, he plunged the jewel back into the pocket of his loose apprentice's robe. Already the cuffs of his robe were grimed and soiled. The voluminous fabric draped around his ankles swished and itched his sweating skin.

His heart skipped with anticipation. He knew his chances of escape dimmed with every passing minute spent in these nighted crypts. How long had he been wandering about these murksome halls? An hour? More?...and yet, something told him he had only a certain hundred or more steps to take before the dank corridor ended and led to safety up and away from the

Archmagrix's private quarters.

He did not know for sure; he just had a sixth sense that there existed another egress back toward the Mages' Hall.

The thought was still skidding about his brain when the clink of a boot heel had him nearly jumping out of his skin.

Footfall? Voices?

A flicker of torchlit cut the eerie shadows.

"He must be down here," came a muffled voice. "Look. Footprints in the dust! A skulker's size."

Skirl bit back a soft moan. He ducked back in the wavering shadows. Sweat pooled under his robe, dripping down his dust-caked brow into his eyes.

Hold forth the jewel! Let the sorcerous light spill into their eyes, smash their brains. Bend their will to yours.

The commanding voice spoke in his mind. But no. The sight of their glinting blades, the memory of the ferocity of those blades in the outer courtyard while training, unnerved him. If the jewel's magic should fail him…

A better idea surfaced. His lips curled in a sneer.

With the desperation of a cornered rat, he doused his candle. Swiftly he nestled his lean frame behind the nearest object he could find: a bronze gargoyle, standing chest-high. The leering face was squashed like a pumpkin. In the dimmest of light the claw-like fingers were outstretched, beckoning any who trod here like an underworld ghoul. The head was missing one rat-like ear. He crouched, breath held, his back to the cold stone.

More gruff voices drifted from ahead of him. Or was it behind him, a trick of deceptive echoes in this loathsome place?

Capture was inevitable lest he come up with some plan. The area below the Hall of Mages was forbidden to novices. He was no swordsman, or master magician. With a last huff of defiance he stuffed the red-flamed sapphire into the cobwebbed mouth of the moldering gargoyle, in the hope that he could retrieve it later.

None too soon.

A torch hissed and flared not twenty paces away. Four of the Mages' Guard stood illumined under the fleeting, feral light.

"There he is."

He flicked his fingers outward. The approaching figure, torch in hand, suddenly stiffened as Skirl sent a push of magic on him. *Poof.* Like the breath of wind, or an invisible creature of the night, the flame flickered out. The guards were left blinking, the ancient hall cloaked in darkness.

There came a weird whistling sound from somewhere above…then a bewildered exclamation.

An anguished cry rang out in the dark. Then a scuttling of bodies and a scrape of boots as men scurried desperately to get away from some horror.

While the guards bumbled about, grunting and cursing, Skirl grinned and made stealthy steps away from the crumbling path and the gargoyle that now hid the Eros stone.

The laugh froze in his throat as a torch lit up and a familiar figure strode out of the murk.

Taranis!

CHRIS TURNER

Chapter 2

The sorceress stooped and lit the smoking torch lying in the molder. With a vehemence known only to her, she thrust it into the hands of the captain of the guards. "Go, you fool! Capture him!" Her eyes blazed with wrath.

Skirl turned and faced them.

The first guard that came at him, he deflected with a wind push that sent the man reeling back on his heels.

A bulbous creature that had shimmied down on some slimy rope of web scuttled across the lifeless body of his peer. A temple spider.

"Pin his arms, you fools!" Taranis cried. "Let him make no more thaumaturgic gestures. I'll strip this wretch of his powers ere the moon sets! The witch-shields and incantations of Dal Sagoth shall see to that!"

Terror seized Skirl's heart. It was one thing to stymie a few bumbling guards, but to go up against the Archmagrix... No... He ran and ran until he thought his heart would burst. But his feet and vision at last failed him as he tripped over a fallen block of crumbling stone.

The disgruntled guard at his heels made a wild lunge and tackled Skirl. With the wind knocked out of him, he had no ability to spring to his feet.

Skirl flailed about but to no avail.

Strong arms hauled him up, rough hands slapped his cheeks and pinioned his arms behind his back. The caching of the jewel had been his undoing. His devious scheming likewise with the wind magic. "What are you doing here, scoundrel?" the captain bellowed. "The Lady told us somebody had broken into her chamber and had taken to the secret ways below."

"The door was ajar," Skirl protested. "I was curious. Take your hands off me, you louts. I'm an accredited apprentice of the Order!"

"No, you're an intruder who's gadding about in forbidden territory. Search him!"

The closest guard gave a rusty snort. He padded down Skirl's loose robe with no gentle fingers. He suddenly came across something solid. He plucked out a strange bone. Smoothly varnished, about six inches long, a pale blue-gray color, inscribed with arcane ruins and script and swirls. The grinning-eyed man held it up in the light for all to see.

The captain of the guards snatched it out of his hand. "So, you're a proven thief. In a place you shouldn't be. Archmagrix, over here!" he called.

The other two hauled Skirl away. At times when he resisted, they lifted him bully-puppet-like a foot off the ground, his feet pedaling in midair.

The troop was not eighty paces down the passageway when there came a clicking sound and faint whistling from above. Eyes beetled upward. A familiar black-haired gangling shape sprang down from the murks above on some slimy rope-loop of fiber. It was the size of a coconut. Skirl's mouth gaped. Another of those temple spiders: a cross between a giant black widow and a wolf spider. Deadly in these climes.

It sank fangs into the neck of the leftmost guard. The man buckled; he let out a hideous, bloodcurdling scream. He loosed his hold on Skirl. Skirl toppled back like a marionette while the man gurgled another incoherent cry. He took six stilted steps before he convulsed and fell, his mailed body arched in a grotesque V. The captain of the guards pushed forth his torch. Under the flickering glare, the man's parched white face lay creased in a rictus of agony.

"Dergath's devils!" He crabbed back, shoving the others out of the way.

Taranis emerged out of the stygian gloom, unafraid of murks or beasts. "Kill it, you fools! Are you so inept not to dodge one single clumsy spider?" In a clenched fist, her stave came whistling down to swat at the hairy thing as it crouched over the body of the dead man. She sent it scuttling back into the shadows on three broken legs. A horrible clicking sound echoed in the coils of darkness in its wake. Angry. Resentful. Brooding.

"My lady, we did not realize that there was only one—"

"Silence!" Her darting eyes flicked across the space at the apprentice. Her shadow fell over him like icy winter. "Skirl! I should have known. Get him to my chambers. One of you can fetch the fallen guards later."

"Yes, Archmagrix."

Taranis stood brazenly, legs spread wide apart. "What have you seen?" she demanded of the cringing man.

Skirl sucked in a breath, trying to straighten his spine to his full height, two inches shy of six foot. "Shadows and murks. Loathsome smells and vulturish spiders. What should I have seen?"

She scanned him through her hooded eyes, assessing the truth of his statement. Not an easy task with a dissembler such as he.

She loomed larger than life, her broad cheeks flushed with anger. The sorceress was lean and slinky as a black panther, her bronze skin oiled and gleaming in the dim light. Chestnut-blond hair dyed to the roots spilled down to the sides like wings. Regal, awesome, intimidating. A dominatrix, in all her domineering majesty.

How to describe the seductress? A figure who struck awe in

the bulk of the citizenry, terror in the rest; promiscuous to the core, a student of black magic, arcane and forbidding, recognized as a power unto herself in all respectable wizard circles.

The top of her chestnut hair was ruffled and a puffiness remained around her eyes and cheeks, as if from a recent love play. No more the sultry murmurs and husky laughs of the boudoir from her throat. A feral gleam lurked in those eyes, as if a black widow had just devoured her mate.

The captain of the guard edged back cautious steps out of her shadow then motioned roughly to his two remaining men. "Leave Farl's body where it is. Watch out for those damn spiders."

The group resumed their journey. Flickering torches cast monstrous shadows on the ancient walls and pillars.

Taranis led the pack back to the moldered staircase; Skirl gazed in a rueful daze at the sway of her hips…seductive under the glare of her snug, skin-tight gown revealing every ripple and muscle clench. From her near-perfect curves there emanated a waft of the unmistakable spoor of animal hide he'd sniffed earlier.

Odd. Down by that criss-crossed stone-block grating. Considering she'd spent no more time down here than he had, was she dallying with beasts now? The thought repulsed him.

As if sensing his obscene thoughts, she whirled on him in sudden suspicion. "How did you get down here?"

"I came to call on you, Lady. To discuss the intricacies of a moon spell. The door in your sanctum was open."

She gave a mild snort of exasperation. "True, it was my fault. I must not have secured the portal's bolt properly. It will not happen again."

The captain of the guards gave a derisive grunt. "Caught

him with this on him." He thrust forth the gleaming bone.

Taranis snatched at it. "That is Keren's wish bone," she muttered. "A femur of one of the young Kyldrie beastlings he used to raise. An obsessive pastime. Mind you, one of his lesser talismans. What else have you pilfered, thief?" She glared at Skirl. "Speak up!"

He gave a diminutive shrug. "Keren, our beastmaster, was not using the bone. It lay in dust for many years. I thought to try an apprentice's spell or two, to see if I could coax more magic out of the talisman. Is that a crime?"

Taranis laughed, not a pleasant sound. "You speak in euphemisms. An attempt to brush off your theft and trespass."

The captain snorted. "I've seen this thief loitering about the beastmaster's trunk of trinkets. Hoping for a bone or two."

"He's a meddler and a snoop," said Taranis. "Make no mistake, Grindar, he will be punished. The question is, how?"

"Maybe cut off a hand, my lady?"

A cat-like murmur purred in her throat. "Crude. But there is a certain poetic justice in the recommendation. Still—" She frowned and her eyes grew duskier. "The matter merits thought. And yet, something is still amiss. The obvious confounds us, a slinking weasel putting his nose where it shouldn't be, skulking in the murk his trademark. I've had my eye on you, Skirl. You must think I'm stupid."

His breath drove quick and sharp against his clenched teeth. *Yes, you are, you dumb wench. You still haven't figured out the Eros jewel is a fake.*

She fixed him a sultry glance then pierced him with eyes that seemed to bore holes right through his skull. "You're holding something back, aren't you? My psychic sense tells me so. You thought to steal another treasure." In a moment of doubt, she clutched the leather strip around her neck. Long fingers touched the amulet. She examined the crimson flame deep within the contours of the jewel, which albeit didn't seem to gleam as brightly under the flickering torchlight. But she did catch the characteristic deep blue flame that was the jewel's taint as it morphed from scarlet to ultramarine.

"If you'd tried to steal this," she said, "I'd have cut off your head and had it shrunken and pickled."

Skirl licked his lips. The sweat pooled down his back. He tried to mask his anxiety but was unsuccessful. "I wouldn't think of it, Lady."

"Don't 'wouldn't think of it Lady' me. You are a filthy liar! You'd steal this talisman in a trice. You're a mendacious conniver. One who seeks to con me at every step and everyone else in the academy with the most forked of tongues."

"I'm distressed that you have such a low opinion of me, Archmagrix," Skirl said unconvincingly. "Were you not enamored with me enough to lay naked at my side the night of the last full moon?"

"Enough of your knavery! For your impudence, you'll serve as an example at tomorrow's prisoners' trials. I don't care if my cousin holds your child in her belly." She snatched at the iron ring to her chambers and shouldered the door open, her last words gusted with such venom that Skirl shrank back into the arms of the guards, trembling.

They all repaired to the sorceress's chambers. Up the last uneven steps and into the welcome light of sconces and guttering candles, Skirl was happy to be out of those murks. But not in the clutches of the witch. Everything had gone sour. Well, not exactly everything. He'd hid her precious jewel in a place she'd never find. One success. Unless of course, she were to discover that he had substituted the jewel, and went on a mission to torture him for the truth.

Skirl swallowed hard. He must never let that happen. If he survived tomorrow's trials, whatever those were to be, he'd sneak back and recover the jewel at a later time.

No mean feat. If he could pull it off...dear Taranis would have a rude surprise awaiting her, the surprise of a lifetime, and then they'd see what they would see.

Chapter 3

The public market of Xalgossa was a noisy and shoulder-jostling experience. Flanked by square stone towers, weatherworn as the dusty hills, the main road passed through its animal liveliness and the central square. Every manner of trader, peasant, hunter, fishwife, thief, priest, peddler and con-artist in the northern capital of Umbria was present.

Sword-for-hire Vetravincus pushed his way through the throng, hoping to snag a half decent meal and some ale after a long journey. He'd been working for a petty baron on the Mercian border for small coin. That had not ended well and he had taken his measly share of silver and headed south.

There was a wolfish hardness about him that marked the lone and wandering swordsman...and yet, a kinship and empathy for the underdog that was rare in these times.

The city was the oldest of such settlements in Umbria and the northern kingdoms, predated only by Lausern in Lvendar and possibly the seaport Syrn farther south and east. Priest kings had given way to hereditary kings and satraps leading up to the 2nd age. The real power lay with the mages who held the stronghold to the west. There, on a low hill within the city boundaries rose the octagonal tower complex of the Magicians. Its bright yellow-white gleam caught the full reflection of the noonday sun, causing Vetra to squint.

The king's castle loomed opposite to the Mages' stronghold on a lower hill east across elegant gardens and shrubberies where stone bridgeworks connected the four-towered palace to the inner city. Slums and dives huddled to the immediate south. Ironworks and smithies, tanneries and brothels ran right up to the southern gate of the city with flanking barbican that protected Alantra from invaders from Lvendar and Sahir farther afield. Here archers stood aloft, keeping watch for outlaws and troublemakers and anyone else who looked suspicious.

To the north lay low brooding hills, topped by evergreens and outcrops of rock, amid the odd slender blackstone watchtower that too looked north for invading armies and protected the winding dirt roads that led to peasant-tilled land, crofts, sheltered woods and at last the inhospitable mountains of the Kyldrie.

The sky was a clear blue and sunbeams traced bright lines through puffy white clouds. A twin gallows stood at the market's side under the watchtower. Already there was activity there: royal guard and city soldiers in red and yellow surcoats over burnished armor milling about and tacking up flags and pennons on long staves and poleaxes, preparing as if for a public spectacle. Not the clear day one would expect for a public hanging, thought Vetra, but this was Umbria after all. Such barbaric spectacles were commonplace. It was nothing that he hadn't seen before. A scar ran down the tip of his left ear to mid chin, mostly hidden by the brown-black hair that rested at shoulder level. Also hidden was the pink scar running from the top of his left shoulder to elbow from a sword slash that had nearly taken off his arm in a border war in Condoria when he was but a stripling learning his craft.

Rutting hogs on one side; on the other, fruit of all colors hanging in baskets in vendors' stalls. Raw meat buzzing with flies, slabs of venison hanging on hooks or wooden slats. Vetra would give that a pass.

Snarls and growls caught his attention past the hanging meat and the butcher's block. Some wolf-baiting was in progress—or some look-a-like cross between a steppenwolf and a wolfhound. A man grinned, let out a squawk of triumph as a wolf yelped, tucked tail and ran to the back of a lengthy fenced enclosure while a larger dog leapt snarling at its throat. The wolf keeled over from wounds. Money changed hands. There came another savage snarl as the same vicious animal sunk its yellow fangs in another's hind leg. The gambler gave another crude squawk as more coins changed hands.

Vetra walked with certain ease toward the fenced-off confines of the wolf-baiting, the gears working in his brain. In places like this he'd walked a hundred times. Never without his hand far from his sword. He gripped the pommel now, a broadsword of crucible steel, of impeccable quality with keen edge. From his shagreen belt hung a Sahirian blade, gleaming and oiled, purchased from a Mosete camel herder on a mission east. The blade was razor sharp, the hilt gilded and thickly scrolled, ever at the ready if his broadsword should fail him. His dark brown hair fell in loose waves upon his gleaming black-scale mail coat over leather-jerkined shoulders. The hair on his head covered by a light bronze helm of matching color, designed for quick movements, lightning fast combat.

The semi-snug leathers underneath the chain mail could not hide the breadth of his broad shoulders, the lean muscle that rippled under the sway of his confident gait as he walked. His thighs were well-formed, his dark brown eyes like a soaring hawk's, wide set in a face usually pleasant but often moody which was his manner of late. Not that he couldn't show a rare mirth at times when the occasion warranted.

His instincts were honed, his eyes sharp, senses alert, ever aware of danger and threat in all cities. Such sixth sense and reflexes had saved his skin more than once. In these rough precincts, the only law was the one a canny man created himself.

A mix of races traversed the market. Lean-shanked Thrules standing no higher than his shoulder in black dusty robes with dusty hoods drawn up around their lean desert faces. With skin as dark, lean and parched as lizards. Pale-faced northerners from Umbria and Mercia. Husky, bearded mercenaries for hire from as far away as Balboria and Tolizia bearing axes, swords, and every weapon imaginable. Hawk-eyed tradesmen with reddish beards from Thrakia. Camel merchants from Membes and far-off Condoria. Traveling gypsies and grifters with slatternly women on pony-driven carts of spice, wine and charms as distant as Behundria and Guiritia. Galashadians, brown-skinned and grinning, and the odd sea traders with gray-green eyes and characteristic bow-legged strut from the seaports, Syrn and Mmos.

All the color and life one would ever want...if it were color and life one was looking for.

Pickings were slim in the central kingdoms in the sword-for-hire department. War was brewing to the north. Good for business, if it were mercenary work and Mercia he was cheering for. He was not. Already skirmishes had broken out between wandering hordes of looters and wannabe glory-hounds in Upper Umbria and Mercia. But it would be a cold day in hell before he'd fight for the Mercians, the treacherous dogs they were. And the Umbrians?...They'd likely get their asses handed to them if war broke out.

So now, with only a chipped silver talon to his name, funds were running low. The prospect of gambling looked better to his eye than perhaps it was in reality.

A commotion rose. In the lower half of the market jeers and rough calls drifted. Curses and bawdy jests. Vetra pushed deeper through the throng, throwing aside hunger and thirst, though tantalized by the smells of frying meat in oil and spice. An interesting, if not brutal tableau was brewing at a rude pen of chicken wire strung on wooden stakes. Wild dogs of mixed breeds and colors in individual cages were thrown in to fight it out, some perhaps to the end. Those in cages or those roped at the back of the pen, paced back and forth, snapping and yipping, some which looked half-starved. The flagstones were stained with dark umber and there was the sharp tang of piss and wet dog in the air. The pen ran flush to the high stone wall that enclosed the market, and served as a backdrop to a butcher's shop and a weapons' dealer.

A thin man with black, oiled mustache and tapered goatee called out wagers. He strutted in front of the pen calling challenges in a brassy voice. Fingers on one hand beckoned, fingers on the other clutched coins. The gamesmaster. Gaudy opal earrings dangled from both ears. He wore a dirty purple caftan and bandanna as if he were some pirate from the high seas. Yet he bore a wicked-looking whip at his side, ends flecked with metal barbs to chastise the dogs if they grew unruly.

"Come one, come all! Betting is open! No one with a dog or *wolfshen* here worthy to challenge my own champion? Be not faint-hearted, friends! Are you all lambs? A bunch of wafflers and chicken-hearts?"

This bravado generated laughs as he crouched low, waddling around like a hen making *bok, bok* sounds.

Very droll, thought Vetra.

A voice spoke in his ear. "That black-furred wolfling there is the one to lay your money on, friend." A heavy hand latched on his shoulder.

Vetra looked into the chiseled face of a tall, muscled traveler in mail like himself with a grin on his face and a scar that ran down the left cheek to his chin. Twin curved blades were sheathed and tucked on his back in a leather dusty baldric.

A soldier-of-fortune, like himself, Vetra thought. The battle wounds showed it—scars, chiseled face, worn leather jerkin. A badly-trimmed, matted beard speckled with the faintest white hairs ruffed his square chin. Vetra guessed his age at about forty. Ten years his senior?

Scar-face gave a small frown and impatient tug on Vetra's shoulder. "Well, what are you waiting for, friend?"

Vetra muttered. "If you're so confident of your dog, why don't you bet your own money?"

"I would, but I can't," he explained with a rueful shrug and twiddle of his badger beard. "My love for ale and women has got the better of my finances." Again, the disarming grin.

Vetra examined the animal in question. It was a shaggy halfbreed, still young, now being roped and yanked into the pit by the comedic gamesmaster. But, would grow into something to be reckoned with. "The runt looks as if he couldn't make it to the next butcher shop."

"*She*, friend," said the stranger. "And looks are deceiving. I've got a nose for this type of thing." He tapped his flattened nose that had seen many a fist fight and taproom brawl.

Vetra rubbed his chin. He set himself to pondering. While he dithered, the fight was on and the runt charged to send the larger russet male back on its heels. There came a flurry of snaps and bites as the larger dog struck back. But too late. It was over before it began. The runt had ripped the other's throat out.

"Told you," the man chuckled. Big blue eyes glinted under bushy brows set underneath a rough mop of black-gray hair.

Vetra made a wry face. "Bet-master!" he called in an impatient voice. "Put three shekels on the black runt. On the next round!"

"Which one?"

"The one with the white line under his throat." Vetra lay down his last talon.

The oily-faced bet-master snatched up the coin in quick, greedy fingers. "As you wish, Sirrah."

"Where's my change?"

"You'll get it after the fight. And more if you win. Stakes are high. I'd estimate 6 to 1 against Wolfsha, the runt. Are you sure?"

Vetra shrugged. "Sure as rainbows lie flat in the rain."

The betmaster grinned. He shook his head. "It's your money."

"Just place the wager."

CHRIS TURNER

Chapter 4

Men thrust their noses in and there came much elbow jostling and mutters, such a stir the bet had created. More prospects pushed their way forward like packbeasts, champing at the bit for a piece of the action. Many wished to take bets: a mix of grifters, idlers, practiced gamblers. Bets were accepted. The black wolfling was clearly not the favorite. The next wolfshen up, a wolf youngling, was almost twice as large and looked mean as a snake.

"I'll put a crown on the white wolf!" cried a bloodshot-eyed Behundrian.

"Another on the white mutt," said a smith whose breath stank of grog.

"Three Mercian pennies on the black!" bawled a squinty-eyed Mercian.

The lone mercenary who'd befriended Vetra chuckled, grinned, as if proud of the ruckus he'd created.

The wolflings were set in motion. A blur of flying fur, a vicious frontal attack. Barks, snarls and flashing teeth. The rivals leapt at each other's throats, fangs glistening under the sun as they snapped and lunged for any purchase of flesh.

The smaller animal with the black fur got a piece of the enemy's nose and ripped. The victim cowered back, set up a hideous yelping. Blood ran from its jowl onto the flagstones. Saliva and foam flew.

Vetra winced, licking his lips in distaste. This was not a spectacle he liked. Ordinarily he didn't go in for this kind of crude brutality—but he was down of coin and somehow he'd gotten himself sucked into the madness of it all.

Despite his disgust, his face brimmed with appreciation. The runt was a clear winner. The fight was as good as over and the coins in his pockets.

The gamesmaster did not look happy. The outcome seemed to surprise even him. Vetra could read from his features, the down-curl on his thin lips, the muttered oaths, that he had saved this runt as a sacrifice to gull in chumps like himself to scoop up spoils when they lost and his poster animal made mincemeat of the other.

But it did not. The gamesmaster bit his nails. He darted shifty eyes left and right. There came an imperceptible tug of sweaty fingers on his left bangled ear.

Almost at once, a hunk of pig flesh came hurtling over the heads of the spectators to land in the pit beside the rearing dogs.

Vetra's head turned. The entrails had been thrown by an accomplice. He caught a brief glimpse of fleet feet, a hooded figure bustling off into the crowd.

The white dog's teeth went for the meat, despite his bloodied muzzle. The black wolfling took opportunity to snap at the dog's belly. She missed, but her teeth went on to snap at his heels. Vetra winced at an audible crunch. The white dog yelped, limped away, tail tucked between legs.

The betmaster snorted his disgust. He leapt over the chicken wire and kicked the black wolfling in the muzzle with his heavy boot.

Vetra started forward, his fist balled. "Hey, leave her alone!" He did not abide by wanton cruelty to animals. "She's done nothing wrong except defend her life. Give me my money, you bullying shyster! You owe me 18 shekels at 6 to 1."

The bandanna-man growled, "Sorry chief, but that meat thrown in declared a foul. Outside interference. The game's forfeit."

"To hell it is!" Vetra blared. "Dergath's cocks! You mean to vouch for a lackey of yours?"

The gamesmaster blinked, but Vetra could see the sly smile behind the narrow face. "You knew you weren't going to honor your bets the moment you started losing, so you had some schmuck toss in meat to throw the fight."

The gamesmaster shook his head. "You're seeing pink elephants, outlander."

"No, you're running a racket here."

There came a rumble of discontent from the onlookers. They looked sullenly and ominously at the betmaster, ready to take fists to him.

The man swallowed but reached for the whip at his belt. He gave another quick signal. A not-so-subtle clench of fist with knuckles brought up to his left ear. From the crowd came a stir as four rough-looking bravos pushed through the mob, wielding knives and clubs. Each had tattooed ears and necks.

Vetra quickly sized them up. Thugs. Hired goons. Likely Mercians. The knobbed clubs and gleaming blades had the capacity for violence in the hands of these burly brutes. They looked mean and meaty, just another routine messy cockup that needed mopping up. The problem was, they'd done it once too often. They had a look of complacency about them. They shoved people out of the way without a backward glance. Those who didn't move fast enough were kneed in sensitive places. The first enforcer plowed his way in to menace Vetra, a two handed grip on his wooden club raised to the right side over his head.

Vetra did not flinch. He treaded slightly to the left out of the line of the club, reading the man's movements. His body moved with a fluid ease, instinctively, automatically, his rippling muscles mirroring the years of training under various sword masters and his father. He pivoted sideways in a crouch to allow minimal surface area and less of a target on his body should the club, by quirky chance, jerk sideways and snap up into his face. Ordinarily it would be foolhardy to face four ruffians like this in close quarters. Better to avoid such encounters altogether. Too many bodies, no room for maneuvering. It reeked of the stuff of broken limbs and cracked skull. Yet no fighter was ever given ideal conditions. Anything could go wrong. One smack in the wrong place with that club or the thrust of a sword and it would be all over.

These thoughts were just bees buzzing in Vetra's mind. Arrogant swine like this cockerel were just begging for a beatdown. These cocky bastards had piqued his blood lust. The game had been rigged which meant the loss of his last coin. He couldn't back down now; someone needed to teach these bullies a lesson. Obviously the town guard did not give a shit. Out of the corner of his eye he could see a few stiff figures fussing about by the gallows off in the fringes, looking busy but doing nothing. They probably pocketed a percentage of the cut that the corrupt betmaster had squeezed out of the people.

At the last minute Vetra feinted left. He drove his elbow with the iron studs into the man's jaw.

There came a crunch of bone. A delayed yelp of substantial pain as the man doubled over, clutching his broken jaw. At the same time he barely ducked the hissing sword of a second man who had a slaphappy, showy style to him.

Hoppy little bastard. He bobbed back and forth like a jack-in-the box.

Vetra was unperturbed. On the balls of his feet, he moved and slashed steel into their comfort zone. Hoppy leaped back with a foolish grin. The third man charged, his blade whirling in time with Happyjack's hops and bobs. With a hog's roar, Hoppy skipped in and Vetra let him advance. Vetra was an old hat at this type of game. He shifted stance, rocked on his heels, jerking head back in time to slash out his blade unpredictably, drawing a thin line of blood on Hoppy's sword arm.

The crowd had spread out, sucking in breaths. Now they moved closer, jeers on their lips. The fire of blood was in their eyes, excited by the prospect of fresh blood with that of the dogs'.

A crude chant had sprung up. "Fight, fight, fight!"

"Three shekkies on the swordmeister!"

Vetra roared over his shoulder, "You owe me 18 shekels at 6 to 1!" He ducked another clumsy strike from Hoppy.

The gamesmaster looked on with an amused simper. "You don't look in any position to claim it, outlander—Think you can get past Dokin and Joki?" He sneered and crossed arms on his thin chest.

A short burst of speed and Vetra sprinted in. Sheathing sword, he picked up the betmaster by his scrawny neck and hindquarters and hurled him into the dog pit. He hopped the fence, unsheathed sword, and came marching toward him, a grim craziness on his face.

The dogs went wild, snipping and biting at their ropes and cages, nipping at the betmaster's shins. One sank its teeth into his lower leg.

The betmaster gave a howl of dismay. He crabbed back on his haunches, spitting curses, much to the amusement of the spectators. Apparently, the animals had no love for their cretinous master, the animal-baiter.

"You bloody boor!" he shrieked at Vetra.

Vetra nodded and did a mock bow.

The victory was shortlived. The third thug had hopped in and rustled up behind him. Now a wicked club came arching down at Vetra's helm. Vetra rolled, but caught the hair's edge of the club on his right ear, a glancing blow that sent a hollow echo ringing through his brain. The club came down for a second, fatal strike but the black wolfling leaped in midair and chomped at the attacker's arm. The man yowled, beating at the dog with his other fist.

The dog would not let go. He dropped his club. The dog ripped and tore, snarling like a maniac. He started to drag the dog around in a circle but couldn't get her wretched teeth out of his arm.

There came laughter and hoots. A new chant had arisen. "Dogfight! Man-fight! Dogfight! Man-fight!"

Vetra's mercenary friend with the scarred cheek laughed. He sauntered into the pen, spread his arms and boxed the ears of the third man wrestling with the wolfling. The man fell to the ground with the wolfling tugging and dragging at him still with her teeth. The scar-cheeked mercenary ducked just as a fourth man, a blond giant Mercian in a steel cap, took a swipe at his head with his curved blade.

Scar-cheek roared and came charging at him with both swords bared. There came a great clang and clash of blades. Steel met steel. Scar-cheek bulled his head in and butted the blond Mercian hard on the forehead, sending the man reeling back with his eyes swimming.

He kicked him in the crotch, jammed his bootheel in the back of his knee, sending him to his knees. His boot came up, lashed out at the arm, cracking bone.

The last man, Happyjack, decided the odds were against him. He licked his lips and snarled. Three of his companions already lay sprawled in grime and blood, groaning and wheezing. Cornered between the two mercenaries, he now tried to edge his way back toward the fence.

Scar-cheek jerked forward. "Boo!"

The man hopped the fence in a panicked leap and turned tail and ran.

Scar-cheek bounded after him, shoving bodies out the way. He chased him for while then decided it wasn't worth it and came back muttering, "Too many weaklings in this world."

"Leave him," said Vetra. "Cowards can run like rabbits."

"Don't I know it. I think I like that black dog," he said, stepping over to ruffle the fur on her head.

But the betmaster hobbled in toward the black wolfling with his flail. Vetra sneered and raised his blade, ready to split his head. The wolfling backed into a corner, snarled, ready to pounce.

"You going to pay up or what?" he demanded, steel bared. "Where's my money?"

"Get lost, you bastard. You've done enough damage already."

"Not nearly enough."

With a cold grin, Vetra hacked at the wooden fencing with his blade. The wolfling charged and when the betmaster's flail fell, the dog leaped past it as the metal ends clacked on the stone. She leaped over the broken barrier and fled into the crowd before the betmaster could get his clutches on her. Vetra hacked at the ropes of the other dogs and freed half of them before any of his hirelings could beat them back.

The betmaster looked on in horror. His setup was a shambles. On stiff legs he limped in, his mouth gibbering. "You loosed my wolfshen! You lost me hundreds of talons of prime dogflesh," he cried.

"All the price for shystering." Vetra grabbed the man's fist that clutched the whip and squeezed, hearing a bone crack. The whip clattered to the flagstones. While the man sank to his knees, Vetra took 20 coins from his pockets. This was enough to pay for a decent meal and lodging—plus four more for extra measure. He spat at the three bully boys lying in their own blood. These thugs would have slit his throat and the betmaster wouldn't have batted an eye. Other disgruntled gamblers surged forth to extract the rest of what was owing to them while the pirate-fake nursed his cracked hand and bitten shin.

Vetra cast a brief nod of acknowledgment at the scar-faced mercenary who stood by surveying the scene. "Well played and fought, old soldier." He counted out nine coins, pushed them into the other's hand. "Here's your half of the spoils."

"That's mighty generous of you."

"Wouldn't have won anything without your help—or your tip on the wolfling."

"The name's Nog."

"Mine's Vetravincus. Vetra for short."

"A fine day, Vetra. Let's try for something a little slower, shall we? A little less bloody?" He chuckled. "Cups and beads?"

"Lead on, friend," rumbled Vetra. "I'll watch."

The big man hefted his broad shoulders in a shrug. "Your choice. But you're missing out on the fun."

"I highly doubt that."

Nog motioned to where a younger man dressed in a loose, gaudy orange smock sat at a table like a fortune-teller. Three cups lay tipped upside down before him. He was holding up one pea in a hand.

A crowd had already gathered. The young man placed the pea on the table, lifted the middle cup over it, then with dizzying speed, rearranged the three cups in the hopes of stymieing the onlookers.

The young man stopped at a certain point. He put the cups back in a row. Which cup hid the pea? One did, the others did not. He whipped back his hair and called out a challenge.

"Anyone, anyone?" Catcalls came from the audience.

"Gather round!" he said in a hearty voice. "Whoever guesses which cup has the pea, gets double his wager. One shekel, a single coin to bet! Place your bets, young and old. Only a shekel. Who's going to match my two shekels for his one?"

Vetra rubbed his chin. Watching with amusement, he gave a knowing smile as he saw the young man laughed when he lost and did aw-shucks faces when he won. He was not wrong to conclude that it was all show to stifle any suspicion of skulduggery.

Nog, after watching for some time, sat down opposite the trickster and threw his coin on the table. He stared at him with grim mirth.

"Oh, ho!" said the young man. "We have a scar-faced brute willing to double his money."

"That you do, young upstart. Shuffle the cups."

The young man obliged. After a time he stopped, looked straight into Nog's eyes.

Nog pointed to the middle cup.

The man lifted the cup. No pea. Nog blinked owl eyes.

"Right cup!"

The young man lifted the right cup. No pea. He overturned the last cup and there was the pea.

Nog bit his lower lip. "Go again!" He laid down two more shekels. The young man tipped his head, matched it with four.

Vetra grinned, hitched in closer, amused by the drama. He stood aside, his arms folded across chest.

Nog lost the next round too, of course, the pea not where he pointed but he laid a hand on the gambler's forearm and shook the voluminous sleeve.

Four dry peas clattered out.

"You're going to retract that bid, aren't you, friend? Give

me back my money with interest?"

The youth licked his lips.

One of the tavern wenches, a saucy maid with painted face, baggy pantaloons and sagging breasts, leaned on Nog.

Nog bunted her away. "I'm busy, woman. Can't you see? Look over there for sport, to my strapping friend, Vetra."

With a toothless smile the street woman now seemed to have taken a shine to Vetra. Or more likely to the glint of silver in his hands.

"You in need of a pretty maid to wile away the time, muscle boy?"

"Not at this hour, missy, thank you. It's too early in the day."

She sniggered. "Never too early to any man I know." She gave a speculative scowl. "Unless of course you are one of those…" She gazed down at his package. "You don't look like a eunuch to me."

"Careful with your tongue, missy," Vetra warned. "Could get you in trouble in these precincts."

She gave a wild snort and bawled out a gravelly oath. "Think I've seen all the trouble there is to see, friend!"

It had Nog near laughing. He was still looking for kicks and giggles. After extracting his money from the charlatan, it seemed he was about to try his hand at some gambits with the mettlesome woman, but suddenly a trumpet blew.

Nog's and Vetra's heads turned. A band of eight horsemen had burst into the square, clearing a path for a small cavalcade. The middle rider, a tall, brazen woman, seemed the point of interest. She rode a sizable steed.

Trouble was afoot, thought Vetra. Trouble with a capital T.

Chapter 5

The woman's chin was held high, her long, flowing chestnut hair tucked in a leather basinet but coved down the sides like wings. Her horse was a spirited one, caparisoned in red and gold silk with the emblem of the six wizards: an eagle facing a dragon with talons clutching stave and wand.

Behind her rode a scowling prisoner in blue robe, handsome in a rebellious way, with hands shackled in his lap. His smaller roan was herded forward by the rest of the riders who were guards, clad in red and black jerkins, plumed morions and high black boots. All were armed with swords and daggers at their hips, maces at their saddle-bows.

Nog gave a soft roar and lifted his bulk from the stool. "What are these bumpkins on about? It's either whores or cheats. Now pompous wizards and royals."

"I'd guess a hanging's about to go down," Vetra mused.

"But why the wizard's templar?"

"They probably run the town."

"That young man looks like he's not enjoying much of this."

Vetra snorted. "You think?"

"Off with his head!" cried members of the mob, piking fists in the air.

"Hang him!" expostulated another.

The crowd's thrum grew to roar as the lead rider, the captain of the guards, dismounted and dragged the prisoner off his mount and up onto the scaffolding. The solemnity of the ceremony was further reinforced by guards and leathered officials who stood by watching impassively.

Nog uttered a low growl in his throat. "Barbaric ritual. They haven't even heard the prisoner's crimes yet."

"Does it matter?"

"He doesn't look like a knave. If I were a better man, Vetra, I'd save his skin. But I'm not."

Vetra exhaled. "None of us are better men. We're just pretenders, Nog. Always leaving the tough jobs for someone else."

"Isn't that the way of it? Still, I don't like to be witness to a hanging. Let's go."

"Me neither, but wait. Let's hear the woman out. She looks like she's the queen bee."

Nog scoffed. "That's Taranis, queen witch of the wizard's order. You're right, I hear she rules the city."

"With a body like that, it doesn't surprise me." Vetra's eyes flitted off her contours with rising interest. "There's a challenge for you, Nog, old boy. Why waste time with these dumpy, pock-faced whores?"

"Don't tempt me, please, Vetra."

Taranis removed her helm and whipped back her lustrous hair. It dovecoted outward, giving her the semblance of some predatorial hawk. She dismounted, touched a brilliant red jewel that hung round her neck.

As the captain of the guards hauled the man up to the gallows, the woman set her black-clad hips sashaying up the stairs to stand beside him, face carved in triumph. She held arms wide to address the crowd.

"This man is a thief!" she called in a husky voice. "A former apprentice of the Xalgossian Order, Skirl Atherlai. He tried to rob the Mage Order of our most sacred magic."

"Not true! I merely borrowed a second-rate talisman from our own beastmaster, Keren. 'Tis you who have stolen the Eros Flame." He lifted shackled wrists to the sorceress. "Look, everyone! As we speak, the Archmagrix flaunts it around her neck. See how it glows blood red even in the noonday sun! An omen, plain to see. I dug it up with the oldest wizard of our Order, Senesch, but two moons ago. The Archmagrix stole it from us and claimed it for her own."

"Infidel! I should cut out your tongue. Your weakling magic is a testament to your guilt. Look! Does the accused, a mere apprentice, dare suggest that as false founder of Eros Flame, his power is superior to ours?"

The young man had nothing to say. He fumed, his long face flushed with humiliation. The dark veins on his neck bulged, now circled by a stout rope. The hangman, a bald, beefy man dressed in gray robes, stood hawk-like nearby with leather sack ready to drape it over the victim's head on the lady's signal.

Another rider on an elegant roan came galloping into the throng: a woman with the likeness of Taranis but not as supple or beautiful. A golden braid in her blondish hair hung full-length upon her shapely back. Slender arms dropped loosely at her sides past her silver-gray gown. Her concerned face was creased in anguish.

For a moment the prisoner held a gleam of hope. But not for long.

"Come to see your paramour off?" Taranis mocked.

"Belgra, tell them!" the condemned pleaded in a hoarse voice.

"Call this off, Taranis," the blond woman said. "Skirl's a sneak and louse, who's betrayed us both, but he's not deserving of a death like this, Taranis. He's served faithfully the Order for two years at Dormoth."

"Stay out of things you have no concept of, cousin," Taranis warned her.

"I will not, cousin."

Taranis hissed, pushed her palms outward in the direction

of the defiant woman. "Go, Belgra! You are not welcome here."

There came an odd gust of wind. Belgra's lips twisted, her hair seemed to fly straight back, as if stricken by a freak breeze, or waft of some more unpleasant magic. She did not waver and countered with a flux of her own, a whistling, forest-like sound that caused her cousin to grimace and cover her ears. But Taranis shook off this wall of spell-sound and pushed harder, outward with her palms, as if pressing against an invisible wall.

A pale green bubble manifested in her outstretched palms. The orb wavered in the sunlight like a soap bubble blown by a child.

A strange warp clutched the air. The faint ting of chime, then the low ring of a gong came from farther off.

The transparent bubble whistled through the air and struck Belgra square in the chest, with enough force to send her toppling backward over her horse. She sat dazed on her haunches, her face waxen, her brow beaded in sweat. A cry was on her lips, terror writ in the slant of her eyes. Slowly she lifted her slender weight, the golden braid slipping from her hair to the flagstones. But Taranis had lost interest in Belgra. To her, the fight of wills was over.

Vetra's mouth pinched in a grimace. Ever distrustful of magic, he was one to wish all magickers to Dergath. His hand wandered sullenly to his sword. Two women mages fighting over a lowly apprentice slated for the gallows? He sensed darker overtones to the history of these bickering vixens under the surface and he did not care to find out more.

Taranis beseeched the crowd, "See what happens when misguided forces attempt to stop justice! But because I am lenient and serve as Archmagrix of the Dormoth Order, and because you, dear Belgra, are my second cousin, I will only have this cur whipped." She turned to the prisoner. "Skirl! I sentence you to fifty lashes, administered by Derk here, our executioner. " She flashed sultry eyes at the plump, ugly punisher at her side. "Derk?"

The hangman chuckled a mean laugh. His lips curled and he snatched up the whip at his belt. He snapped it on the oak slabs at Skirl's feet and his hairy hand reached over to tear away the dust-caked robe, exposing naked shoulder and back. Skirl saw his chances diminishing to zero for an escape. He lashed out with his tongue, "You can take your whip and shove it!"

Had the prisoner been smarter, he would have kept his mouth shut and accepted his fate, for, as most men would agree, a flogging was better than a hanging, but Skirl was churlish and not one to accept any punishment or humiliation.

The hangman's fist wiped the surly words from his mouth.

The prisoner spat out blood. His pride was shattered, his honor smirched. Never would he be able to walk in the public market again without the ridicule of commoners in his ears. Even as the executioner's lashes came stinging his back, laying bare his youthful skin, he wished he had not been so prideful.

As he howled and writhed under the lashes, fighting the guards' grip, trying to bite at their bare hands, he cried, "You faithless, conniving bitch! Do you always whip the men you lay with…as numerous as fleas clinging to a dog's back? You're no more than a common tavern slut."

Taranis teeth showed white. Her eyes glinted with a dangerous fire.

Skirl spat further, "Belgra there, the woman you despise, is a woman a hundred times better than you. Let it be known, I shout it out to the world!"

Taranis shrieked, "Off with his ear! Now! Grindar! Derk! I don't care which of you does it."

Grindar, captain of the guard, held Skirl while Derk flashed a knife. The apprentice's blue-black hair was drawn back and a quick stroke and the left ear was sheared off.

Blood dribbled down his neck, staining his torn robes and the planks. Derk held it up with a hangman's flourish for all to see. He threw it out in the crowd with a laugh for the dogs to chew.

The mob chanted for more blood. Taranis's lips curled cruelly, as if a black part of her heart was fed. She could endure shame no more than Skirl could.

The spectacle gave Vetra cause to grimace. He turned away.

"Now, thief," intoned the sorceress, "consider yourself exiled. If I or one of my guards sees your smirking face again in this city after sundown tomorrow, it's off with your head. Do you understand me?"

The prisoner gave a sullen yowl. His shackles were removed from his wrists and he nestled his head against his shoulder to stop the blood rolling down his cheek.

"Withal, you are hereby ejected from the Mage's circle. You are an embarrassment to this Order. Your magic has been stripped. That I saw to earlier today with the Eros stone. Go forth and redeem yourself, then come back no less than two years hence when you feel you are worthy."

Taranis and her riders mounted and rode out, leaving Skirl tottering and trembling on the dark-stained planks. He clutched at his head as blood dripped. Someone threw him a rag which he snatched up and pressed against his ear. Belgra looked at him in despair then with tears of rage and frustration in her eye, she hopped on her mount and abandoned him too in the dust.

The apprentice moved weakly down the scaffolding's stair. He stumbled and fell, picked himself up again before he tottered amid the crowd. Others avoided him, as if he were a leper. He glared around at the many mooning faces about him, sulfurous curses on his lips. He seemed to be in a trance, a red daze, looking for someone to blame, someone to unleash his aggressions upon…or perhaps someone to champion his cause. It was an odd juxtaposition of emotions, considering his state and condition.

Vetra frowned and felt some kinship with the wretch, if not some pull of fate beyond mere curiosity.

Their eyes met.

Nog gripped Vetra's arm. "Let's get some ale, Vetra, call it a day. This drama has soured my zeal for gambling."

Vetra lifted his arm from Nog's clutch. "Hold on."

The riders were trotting under the east archway back to their hillside stronghold. The trumpet blew again. Vetra stared after them with reflection. What need for a public spectacle? The woman was grandstanding. Obviously flexing her muscles in the absence of the king. Easy to make an example of a rebellious apprentice and a rival sorceress.

Standing five paces before Vetra and Nog now was Skirl, his chest heaving. His eyes burned like oil-fired lamps. The look and thought behind Vetra's musing seemed not wasted on the apprentice. He gazed at them not without some wiliness and interested motives. "You are a mercenary?"

Vetra afforded him a curt nod.

"I sense you hate them as much as I do."

Vetra shrugged. "What of it?"

"Just this. I have a proposition for you…the two of you." His tawny eyes narrowed on scar-faced Nog.

"What, that you'll travel along with us to shine our boots? Sorry, boy, we've no time for miscreants. There're many ale games and young girls to entertain yourself with down at the *Goshawk Tavern*. They don't mind a man missing an ear either, I hear."

"Very witty, mercenary. But no. Ale rooms are for drunkards." He glanced at the lean layers of sinew rippling under Vetra's leather and accouterments. "With your swords and my magic, we can go far."

"Oh?" Vetra leaned on his blade in amusement.

"We can take revenge on these upstarts…these arrogant implings who call themselves wizards."

"You might. We wouldn't."

"Vetra and I are here to drink ale and win money, aren't we, Vetra?" Nog emphasized.

The apprentice's eyes gleamed through his winces of pain. "There's wealth to be gained."

Vetra gave a grunt of some interest.

"We strike at night, raid the wizards' coffers. We steal their magical talismans then take off with the most fabulous of all, the Eros Flame…a sapphire old when Sarkala, the sorceress-priestess, made charms to ward off the dark gods."

"Aye, and what if they strike us down with lightning bolts and fire bombs?" Nog asked.

"I will create counter spells to thwart them."

"With your stripped magic?" Vetra snorted. "Sure you will. The same that saved your ass from getting your ear chopped off."

"I can spite them," Skirl hissed. "If we can sell the jewel in the black markets of Lausern or Alantra, we can split the profits."

Vetra looked him up and down, musing. "You could be one of those magickers, masquerading in the form of a trap. Why should I trust you?"

"Because you could be filthy rich…"

Chapter 6

Vetra turned, was about to take Nog up on his offer of ale when Nog gripped his arm. "Hold on, Vetra. Let's hear the wretch out." He motioned toward the east gate where horse caravans were moving on to Alantra before the afternoon grew old. "Let's walk. Too many prying ears about this place."

Vetra shrugged. He examined the bloody-eared apprentice for another time. What did he see? A youth of tousled hair the blackest of black, a narrow face, jaw, small trim mustache, the beginnings of a trendy scholar's goatee. A wide, smiling mouth affected with an oily tongue, a charmer who may or may not be inclined to tell the truth. Like at the present instant.

"Those robed cretins have disfigured me," the apprentice muttered angrily. "Now they'll pay." He gritted his teeth against the pain of his shorn ear. Luckily, the rag he pressed against the side of his head had somewhat staunched the flow of blood. Though Vetra was not sure if it was enough to stave off infection.

The mercenary gave a sad smile. "I admire your spirit, boy, but you must know, you are one, they are many, with more means at their disposal than you. What chance do you have?"

"No matter. I will strike when they least expect it. I will roil them with spells, I will—"

"You are capable of no such thing," Vetra scoffed.

"Since we're short of funds..." Nog said, grabbing a cheap shawl from the rack while the garment-monger was looking the other way. He tossed it at Skirl. The young man nodded and unpeeled the rag gingerly from his ear then wrapped the shawl around his head.

"Stealing from the locals?" Vetra inquired.

Skirl clicked his tongue. "Such pure-hearted rogues." He

shook his head, a sardonic grin on his lips.

"Get moving, you thief," Nog growled.

Vetra frowned at a sudden thought. "How did you raise the malice of those two squabbling vixens? That was one of the most spiteful displays I've seen, never mind that bit about your ear."

Skirl raked at his prickly goatee. "I impregnated the woman with the blond hair who came riding in after. I got seduced by Taranis, the witch, and her Eros stone at about the same time. Belgra found out I'd lain with her and well, you can imagine the rest, me almost getting my nuts cut off. The two initially opted for castration, but Taranis opted for something more lenient, a hanging."

Vetra rolled his eyes. "You sure know how to piss off the ladies."

Skirl's lips pursed in a scowl.

Vetra jerked a thumb back toward the wizard's stronghold. Four towers rose ominously among high domes in the fading light. "Why did the mother of the child do no more to save you?"

He lifted his shoulders. "I think Belgra stews and broods upon my betrayal." He closed his eyes and hung his head in something of penitence. "She sees me as the cause of her problems when really it is that tyrant Taranis."

"What of this Eros Flame?" Vetra pressed. "What in Hades is it?"

"'Tis a love charm, but more than that. An elixir of power. One of old relics of the Age of Magicians. Sarkala, the sorceress, kept it as a periapt of the 3rd Age, to be precise. One gleam of the amulet's light, and the first suggestion the bearer speaks, becomes the recipient's desire to fulfill."

Vetra frowned. "I didn't see any of that back there at your

ear-cutting."

Skirl's lips curled. "That's because I hid the real jewel. Taranis flaunts a fake. She does not know it."

Vetra and Nog both blinked.

"Sounds a little farfetched to me," said Nog. "You don't look like the type to be running after any love charms."

"You insult my honor, mercenary. There is nothing more important to me than love."

Nog gave a bark of wolfish laughter. "You're in the wrong world then, friend. The mage-sisters or cousins look like they rule over Xalgossa—no lost love there—and the curvy chestnut-hair looks like the winner. No doubt they have the ear of the king."

"And more."

"Listen, boy," Vetra began, "I appreciate your offer but we're fighters, not thieves in the night. Better suited to bashing skulls with sword and axe on the borderlands. You're better off hiring a poisoner to deal with the witch, if it's vengeance you seek."

Skirl hitched in with a murmur of frustration. "Listen! My father was a soldier. A swordsman like you. He died splitting Mercian skulls. War pigs. Brigands. In the end, he was slain by a Mercian hetman. I know who you are and what you are about. My mother was a beautiful woman, exquisite beyond belief. Golden hair, the most tawny amber eyes, lissome as a sapling in the wind. The army came and sacked our village. The war was savage, brutal. Umbria and Mercia have always been at each other's throats. They took her away. She was taken into the seraglio of some southern kingdom, I don't know where, sold likely for a few coins to a rich scum lord. I was a boy of 7 years old. Nothing I could do. A tousle-haired, rowdy guttersnipe. Having to fight my way among the other urchins for scraps of food.

"An old conjurer, Nistis, hobbling on a crooked leg with a varnished gnarled cane, took me in. There I learned the arts of gray magic, secret arts. First in prestidigitation, then in higher forms of spellweaving. Then, to a craft more secret and darker. By 12, I became his equal. By 18, I was his better. Nistis had ambitious plans for me. How wide his grin split upon seeing me grow and flourish when he realized I was to become his champion—to fight for a place in the Mage's Circle at Xalgossa.

"But he died, stricken by a rare illness of the spleen. I suspected he was poisoned—by certain jealous individuals within the Circle, and I was left on my own again, pondering, brooding, leaving me with a thirst for magic that I'd never known. I dabbled and delved deep and sought that which was unseekable—the wisdom of the ancients. Forbidden to mortals. I dug for the serpent, the golden apple—the philosopher's stone—the eros of the lost kingdoms…and I failed.

"I was close but far," he sighed, "and to my bitterness, I knew that I had scratched only the surface.

"I wandered the regions far, seeking out country witches, tarot readers, philosophers, spellcasters. I was taken in by croftworkers, wine merchants, alewives, blacksmiths, only to return to Xalgossa as bereft as a wandering vagabond. I applied to the Order at Dormoth. I showed them tricks they hadn't seen before, I answered their questions: 'Who was the archmage of Titon? How would you create a spell to ensnare a conjurer and deflect his magic of the Winds? Who is the maker of the Magic Mirror?' Things like that. The Order accepted me as a lowly apprentice as I showed promise.

"I learned many things. You are right, mercenary. The two cousins rule over Xalgossa. Or should I say the one cousin, Taranis.

"The great library of Linderlore became my home during the day. I crammed every bit of lore, sorcery spells, incantations I could into my brain, till evening when the great iron door was closed. But because of my zeal, I was granted permission to stay on after hours, poring over old musty scrolls, tattered tomes, screeds of the philosopher-historians to my heart's content. I worked uncountable hours into the night, taking notes, pondering, scribbling, pulling at my beard which grew ragged and unkempt. My eyes were red-rimmed craters...

"And then I stumbled on something... Yes! The hidden key to which many a philosopher and grizzled mage had missed over the centuries."

Nog shook his head. "You're either obsessed or crazy."

"Both, mercenary," croaked the apprentice. "I am a cursed man. I drank the potion, and bit into the poison apple and swallowed. Born under a dark star, a shadow living among men haunted by an illusive dream. But with some strange purpose I still cannot yet fathom."

"Cephala's tits, Vetra!" Nog cried. "We have a poet in our midst."

Vetra slapped his arm. "Quiet!"

Skirl scowled. "Do you always take up company with boors, Vetra?"

Nog pushed the shiny blade at his belt under the mage's chin. "Mind qualifying that statement?"

Skirl coughed. "I only jest. No hard feelings. Withdraw your blade, if you please."

The brawny Nog reluctantly sheathed his knife.

"All fine and nice this history," muttered Vetra, "but what does it give us? A disgruntled, disfigured mage, thinking more with his embittered heart than his brain."

"The jewel's worth a fortune!" Skirl hissed. "Unloading it to the right merchant or ambitious wizard, we can live as rich men for the rest of our lives. Do you not see? Taranis has maimed many on her path and now I will thwart her for the rest of her days."

"Revenge, eh?"

"The dish best served cold, as a man of the sword like you, can understand."

Nog's mouth twisted. "If they catch us, it will be all of our necks they will slit, not just an ear."

"Life's risky, mercenary—" Skirl showed a thin smile of fine white teeth and upturned palms. "I need muscle to deal with the guards in and around the Hall's exits and entrances. From there, I know the way to retrieve the jewel."

Vetra gave a skeptical murmur. "No spells? Potions? A big, bad, powerful magician like yourself can't even get past a couple of guards?"

"You heard her—" Skirl flourished icily. "My magic has been stripped. The witch Taranis so brazenly bled off my powers and boasted about it to the crowd. I am missing an ear! I'm in rags and penury and half starved. What more can I do? I have not many props to fall back on. One glimpse of a leper-like beggar at the gates of Dormoth and sure as Aramis's tits they will lop off my head."

Nog frowned, pulling at his beard. "Risky, clubbing down a couple of grubby guards at the castle, Vetra. More'll be prowling around the interior of the apprentices' hall. They'll cut us down in instants. I've heard the Order is well protected—like a Knight's Templar or Crusader's Haven."

"You make a good point." Vetra stroked his chin. "If the jewel's as valuable as you say, it could be worth the risk. We'll need some well-wrought plans."

"Get young Skirly here to turn us into mice then," Nog

muttered. "We scamper through a hole, change back to fighting men, grab up the jewel and bust our way out."

Vetra rubbed his chin. "The idea's not as preposterous as it sounds." A wide grin settled across his face. "If we appear as harmless as mice to them, we might be able to make it work."

"I didn't mean it literally, Vetra," Nog protested. "You've been smoking too much poppy."

"Fool! I mean, why not apply to the Order as guards? A couple of strapping fellows like us, we'd be snapped up. We'll sell ourselves cheap, give the impression we're down on coin. We get in there, dress our mage up as some harlot or cripple, sneak to his hiding place, recover the Eros jewel then off into the night."

Skirl's eyes widened. "This is the spirit, gentlemen! I knew as soon as I saw you across the crowd, you were my man, Vetra. I don't even have to go into Dormoth. You two can get to the gargoyle statue in the combs, then—"

Vetra shook his head. "Not going to happen, mage. We aren't doing all the heavy lifting while you sit back on your laurels sipping wine and collecting the spoils."

Skirl gave a stiff wave. "As you wish."

"It boils down to this," Nog said with an impatient flourish, "we need lodging, a good rest, a good start tomorrow. If we are to sneak our prodigal black-sheep magician into the wizard's lair, we need to set our heads together."

Chapter 7

They were half way across the footbridge over the canal when the half wolfling came snugging up behind them, giving a happy bark.

Vetra knelt down and gave her a good pet. Her matted fur was caked with dried blood. The bloody wound on her back would be long in healing where the other dog had sunk its teeth. "You sure are a scrapper, aren't you, Wolfsha?"

She whined, licked Vetra's face. His lips curled in a smile. The first genuine smile that day.

The magician looked down at the wolfling. "Seems to me the half wolf and I have something in common—fresh war wounds."

Vetra gave a brief mutter. He seized the dirty leather collar with the iron spikes and used his sword to saw through it.

"There you go, Wolfsha, whatever your name is. You're a free wolf, your own master."

The animal gave an excited bark and circled around Vetra, jumping up at his waist. Her tail wagged as if it would fall off.

Vetra looked at those around him: three oddball loners, all met under the oddest of circumstances.

The sun was a shimmering orb over the western towers, burnishing stone in crimson. It'd taken till sundown to find a place affordable enough for the three to rent a room. Their searches took them to the *Rat Peacock Inn* on the dingy south side of the canal. Legend said the brick-walled canal had been built centuries ago to separate the slums from the royal grounds and the wealthy landowners and tradesmen. Either way, it was not the most pleasant of surroundings. The sour smell wafting from the stagnant, blue-black waters now emphasized this disparity clearly, but in these quarters the prices were much lower, and neither of them could foot any bill for modest-priced accommodation. Vetra grumbled ever more loudly at his lack of coin. He voiced his amazement anew that after the wolf-baiting they'd managed to walk out of the market without getting their throats slit.

"We can hole up at *Madder's Pike* down the alley for 10 shekels," Nog said, "but I'm not keen about the roaches and bedbugs. This *Rat Peacock* place looks and smells better." He spread his palms, nodded approvingly. There was a convivial glow of the taproom and an aroma of roast venison. Inside, men huddled over tables of dice. "Looks like some easy pickings here, Vet. Perhaps we could throw down a few more coins later in the evening?"

"And attract more attention?" Vetra scoffed. "No. You can gamble your last coins, not mine. I've risked enough already back at the wolf-baiting."

"You an edgy bird today, Vetra? Turning into a killjoy?"

"No, just not stupid. Fool me once, fool me twice, blah blah blah, call me a damn simpleton, Nog, you know the saying—"

"Yeah, I know the saying. It was your choice. You were as eager as me to make some quick coin, so stop your grousing."

Vetra was about to object when a bustling, barrel-shaped figure wiping his hands of meat and kitchen grease squared himself solidly before them. He took one look at their dusty leathers, mail and soiled, blooded garments—not to mention Skirl's bandaged head—and shook his head.

"No lepers allowed—" he motioned to the door.

"He's not a leper," Vetra explained. "He's a friend, in a jam—*Skrill*. His face is disfigured from an accident."

"Sword fight?"

"You could say."

"Axe?"

"Not quite." Vetra licked his lips. "Let's just say a vindictive woman was involved."

"Oh. The worst." The innkeeper grumbled an apology. "Well, we have one room left that'll fit the three of you roughboys, but it'll be a squeeze. It's neither pretty nor clean, but is going for 13 shekels. Includes a meal each."

"High for this neighborhood," Vetra mumbled. "You have any other cheaper lodging—"

"Sorry, fellows, rooms all booked. Only suites left are deluxe, at least deluxe for the Canal District—100 shekels per night—and you boys don't look like rich merchants to afford 100 shekels."

"Grand larceny," muttered Vetra.

The innkeeper cast him a sober look. "It's a supply and demand world, friend, run by complex mathematics."

Vetra huffed a sardonic breath. "We'll take it. Beggars can't be choosers."

Wolfsha had snuck past the door and came creeping around Vetra's legs, wagging her tail.

"No animals either!" the man said testily.

Vetra gave a resigned nod. "Okay. Go on, girl. Get!" He clapped his hands. "Find a home, or at least some dry place safe from flails and baitmasters. This world of men is not for you."

The half wolf whined and seemed to understand the gist of Vetra's words. After some backward hounds' eye looks, she trotted back through the open door and off into the alley.

Vetra shook his head. "I swear that animal knows the human language, Nog."

"You'd have to, fighting those lowlifes for masters, who pit her against wild she-hounds."

The landlord flourished. "Come upstairs, I'll show you your room." His eyes lifted in a wise look and he wound his burly frame up the narrow staircase and down a hallway past the landing. They saw he walked with a jerky limp.

The room was small and stuffy with the lingering odor of sweat and grog. White paint peeled from the walls. A small window overlooked the canal, much as they would have liked a room at the back of the inn. A clink of coins came as Vetra thrust the shekels in the innkeeper's outstretched hand. He limped away with a contented murmur.

Nog flopped out, boots and all, on the far cot. "Only two beds. Someone's got to take the floor. And no way I'm sleeping with mageboy here."

Skirl grimaced. "Fine, I'll take the floor." The apprentice hunched amid the dust balls.

Vetra slumped on the other bed, stifling a yawn. "Tell us now where the jewel is, Skirl, in case we can't smuggle you into this Dormoth place."

"It works both ways, mercenary," said Skirl coolly. "What's to stop you two from getting the jewel and cutting me out of the deal? You don't trust me, I don't trust you."

"Fair enough, mage," Vetra growled. "But you'd better not be scamming us. Be ready. Await our signal. We'll set a light, torch or some candle in one of the courtyard towers. Three flashes when the guard changes. Watch for it—say between midnight and two."

The apprentice grunted.

"I'm going to the taproom to see what I can learn from the locals and get some eats."

Skirl jumped up. "I'll go with you."

"No you won't. You'll stay here and keep Nog company. I don't want you drawing attention to yourself."

Skirl rolled his eyes. "Spare me the sentiment, Vetra... You think anyone cares about a bloody-eared apprentice? I think I'll go mad if I have to listen to Nog's chatter any more."

Nog leaped off the bed, shoved his blade under the apprentice's chin. "Care to revise that statement?"

"Knock it off, you bozos." Vetra shook his head, rolling his eyes. "See that you two don't kill each other while I'm gone."

Chapter 8

To the tune of a lively hornpipe and bawdy lyrics of half drunk minstrels, Vetra drank ale and mixed with the locals. He played dice in the taproom with the last of his shekels. He learned several salient facts. That Xalgossa was in decline and that there was unrest in the kingdom. The king would likely be deposed before long, if not full-scale war to come first.

The bawdy melody was not to Vetra's liking. Though he endured it: three troubadours with lyre, pipe and fife, red faces shining and grinning teeth. He preferred the soft, slow melody that harked of country forests and trout-filled brooks not slutty limericks of dancing vixens and lecherous lords. About twelve patrons milled about or sat at tables in the dim sconce light: a mix of men and women. The smell of varnish and sour wine hung heavily in the room. Notched blackened beams ran along the low ceiling. Various heads of stuffed animals were bolted to the walls: elk, boar and goat, including a large green peacock, inspiration for the pub's name. A plunk of darts echoed from an old warped board not far from where the minstrels sang, along with the clinks of mugs and low laughter, some hearty, some bitter, amid the usual barroom murmur.

A sheep trader sat on a stool next to Vetra, chugging a tall tankard of dark, warm ale. He spoke in a moribund tone, wiping his drooping mustache. "King Grinas has decreed all firstborn males to fight in his army, can you believe it? Outright banned deserters who buck their duty. The Mercian dogs encroach on our borders and have put spies in the city."

"Aye," said another, a sad-faced man with droopy eyes and threadbare cloak. "They use Alantra in nearby Lvendar as a base. Taranis is his new advisor. Probably whips his naked ass at night. She has no love for this city. At least not more than that fancy jewel she totes around her neck can give her. Devil's beards! Like a sorcerer's ring, drawing people googly-eyed to her side."

Vetra recalled how the sorceress had twirled the stone in her fingers while addressing the crowd. "She seemed not to have the ear of the crowd today," Vetra said innocently.

The trader looked away and winced. "That was unusual. I'm at a loss to explain it. Maybe the bitch was having a bad day. Or the magic had deserted her for a space. I hope both."

Vetra absorbed the news with a thoughtful rub to his chin. The trader's words gave more credence to Skirl's story. That he had stolen the real jewel and cached it somewhere in the crypts below the wizard's hall did not seem so farfetched. To have that amount of power... Vetra marveled. The value must be beyond worth.

He spoke in a cautious tone, "From my eye, it appeared the Archmagrix wasn't much in control of that crowd."

The sheep trader grunted. "'Twas odd. The jewel usually turns people into obeisant sheep. Fawning and fumbling over her every word. This time—" he smacked his lips "—I always look away from the thing or turn my head, or better yet, I don't attend any of her pompous public ceremonies."

"A wise policy."

A hunter in a red-and-black-checkered trapper's jerkin sat cleaning his nails with a hunting knife. "War's brewing in the north," he said dourly. "Up Davilnook way, where the hillside barrows separate Umbria, Mercia and Lvendar. Just came from there. Seen it with my own eyes. I checked the rabbit and mink traps while scouting for elk. Border raids, skirmishes in the night. Mailed men with fine broadswords, some with mace and evil on their minds. They slaughtered horses and livestock, set fire to barns and sheds, killing hens and goats, the odd ravage of a farmer's wife. Anything to try to goad Umbria into a war."

"They'd love that," spat one of the barflies familiar with the other two. "Give them more of an excuse to come in and take over our lands. 'Annex' it. For the safety and security of all. Whether they be fighting Umbrians or Lvendarians, it doesn't matter. Let's face it, fellows, Umbria's weak. I doubt she could hold even with our good King Grinas's horse guard and pikemen."

A quasi-fortune teller and palmist put in her two bits. "Mercia's in for a humbling, I reckon. A great flying beast'll come from the west. It'll smite her. I've tossed the bones, I've seen it. 'Tis foretold—in the scrolls."

"And unicorns'll fly," scoffed the innkeeper. "What island world are you living in, Zelda?"

"I've seen it in the cards!" she protested. "The cards, the bones, they don't lie."

There came boos and hisses from the motley mix of patrons in the dingy room.

A man with a red face and purple veins on his nose raised his mug. "Three tankards for the lady! A great winged flying beast! Hearken, all." He waved his peaked hat to the minstrels who stood at the front of the room. "Relph! Can you do us the honors? Ode to the dragon!"

There came hearty roars.

The minstrels obliged; the instruments changed hands. The tall man with the green jongleur's cap sang in a high, jaunty tone:

"There came a dragon from Whistling Woods,
All scaly and glistening with plates he stood,
Hey diddle diddle and play my fiddle!
Flame and feather, whither, thither!

Hi hi ho and a bottle of rum,
To fire the city under a darkened sun,
Hell's fire and ruin. Smoke and cinder. Beyond huntsman's ken,
Came the crusty dragon from the sorcerer's den!"

Vetra rolled his eyes. "Dragons and kings, wizards and rings," he muttered, "who needs them?" He gave a ragged sigh. Time to call it a night.

A jaundiced-faced drunk bumped his shoulder, scowling. "You don't appreciate our lore, outlander?"

Vetra just shook off his arm. Better he use the time to plan an early attack for tomorrow. They'd have their work cut out for them. He drained his mug, raised a hand to his new friends, pleading fatigue. He was about to saunter off to bed when he turned to see the skulking figure of Skirl stealing down the stairs. The apprentice's face was flushed. A wide grin split his face as he assessed the liveliness and movement in the taproom.

There was a jingle of coins over by the dartboard. Vetra saw the apprentice's eyes narrow shrewdly as they passed over the three men playing darts.

Vetra strode over to intercept Skirl. "Shouldn't you be resting, Skrill? That split head of yours needs some healing." His voice was cheery but gruff.

"By no means, my good man. I feel spry as a dunghill cock! And thirsty too. Ale, bartend! A cup of your finest, if you please!"

The innkeeper finished wiping down a glass and cast Skirl a cool glance. "How will you be paying for it, sir?"

"Put it on my tab. I'll give you coin, plus half more by the end of the night."

"We don't do tabs or honor here, sir. Too easy for unscrupulous patrons to play jiggery-pokery with us." He blinked. "Half more, you say?"

"Indeed."

"Coming right up then." The landlord poured a foaming jack and walked it personally over to Skirl who downed half of it in one gulp and wiped his thin mustache of amber foam.

"Another!" Skirl cried as he sauntered over to the dart board.

Vetra shook his head in amazement. He murmured some unkind comments about apprentices missing ears under his breath. "It's your neck, Skrill."

"My neck is fine, Vetra," he called. "As is the rest of my innards, skull, brain, wits and heart!"

Skirl was invited into the game without question, despite his crude bandage. Apparently he was a man of importance having gained the innkeeper's vote of confidence.

Nog had come down to briefly watch the dart play before he drifted off to the back where he started chatting up a shifty-eyed, slatternly woman in the shadows.

A fat man who did most of the tossing and talking at the dart board, name of Jaksi, swore and fretted and took a furious gulp of his arrack. "These darts seem flying cockeyed! Missed the bull's eye three times now."

"You've missed not only bullseye, but the inner ring and outer ring," laughed one of his lank-toothed pals.

Skirl clapped him on the back. "Tough break, master Jaksi. Those darts seem to be your enemies."

"Damnedest thing I ever saw. As if there are magic elves skittering about this room, magnets turning my points."

Skirl's eyes widened. "Elves? Today the Archmagrix accused a young man of theft and witchery. Had his ear lopped off in the market, can you believe it? Perhaps witchery's in the air?"

"And spooks fly on the full moon," crowed a man from a nearby table. "You dart-mongers utter mere wives' tales. You don't believe any of that mumbo jumbo, do you, Jaksi?"

"Most of it, no, but I remember when old Darv, the carnival-monger, brought in a witch and an ape to the midsummer show. The moon and stars turned red and—"

"Spare me," the man said. He made a cut signal with his hand.

Skirl lost a few rounds then went on to win sizable coinage which he attributed to 'beginner's luck'.

Vetra knew better. He'd seen the apprentice move his fingers in a weird way then mutter some unintelligible syllables as Jaksi and his peers tossed. He wondered just how much of the young man's power had deserted him.

With a happy cluck, Skirl sidled over to Vetra sitting sullenly at the bar. He thrust 4 shekels into his hand.

"There you go, mercenary. Don't say I didn't gift you anything."

Vetra eyed the mage under narrowed lids. After some muttering and small talk, he rose to leave. Skirl elected to stay and quaff another round of ale, try his hand at some more darts. Vetra gave a sigh of moderate exasperation and wished him all the luck.

Halfway down the hallway back to his room, he could not help feeling dissatisfied with the day's events. The feeling puzzled him. Things could pay off well in the long run with this jewel heist. *If* they could pull it off and pawn the gem in Lausern or some city. It could be the best thing to fall into his lap for months. A lot of ifs. No, there were strange things in the works. Trouble was brewing. He was no psychic, but he could feel it in his bones.

He opened the door to the room and in the dim candlelight he saw Nog lying on the far cot snuggling up to the buxom tavern whore he'd been schmoozing earlier. He gave a sour curse. Definitely bottom grade, this unkempt slatternly maid with dirty dress tossed on the floor and cuts on her face. A shekel at the most. And why not? Nog didn't appear to be too choosy about his bed-mates.

Vetra sighed and lay on his cot. He turned his back to them.

There came a half hour of noisy tumult—creaking cot, slap on slap of bare skin and vigorous play before Vetra finally had enough. He launched himself up and marched over to the bed and shooed the woman out bare-breasted into the hall. He bolted the door, oblivious to her curses. There came insistent bangs on the wood.

"Foul mouth on that wench," Vetra grumbled. "You certainly know how to pick them, don't you, Nog?"

"Still had a half shekel's worth from that moaner—Why'd you have to go and spoil the fun?"

"Because I'm tired and need to sleep. Do it somewhere else. You're forgetting who paid for this room."

Nog gave a reedy sigh. "Too knackered anyway." He yawned and grinned. "Probably for the better, Vetra. Dame smelled of fish anyway."

Vetra grimaced.

"Where's our mage?"

"You mean the one you let downstairs despite my instructions to the contrary? Still down darting. Amazingly seems to be winning." Vetra frowned. "With whatever faint whiff of magic he has left."

"Magic, you say?" Nog reached for his jerkin. "Maybe I should tag team with the rogue."

"Be my guest. Just don't be bringing any more of those hosebags up here."

"Sure, sarge." Nog tipped fingers in a salute.

The next day, Vetra awoke at the crack of dawn to the squawk of crows and the snort of hogs outside their open window.

Bright sunshine streamed in, causing him to squint. He stretched his muscles and cracked his joints. In his bones he felt a vague stiffness he didn't remember in his youth. *Dergath.* He was getting too old for this.

He tied the laces to his black leather boots then did his regular fifty push-ups and forty deep knee-bends, a vigorous routine...to the bellow of a fishwife, the various odors wafting from the window, the rolling of beer barrels down the street and the yowl of stray dogs.

Nog had his mouth half open as if collecting flies. The man had dark circles under his eyes and smelled of sweat and sex. He was snoring loudly. Vetra scowled. With a forceful swat, he nudged him awake. The mercenary jolted upright, clutching for his sword.

"Hey, wassup?"

"You snore too loud."

"Sorry for being alive."

Skirl was just rousing, blinking like an owl from his perch on the floor. He groaned and clutched his ear.

"Still hurts?"

"What do you think?"

"A little pain never hurt anyone," Vetra said.

"Sure, I'll trade my ear for yours."

"Let's not get hostile. We've got work to do. If we don't return to the *Rat Peacock* by noon you'll know we made it into Dormoth."

"Or you got your throats cut."

"Fine. But let's not put too much energy into that thought."

Skirl nodded. "I've been doing some thinking of my own, Vetra. I'll meet you two at the north junction of the Hall of Wands where the corridor widens—you'll see the wizard's emblem hanging on the wall, the Dragon and Eagle. At midnight. No later. The tower gong tolls on the hour. If you can light a candle in the North or West tower where I'll see it, I'll know I'm not wasting my time. From there, we'll proceed to the place where I hid the jewel."

"You seem confident, mage," said Nog, "for one with only one ear. How are you going to get in?"

"Never you mind. I'm not without my tricks."

"From last night's dart play, I don't doubt," Nog quipped. "How much did you rake in anyway?"

Skirl gave a cryptic smile. "A wizard never tells his secrets."

Chapter 9

The shadow of the sorcerers' stronghold fell over them in the mid-morning blaze. Vetra squinted up at the high stone wall and the forbidding, blackstone towers. He and Nog had approached the 10-foot spiked iron gate at a cautious pace to find it partially ajar.

Vetra frowned anew. The doubt in his mind grew about this mission. A guard outfitted in steel hauberk, bronze morion and red plume called out a challenge. "Who goes there?" His sword swept up past leather greaves and mail shirt.

Vetra saw the hints of an open courtyard beyond him and the gate. Three mage guard in red and black surcoats practiced with sword, axe and mace. Gaudy coats covered their leather and mail.

"We're mercenaries for hire come to offer our services," Vetra said. "We were impressed by Taranis's speech the other day in the market. Her call for law and order and a crackdown on knavery is a good one. We figured your Order of Dormoth Mages could use a few more fighting hands." He spread his arms, gestured toward the sparring figures who grunted and smashed mace on heavy shields.

The man's sunburned face creased in a grin. "Well, you've come to the right place. The Archmagrix has put the word out for more men-at-arms. I'll pass your request on to our captain."

"Very well. We'll wait here and not disturb your training."

Before long, a tall figure made swift strides over toward them. Vetra recognized him as one who'd helped in the ear-cutting at the market. Grindar. A grim-faced bully with dirty blond curls and weathered war gear.

He looked them up and down for a few seconds then snorted with a practiced eye. "Mercenaries you say?"

Vetra gave a smiling nod. "Of singular quality. We are willing to work for a decent wage." His eyes roved past the iron bars to see that one of the fighting men was down, his shield battered by repeated mace blows. His partner-in-arms lifted a hand to help him.

"Where did you fight and who did you fight for?" the captain demanded.

"Tolizia, Mosete and Condoria. Border wars mostly."

His stark, blue-eyed gaze turned to Nog. "And you?"

"The seaports of Syrn and Mmos. Mostly guarding ships and cargo from raiders."

"What are you doing this far west?"

"What any other mercenary would be doing," Vetra interjected. "Seeking work."

The captain gave a brief mutter. It was something he could understand. "This way then."

The gate was pulled wide and they followed the thickset man into an even wider expanse, a grand octagonal court bordered by arched doorways of shaded colonnades. Plumed winter palms rose close to the inner walls.

The other guards paused for a brief moment from their practice but paid Nog and Vetra no heed. To see mailed men coming and going in this court was not uncommon.

Grindar's quick heavy tread brought them under the shadow of the south tower. Six high-looming towers of black stone flanked the courtyard, two facing each of the four directions. In between each set of towers, gilded domes rose over elegant halls. The southern-facing dome was twice as high as the others. Twice as opulent too. Inlaid with bands of pure silver and crowned with a spiky spire looking like one of the mysterious, stepped pagodas he'd seen in his travels far east in Membes. Atop the walls surrounding the stronghold ran a wide stone parapet where archers could rain fire down in case of attack. Two men walked back and forth across the sun-warmed stone with arbalests pointed downward.

In the center of the court rose a circular stone well. Two plain-faced women dressed in peasant smocks bore buckets of fresh water suspended from ox-yokes about their necks. Likely to the kitchens, Vetra mused.

Nog tipped his helm with a cheesy grin on his face as they passed.

There came the scurry of feet as a young apprentice dressed in blue robe and conical cap with a spellbook tucked under his arm almost ran full tilt into them as he hurried across the cobbles. He was mumbling words to himself, his mind clearly elsewhere. Grindar swatted out an arm and muttered a curse at the apprentice's lack of attention. Another scooted by in a red gown and loose hood with wand in her hands. She had close-cropped sandy hair, a young maid in her teens. One with short legs and budding hips, making quick steps toward the north-facing, domed hall.

A big place, thought Vetra. A conservatory of sorts? A place that held a small student body and fighting force? Self-contained, independent? Perhaps a cover for the tyrannical reach of the head sorceress? Every cell in Vetra's body told him this was likely so. His mind churned over the possibilities, likewise how the situation could be handled. The gate was well guarded, the courtyard occupied and friend Skirl would have a hard time getting past the watchmen. The apprentice had been overly optimistic. Perhaps a change of plans was necessary? Skirl had lived and worked here for several months. Basic logic would dictate he'd have considered all this before boasting that he could gain entrance on his own. A conundrum that Vetra himself couldn't answer. He sank deeper into doubt.

Grindar led them through an archway into a private, enclosed court. Shaded porticos rose on either side. At the center to the back, a marble fountain tinkled into a small pool. Snub-nosed goldfish lazed in the water. To the right grew a garden of shrubs and flowers. Most disturbing was the squat gargoyleish statue by the pool, a great ugly brownstone mass with scaled wings tilted in flight, hideous bat face, glaring eyes, ratlike teeth and enormous peaked ears. The statue guarded the waters, where incongruously someone had thrown a few rusty coins.

"Wait here," Grindar instructed. He left, tipped his massive head under a low archway and disappeared into the cool darkness beyond.

While they waited, Vetra prowled the perimeter. Nog was content to study the fish.

So, a secluded garden courtyard... Beds of flowering myrtle, rose bushes and faint scent of myrrh in the air. Very pleasant, but all tainted with an unspoken tension...no less, the gruesome and grimacing statue. What was the purpose of this grotesque symbol of the underworld that looked so out of place? In Vetra's mind, one that should be blasted to ruin? The sun slanted down between lazy clouds warming his helm. He rubbed his cheek. He wondered how nuanced Nog's playacting would be during this interlude. No doubt their easy entry was an audition. They may be testing them right now: silent watchers gazing from the darkened, upper windows.

Nog and he traded uneasy glances. All was quiet in the court but for the tinkle of waters and the soft rustle of morning breeze through the fragrant shrubs.

"So far, so good," Nog said. "Everything going to plan, Vet."

Vetra cast him a distant nod. "Let's keep it that way, Nog.

Just follow the script."

Nog made an easy gesture. "No worries, Vet. I have everything under control."

Vetra's lip curled and gave way to a scowl. "That's what I'm afraid of."

Bootfall echoed from the arched doorway. Within moments Grindar returned with another man just as big. He was unsmiling, lumbering and rangy and curled fingers gripped the pommel of his broadsword that hung from jeweled scabbard past hips and greaves.

Vetra turned to the sound of a husky voice to the side. "Gentlemen." A familiar feline figure sashayed in at them from a side archway. She tipped her head in brief acknowledgment. With an exaggerated and brazen swing of hips she strode past the two guards and came to a halt before them. A blazing heat radiated from her body.

"Lady." Vetra and Nog dipped their heads in unison.

She wore a skin-tight black leather gown with a silver tiara which held the chestnut sweep of shoulder-length hair. Her oiled cheeks were powdered with the faintest rouge. Dark kohl accentuated the mocking mystery of her gaze. Brass cups adorned her perfectly-sculpted breasts. Her bare forearms, brow and neck were oiled and gleaming to perfection.

Even more striking was this she-panther in the flesh than at a distance in the chaos of the market.

The Archmagrix waved an uplifted, jewel-fingered hand. "I hear you are seeking employment in my conservatory."

Vetra gave a swift nod. He could not help his eyes straying from the supple thighs and camel-toe crotch to the disturbing statue staring out from before the pool, guarding the precincts like a scavenging basilisk. The black glaring eyes seemed to follow him wherever he went; the ratlike teeth threatening to champ at his limbs like a living fiend.

Taranis saw where he was looking and gave a brief chuckle. "Do you like Besemooth?"

"He is charming," Vetra said. "A regular Sarkala's bane."

"Isn't he? He is—" Her eyes clouded and suddenly grew chill at the name. "Sarkala? Where did you hear that name?" she demanded.

Vetra licked his lips. He wished he had not spoken. "I am not unfamiliar with lore," he recovered, knowing full well the name of the sorceress priest had been dropped by Skirl.

"There is more to you than meets the eye," she mused. Her red ruby lips curled once more into a playful cast. "The statue is a likeness of the one who is the winged messenger of Dal Sagoth, the Elder God. I recently had the statue moved here— from a distant ruin our students were excavating at Cuiros. Not far from Mmos on the sea. The god was transplanted in this garden to commemorate the darker arts and their implications. See how Besemooth's ears peak like an attentive hound's? As if waiting for his master's command…and the wings, so far outspread! Ready to carry him off and deliver a dark message across kingdoms on the whim of a god."

"A fascinating history," Vetra murmured, "and I'm sure you will regale us with more later but—"

She cut him off with a curt wave of her hand. She seemed pleased with Vetra's reaction, as if it were part of her plan to unnerve them. Nog only seemed to give the statue brief notice. His eyes were glued to the vivacious figure of the black-clad sorceress who flaunted herself before them.

Vetra glanced over at the ruthless face of the captain of the guards. The same mean-ass mongrel who had helped carve off Skirl's ear. Whose ear would be next?

For a moment, the two appraised each other, each reading

the other's thoughts. Somewhere in all this interplay, they divined there would be a clash of arms.

Taranis moved in closer to Vetra, so close he could feel the animal heat of her. "You seem sturdy and quick, mercenary, and carry good weaponry. Judging from the cast of your sword and its silver guard, I wonder where you hark from? What are your qualifications?"

She came up behind him and traced a slinky finger along the edge of his shoulder then down to waist in a flirtatious, if not provocative way.

Vetra did not like that touch. There was a hint of snakes about it, cold and sinister.

"Well built...handsome, in a rugged, no-nonsense way," she said.

She circled him the other way as his head turned. "You do not answer me, mercenary? Has the cat robbed you of your tongue? Where did you learn to fight? The Umbrian army?"

"No," Vetra rumbled. "My father's school in Tolizia. He was a harsh taskmaster. We had a riding school there where he trained swordsmen and bred destriers."

"Oh?"

"I was on the road to becoming an elite defender myself. He wanted me to fight for the Royal Guard in Vulfryn. I despise all those powdered nobles and refused. I objected to the fatebringing he proposed for me. We clashed. A vicious argument led to blows. I finally fled my homeland, journeyed east by foot, where I trained under three sword masters, the first, the mad hackman Lu Zu in Mosete. He lived in a tree and ate only papayas."

She let out a snorting laugh. "Very droll, swordsman. How do I know you are not feeding me a bunch of malarkey?"

He shrugged. "You don't."

For a second her gray-green eyes flashed, perhaps taking the remark as an insult. Then her gaze veered on Nog. "What about you?"

"A boring story. Look to Vetra, he's the one with the history, not little old Nog."

She gave an impatient mutter. "Enough evasions. Why come here and appeal to the Order of Mages? You two would do better with jobs as bounty hunters or swords-for-hire at some rough outpost in the hinterlands, as suits your looks."

"I remember your quick punishment of the feckless wretch at the market. He deserved the gallows' rope but got only a cleft ear. We figured it would be less tasking to our hides serving the mages of Dormoth than cleaving heads on the frontiers."

She seemed pleased with the logic and his denigration of the renegade apprentice.

"Can you two fight?"

"We would not be here if we couldn't."

A flash of eyes and a brief tug on her left earlobe had Grindar leaping forth with blinding speed. His mailed bulk hit Vetra like a battering ram. He was smashed sideways. Grindar's blade flashed in his hand and there came an attack as furious and merciless as Vetra had ever faced. Like a well-trained assassin or the deadly assault of a wolverine.

Vetra's sword was in his hand, parrying death. Steel rang left, right, backhand, overhead with Grindar's intent to beat down Vetra before he could lay a single stroke.

Vetra had no shield. He must rely on pure footwork and clever parrying. He dodged back, giving himself enough room, parrying skillfully. All too aware he must allocate his energies optimally if he were to defeat this foe and not get spitted and bleed out before this sultry sorceress. But he could feel his lungs already working, his arms beginning to feel the shock of

Grindar's hammer blows on his Sahirian blade. Grindar's blade was half a foot longer and probably three pounds heavier, and he had no doubt the bigger man was his better in terms of strength.

But speed? Vetra gave a cursing laugh. Never.

The captain's attack was iron savage, though he lacked a certain finesse that should have ended this fight moments ago. Somehow it was all by rote. Hammer blows, grunts, cuts and parries.

Vetra, responding in kind, parried his steel and followed all the standard sword moves, feeling the ruffian out, noting Grindar was always a step ahead of these practiced maneuvers, as if anticipating such rehearsed moves. This was good. But it was uncanny. An odd mix of luck, technical skill and brawn that had Vetra for a time hard pressed to keep him at bay.

Grindar spat and laughed at Vetra in glottal mockery. "That all you got, mercenary? You'd be dead in a whore's breath in a real fight! You'll never work at Dormoth. I'm only toying with you!"

Vetra's lips curled. There radiated a pompous arrogance about this man, also some shame in his own performance, for there was truth in the captain's words. If shock and awe and number of strikes were what kept score then he was losing. He tried to convince himself that he'd underestimated this captain of war, that he'd been unprepared for his lightning attack and that he'd not be paying for it in the end, but he could not kid himself.

Grindar grinned, seeing he'd struck a nerve. Doubtless a psychological trick he'd pulled a thousand times on lesser men. He advanced, pushing Vetra back and back until his mail coat was nearly flush to the statue. A quick glance behind and Vetra could almost feel the thing's evil breath on his cheek. *Dergath's hell*…if such thing were living it would freeze the blood of the living dead.

A stone or chip turned under Vetra's heel. He felt himself slipping as his weight shifted from under him. What? This was unnatural, as if something had hexed him. He caught for a moment the cold lazy grin of mischief on the sorceress's face and the sardonic twinkle in her eyes…as if she'd been hatching a spell.

Nog saw it too.

In a blinding spurt of speed, the scar-faced mercenary's twin blades sang forth and his throat rang with a fierce cry.

His three-foot blades scissored overtop Vetra's head and caught Grindar's descending sword and a clangor of tempests rocked the courtyard. It was a ringing blow that would have ended Vetra's life then and there, one that could be heard in the nearby octagonal courtyard.

Panting and gasping, Vetra crabbed back on his hindquarters. His first thought, an unkind one to himself, was that Grindar was the better swordsman. If not for Nog's razor-honed reflexes, he'd be an eye-staring corpse right now lying in a pool of his own blood.

It was a horrible feeling, shame. Vetra felt it worse than anyone. If he had a flaw it was that. Pride.

On a diminutive signal from Taranis, the remaining guard gave a cry and launched himself at Nog. Nog'd interfered with the sword fight and now he was there to fix it.

Such a stream of sword blows had not been seen in the garden for an age. There came a flurry of steel from the guard that would have rivaled Azlek of ancient Mercia. Nog's blades crossed out to block then unfurled in savagery to strike wicked arcs at the guard's head. He fought bent-kneed, in a pirate's crouch, as in the panther style of the Thrakian mercenaries. But he was as surprised as Vetra when he found himself pushed back to the farther wall.

Grindar now worked to the left on Vetra. Denied his win, he gave a feverish bellow and came chipping in with a vengeance, sword seeking any pocket of Vetra's flesh to end this fight swiftly.

Vetra stepped back, parrying calmly. He let his heartbeat slow. It was a skill he'd learned over the years, taught him by his old sword master Thorian, his belated teacher from Mosete, the Ring-gast.

Whose voice from the past now echoed in his ear, *The distracted warrior is dead, Vetra. Stay focused. Stay alive!*

CHRIS TURNER

Chapter 10

Vetra's breath was controlled, his mind alert and his senses focused. Beads of sweat pooled down the back of his spine. While the sorceress watched on, her eyes gleamed with a catlike expectancy of a waiting sphinx and Vetra felt the cold thrill of death tickle his back, like a reptilian specter lurking over his shoulder, ready to pounce.

Grindar bulled his way in. An impulsive and risky move. A bold and winning one too, if he could pull it off, were Vetra half the man he was. But he was more than half. His thews flexed. He ducked wide, avoiding an arching sweep and a certain beheading. Grindar's blade kept traveling and the sharp, gleaming tip struck the statue's ear off.

Taranis hissed air past her lips. "Fool!" she cried. "You're not fighting statues!"

But the Archmagrix's outburst had unnerved Grindar. He swatted at air for a moment as beads of sweat dripped into his eyes and Vetra slashed in a wild arc. Sword and steel clanked as Grindar's blade barely made it up in time to stop his strike. A twist of body and Vetra's elbow was in the captain's face. His back leg tucked under Grindar's knee and with a wicked shove, he sent the captain tumbling back on the paves.

The mercenary hovered over him like a wraith. He shoved the tip of his blade at the crook of Grindar's neck. "You yield?"

"I yield, damn you!" Grindar rasped, shaking with rage. Vetra withdrew the blade. The captain scrambled to his feet, blasphemous curses on his lips.

From across the court came a clink of steel. Then a painful cry. Nog's twin blades hovered high in a murderous clench ready to shear off the man's arm as he lay sprawled on the cobbles. A bloody gash marked Nog's left cheek. A look of madness was in his eyes.

His blades whooshed down to take off the man's arm, but Taranis pushed forth palms. A vague pulse seemed to snap at the air. In one swift movement, there came a blue-purple globe that hurtled toward Nog's chest. The semi-transparent missile struck his chest and sent him reeling back and his swords clattering to the ground.

"Enough!" she cried. "This was to be a test! Not a full out bloodletting!"

"Seems as if you thrive on the sight of blood!" Vetra growled.

"You are not mistaken."

The man sprawled before Nog was lurching to his feet. Sword in hand, he was bent on skewering Nog.

Vetra moved faster. Like a cat, he sprinted in and smashed his boot into the man's face, sending him flying back along with two of his front teeth. Vetra brought back his sword, ready to despatch him.

But Taranis gave a shrill cry and gesture before Vetra could drive the sword tip through the man's brain. "Hold up!"

Nog sneered, shaking the daze out of his head. "The fight was rigged!" He cast her a baleful glance. Vetra, he graced a nod of gratitude. Gathering up his blades, he looked on in disgust at his bloodied adversary. The man still groaned on the cobblestones. He tore a strip off the hem of his undershirt and stuffed it under his helm as a crude bandage. All the while he kept an eye on his defeated opponent.

Taranis stood squared before Vetra. "I just wished to preserve good fighting men." She stared at her desecrated statue, fingers tipped to lip, as if in deep reflection. "A strange synchronicity here. One man wins, one man loses. Vetra clearly the loser, the famous swordster, with a veiled pride higher than a mage's tower… yet he seems to have a guardian angel hovering at his back ready to die for him."

"There's no such thing as guardian angels," he sneered. "Fate and the gods are all crocks of shit."

"A heretic?" she crowed. "I'll have you a believer before the night's over."

"You think? Like your two dogs here?"

"Sword fights are like cards overturned on a tarot deck," she lectured enigmatically. Her brows rose. Her eyes took on a dreamy cast. "This pantomime today—it is enough to stymie the most astute tarot reader." She gave an uneasy laugh. She cast a moody gaze at her shorn statue. "An omen, and a desecration, which the captain must answer for."

Grindar hung his head. He was unable to meet her eye, and unwilling.

Vetra wiped his mouth and frowned. He liked not this truckling and pandering to this sorceress. Was she a deity that everyone must bow to?

She swung her inscrutable gaze upon his truculent stance, then Nog with the blood-dripping face, as if pondering whether to kill them outright.

Then she smiled. Her cat-like ease was back. The spring and lithe immediacy of a seductive monarch working in full form. "Well fought, gentlemen. Welcome to Dormoth!" Like a royal courtesan she sashayed over to each of them, gave them both sensuous kisses on the lips and a full embrace.

Vetra tottered slightly backward, immediately struck by the woman's sexual magnetism. Nog stood frozen, his square jaw hanging agape. His tongue lolled like a lovestruck schoolboy.

Taranis licked her lips clean of Nog's blood. She smiled. "Now, to business."

Chapter 11

Vetra was not overly pleased with the way things had turned out. Yes, they'd survived the audition, but they both'd almost got their throats cut. Unless Vetra missed his guess, Taranis was a woman who got a kick out of men scrambling about bloodying themselves, while she wasn't shearing off the ears of those who irked her. Cordiality would always be the operative word during this mission. He would trust this she-vamp no more than he would a grass adder.

Taranis gestured. "We run a tight ship here, gentlemen. A school for young talent to develop their skills. A place our practicing mages can explore their craft and build on the wisdom of their forebears. It is for the security of Umbria that we offer this service and not for our own ends."

Vetra could barely refrain a sardonic laugh. Really? The vindictive, ear-shearing she-mage, a philanthropist? A protector of the realm and the common interest of her citizens? Hardly.

"No shenanigans here," she said. "No roughhousing, no abusing of the women of the compound. If you see anything suspicious, you report it. Including aberrant or unseemly behavior, unfamiliar or unauthorized persons. You understand?"

"Clear as a bell, your Excellency." Nog saluted, two fingers at his brow.

Her lips curled in a scowl. "Wipe that snigger off your face, mercenary. This is serious business here."

Vetra gave him a nudge hard in the ribs. "Nog had a bit of a rough night with some mettlesome maids and a cask of ale."

A husky murmur rumbled in Taranis's throat. "There'll be no consorting with harlots here at Dormoth," she warned. "I can see that's a regular pastime of yours. Drink is strictly regulated: a dram of wine and a half flagon of ale per evening, no more."

"What is this, a nuns' convent?" Nog cried.

"It's a place where we adhere to strict discipline. Punishments are meted out accordingly for breach of conduct to maintain our integrity. To both guards and apprentices."

Vetra heeled Nog in the talus and passed his mouth close to his ear. *"Don't push it. You trying to blow our cover? Keep your mouth shut."*

Nog gave a sullen grunt.

Taranis made a lithe movement. "Keep a watch on your dog here, Vetra. He seems the least sensible of you two." She swung her gaze back on her captain. "Outfit them, Grindar. See them to the barracks. Clean up that reverse thrust of yours too. Today it was a bit slipshod."

"Yes, my Lady." His teeth clenched with a sullen sheepishness that Vetra did not miss.

She turned on her heel and disappeared through the archway from where she'd come.

Grindar glared at Vetra and Nog as his henchman slunk off to deal with his bloody teeth. "I'd slay both you here now if the Archmagrix wouldn't skin my hide first. You'll stay in the barracks with the others. Cleanliness and etiquette is our watchword. Slobs and boors will not be tolerated. Pay attention—particularly you, Nog. Slobs'll be beaten. You are part of the Knights Mondalar. The wage is two silver crowns per week. Training maneuvers progress from 4 to 6. Dinner in the Guards' Hall at 7. Got it? Can you ride?"

Vetra masked a grin. He'd been riding horses since he was six. "I can manage."

"What about you?" His hard eyes swung on Nog.

"I know a black one from a brown one."

"Well, you'll be put on training detail bright and early in the morning. Six bells."

"Why not 5?" Nog suggested. "I'll be all ready and saddled."

"Is that being a bit smartass?"

Nog gave an impudent shrug. It did nothing to alleviate the captain's resentment of him.

Grindar led them out of the garden back into the main courtyard. His boots clopped noisily down the colonnaded walkway parallel to the main court. He motioned to the nearest gold-chased dome which caught the bright glare of morning sunlight. "That is the Hall of Wands. You'll not need to go there. To the south, are the Hall of Mages, to the east the Hall of Winds, to the north the Hall of Mystery. You'll become familiar with all the Halls as the days pass."

He led them down a stairwell into the outfitter's room, a miniature armory cut into the stone. It was unadorned, permeated with dampness. Weapons, helms and various gear hung on hooks, including crooked staves, polearms and maces.

The captain plucked one of the helms down and thrust it into Nog's hand.

Nog stared at the plumed morion with wonder. "I'll pass."

"You?" He thrust one at Vetra.

"My helm's fine."

"Suit yourself. But the surcoats are mandatory. We need to be able to recognize our guards from enemies should it come to a skirmish."

"Understandable," Vetra said.

Nog and he withdrew coats of appropriate size and slipped them over their mail. They had the Dormoth Mage's emblem of red dragon and yellow eagle on the front. Both were of good quality, the wool trailing just past waist.

"Do you have a mirror?" Nog asked, batting his eyes while peering over his shoulder.

Grindar gave a curt grunt. "This way, clown. The dining hall's across the hall. Supper at seven…and ends at seven thirty. If you miss the window, too bad. You go hungry for the night."

The irascible man had given them only the briefest tour and the most hurried one. He seemed eager to secure them cots at the barracks then hand them over to one of his underlings to see them to their posts rather than waste time coddling them himself. He sped off down the shadowed hallway to the barracks, but Nog lagged and stared through an open arched doorway.

"Over here, ape face," Grindar called back at him. "Barracks are this way."

Nog paid him no heed. He stumbled in, jaw agape, on curious feet to wander about the sunlit Hall of Mages, much to Grindar's dismay.

The captain strode after him and Vetra was on his heels, a grin pasted on his lips.

Vetra's eyes widened at the grandeur of the place. Crusted jewels banded the upper rim of the cavernous dome: carnelian, rubies, emeralds, rare crystals. Many magical creatures etched in soft, colored stones were depicted on the high dome, itself like a hallowed chapel—of dragons, mages, trolls, witches, crowns, wands, swords. There soared a pantheon of battle scenes. A slain wild boar with hunter tipping a chalice to members of the hunt; a wizard with yellow conical cap tapping a wand on his apprentice's shoulder; a fierce dragon swooping low over a castle, razing it to the ground with tail and fiery breath. Each scene told what Vetra guessed was an epic story of the myths of the lands far and wide. Below the crusted gems, ran a band of high engraved runes. The symbols circled the hall, citing the stories and parables of the heroes of old, in some forgotten tongue. Two stained-glass windows faced the court. These were crafted in the shape of two mighty dragons, from which filtered rainbow hues—blue, red, green and yellow. Dozens of sconces and candles lit what otherwise would have been a gloomy hall, but for the double doors that were thrown wide open, admitting light from the courtyard.

"Nog!" Grindar called. "This way please." His voice echoed across the marble floor.

Nog was not listening. He was more interested in the figures huddled to the side, particularly the slinky Taranis who was bent over, offering one of the young apprentices assistance with a wand. Eight of them gathered in various garbs of robes, hats and wands while two of the older mages stood by, arms crossed on their chests. One was snowy-haired and hunched in an old brown monk's robe, the other was tall and saturnine in midnight black with a cadaverous face and hollow cheeks. Taranis gave the young apprentice they'd seen earlier in the blue robe a caress on the cheek and a wink. Then a husky laugh as she let one of the bluish-purplish globes drift up to the domed ceiling.

The apprentices cooed and cawed. They waved their hands, flapped their wands. The sorceress materialized another globe from her agile fingers. One of the other apprentices seemed hopeful of snagging the Archmagrix's attention. He made a fancy leap up to grab the globe, as a dutiful hound might bring a thrown stick back to its master. The youth fell back with a shriek. What seemed to be a lightning-like tinge had charred his fingers. He rolled on the marble floor, groaning in anguish.

Taranis seemed unmoved by the accident. She did not offer assistance. Instead she muttered under her breath. "Fool." She did a strange leap in the air to catch the transparent globe, catapulting herself catlike six feet up, before it could do any more damage.

The other apprentices took deep breaths. The two mages watched like owls.

"Harpies Horrors! Did you see that?" Nog grunted. His eyes widened into pools. He nudged Vetra. "Imagine her snug in bed showing you a trick like that?"

"Are you insane?"

"What's that, soldier?" Grindar rasped, striding over.

"Play the dumpling, you fool," Vetra hissed at him. "Remember the plan."

"I asked you a question, mercenary," Grindar bawled.

"I heard you, Cappy," said Nog. "When you start saying something worth listening to, maybe I'll answer."

The captain's face reddened. "You and I are going to get into some skull-bashing before the day's done."

"I'm shaking in my boots," Nog jeered. He pushed thumbs in his ears and twiddled his fingers.

Vetra hissed at him. "Don't antagonize the rascal."

A man-at-arms strode up to give Grindar instructions. It distracted the captain from further violence. It seemed reinforcements were scheduled to arrive on the morrow at sundown from King Grinas's garrison. Grindar and he talked for a while in low murmurs, leaving Vetra and Nog to their discussion.

Nog was still staring at Taranis's body as if the wench was all he could think of.

"Dergath, man!" Vetra muttered. "You're like a lank hound chasing a bitch's scent. Get over it. Get with the program. She almost got a yard of steel shoved into your guts, remember?"

"I know, Vetra, it's messed up," Nog said, flush-faced. "But it's like I can't get the wench out of my mind. What I wouldn't give to hop in the sack with that luscious—"

"Why, when you can have any of those ugly mutts down at the *Rat Peacock*? Cheaper and less chance of getting your throat cut."

Grindar turned their way and pushed irascibly in between them. "Talking to yourselves again?"

Vetra cast him a chill smile. "I was just commenting to Nog how fortunate we are to be in such venerated company in a hallowed hall. With local men of such high repute. The view is extraordinary from here. The inlaid jewels, the lush art, the panoramic scenes, the—" he extended an arm which swept over to Taranis.

Nog grinned and mouthed the word, 'bedroom'.

Taranis clapped her hands, sending echoes around the hall. "Enough play, apprentices! Jemin has had his finger burned, but he will survive. I trust this is a lesson to all." She drew herself up to her full height.

She turned and scowled on sight of Grindar and the two new recruits. "Why aren't they at their posts?" she demanded.

"The big one," Grindar began, "snuck in while my back was turned."

"I don't want to hear your stupid excuses, Grindar." She stroked her chin, as if musing further. "Well, now that you are here, I may as well introduce you to our other mages. But first! I have called you all to this assembly to alert everyone to certain changes. Upon Skirl's insubordination, I have no choice but to enforce stricter security. No one enters or leaves Dormoth without my permission. All suspicious activities and movements are to be reported. No matter how innocuous or benign."

There were grumbles, but everyone agreed.

"I have requested more guards from King Grinas. A dozen will swell our numbers by tomorrow. This is important timing.

Five of our own guard will escort Yarne and Hodus to protect the archaeological caravan that travels to uncover more relics at Syrn. A goldmonger, my agent from the moneylenders' guild, has alerted me to recent discoveries when the new silver mine went up. I have no doubt Senesch, our elder mage, will wish to tag along and oversee the operation." She glanced inquiringly at the old man with the snowy white beard.

"I think you are correct," Senesch said with a serene nod.

Taranis looked on with approval. She lifted her hand to Vetra and Nog. "The resident mages, five of us in total, have their own workshops. Each of us is adept in a particular aspect of thaumaturgy. Senesch here is our eldest mage. A guardian of history and philosophy. He is a hundred and four years old. A loremaster." She gestured. "One cannot miss this long, white-haired gentlemen with the philosopher's face, grinning so astutely at Zena, our youngest and most attractive apprentice. His specialty is arcana of the magicians of the Third Age and the overall gamut of spellcraft. Once a powerful spellcaster himself, he considers himself now retired, and devotes himself to the esoteric study and classification of magic—and its unification into a cosmic whole. Whatever that means." She gave a facetious laugh. "Senesch's only mistake has been to take a traitorous thief named Skirl under his wing and dutifully scour the old tomes for lost tombs, relics and amulets."

Senesch pulled at his beard, "I'll remind you, Archmagrix, that the search bore fruit."

Taranis fidgeted with the stone on her neck hanging from its leather strap. "Yes, it is you and Skirl who discovered the Flame of Eros—in a forgotten tomb fifty leagues from here between the sea and the old acropolis of Nespion." Her fingers hooked into claws around the red-shining gem.

Senesch raised his brows in curiosity. "Does the stone make

you itch, Lady?"

"No, it is just functioning in an odd way—" she frowned and glared at the old man.

"You are always twiddling it like a child with a broken toy. It seems to have a hold on you."

Her eyes bored into Senesch shafts of ice. "Meaning? What is your interest in the gem?"

Senesch shrugged. "Nothing. Only that such things and objects of power are not without dark histories and have the tendency of corrupting human souls and bringing ruin to those around them."

"A pessimistic philosophy, Senesch. I'll say that as crude as that assertion may be, it is not without some truth. Please, let me continue my introductions."

"Proceed as you wish."

"Voydred over there, is a similar scholar, though more gloomy in temperament. He is a wanderer, thaumaturgist, and the closest to a warlock you will find in the lands. Do not look to Voydred for humor. He is dour. He specializes in incantations and pentagrams. Look to the tall, sallow-faced fellow beside Senesch, dressed in the black satin robes and the skull cap and you will see Voydred. Many have likened him to a black-robed heron on stilts."

Voydred did not appear to care for the joke. He muttered words under his breath from a language long dead and seeming unintelligible to Vetra's ear, lost as they were in the echoes of the hall. But all of a sudden the mage seemed to grow taller and an inexplicable wind entered the hall, tousling everyone's hair. A low moan came from the shadows and the keening cry of what might be witches, frightening the apprentices. The ghost of a smile touched the man's waxy, cadaverous lips. Taranis merely smiled.

"Keren is our resident beastmaster," she said. "There he is over there. His specialty is falcons and hawks. Look! Even now he tries to tame that feral goshawk and teach it not to gouge out his eyes on a bidden command."

Vetra peered off to the side and saw a short, beefy, ruddy-cheeked man garbed in a hunter's vest and peaked cap. He seemed of no determinate age with flat nose and large, slightly balding head. On his left shoulder a large falcon perched, staring serenely. On the other arm, a goshawk, wild and feral as the wind, clutched the leather grip with ever-tightening talons. It eyed the falcon aslant.

The beastmaster tipped his arm. He muttered a gloomy set of words and the bird took flight, sweeping up to the very dome of the ceiling then came swooping straight down at the mage.

The beastmaster did not flinch. Even though the hawk came within inches of his glaring eyes, the breath of wind from its wings only tousled his hair, flipped off his hunter's cap. The bird flattened out its dive inches from the beastmaster's staring eyes.

"Old Keren is a martinet," Taranis exclaimed idly. "It is said he can take the form of any bird, the best of birds, and fly to all corners of the lands. But he hides his magic and no one has seen him take the form of a beast for an age, though he speaks of events and things beyond the knowledge of men. Chiefly in the border kingdoms and faroff lands which none could know without a waft of sorcery.

"There are others. My cousin, Belgra. How could I forget her? There she is now, at last making an appearance to stand beside Voydred, our wandering thaumaturgist. Belgra is the closest to a master herbalist you will find." Her voice took on a mocking tone, a barbed resonance that Vetra did not miss. She flicked a hand toward an unsmiling blond woman who Vetra remembered from the market, still wearing her gardener's apron overtop her white woolen gown. "She dabbles in herb lore, potion-making and healing salves, the lowest of the thaumaturgical arts."

Why they were lower, Vetra did not know. He thought to ask, but stayed his tongue. He was more curious to hear Taranis's take on her cousin.

"She deals with plant medicine and nature lore and is a dear student of woodcraft. She reads the signs of the trees, the bend in the boughs, the cast of the leaves, the play of winds, skies and clouds. Her nickname is 'Skywatcher', though I find the title pretentious."

"And you, Lady? What is your specialty?" Vetra asked.

Bedroom. Nog mouthed the words, grinning.

Vetra gave him a hard nudge, though fighting to stifle a chuckle.

"You ask the most frank questions, mercenary. In reward for your bluntness, I will answer this: I encompass all. Whatever the mages of Dormoth come to know or attain, I siphon that power from them."

Vetra blinked. "A most fortunate skill, Lady. I commend you for your resource. While you hold the keys to the castle, binding all the power and talent of your peers to your will, you, as head of the Order, can capitalize."

She peered at him with a tang of coldness. "Is that a sarcastic remark?"

Vetra gave a faint smile. "You read too much into my words, Lady."

"Perhaps." She brushed a pale tongue over her lower lip. She drifted over to look at him with shrewd deliberation. Her penetrating, gray-green eyes did not hide their travel to his muscular thighs, his groin. She took Vetra aside.

"Since you express such 'astuteness' and interest in the subjects well beyond the ken of a layman, I invite you to our conclave this evening after dinner."

Vetra hesitated for only a brief instant before nodding.

"I am sure you will find it intriguing."

"I'm sure I will, Lady."

Nog was about to utter a cheeky comment but Vetra dug fingers into his shoulder. "Nog would like to attend too and he promises to be on his best behavior. Isn't that right, Nog?" He shafted him a meaningful glance which the mercenary seemed to heed for once.

While the dim afternoon light drifted in from casements tinted light purple from age, the score of men from the Mage Guard sat at the long, scarred table in the Guards' Hall. Some ate their venison greedily, like trenchermen while others quaffed half flagons of ale frugally, occasionally glancing at the two new recruits and muttering the odd remark or uncomplimentary jest.

Vetra and Nog ignored them. The dusky plumes of their morions dipped as they tucked noses into stew and venison. Vetra could hear the scrape of a chair, the noisy mastication of meat. Not a lot of idle banter among these men, for hired guards with no women about. No doubt a result of Grindar's constant watchdogging and queen Taranis's tyrannical strictures hanging over their heads. He would be happy when this mission was over. A sentiment which Nog shared.

Though the venison was fine.

Chapter 12

The five mages of Dormoth sat on grand chairs in a rough semicircle. These were heavy, ornate seats like thrones of carven oak in the high-domed Hall of the Mages. Taranis sat in the middle upon a larger, more elevated seat to emphasize her status. They all wore ceremonial robes and heavy ornate rings and medallions and charms on necks, wrists and fingers, as was the custom of their ilk. Per usual, Taranis wore the sapphire jewel round her neck. It gleamed like a sinister beacon, announcing its presence to all. It hung on a leather thong, heralding her championship of the Eros Flame.

Nog and Vetra shifted from foot to foot at the back of the hall. Grindar stood, feet planted beside them, indifferent to the mages and their ceremony. His eyes were lazy but watchful, his enormous broadsword slung loosely at his back.

The flickering candlelight lit the crusted jewels, adding rainbow hues to the hall. The band of engraved runes glared with an ancient power of their own.

Across from where Vetra stood, the heavy brass double door adjoining the inner courtyard was barred and bolted. The only other exit lay at their backs through which Vetra and Nog had entered the Hall of Mages under Grindar's command. This exitway led out to a corridor that branched into various other areas of the complex, the main branch which ran parallel to the octagonal courtyard.

A gnarled hand lifted from the man seated to the left of Taranis. Senesch. "Why are they here?" he demanded.

"Because I asked them. They are new additions to my Mage guard detail. As a reward for their besting my two best captains in a sword fight, I thought to give them an insiders' view of our council. Vetra, as you recall, is the one to the left. He seems to know a thing or two about thauma-history and lore, also, to have a good head on his shoulders."

"Really?" snorted the blond woman, Belgra at Taranis's other side. "More like another concubine for your bed?"

Taranis brushed her cousin a cool stare. "And are you jealous, cousin?"

"Hold off," Voydred intoned. He gestured idly, shaking his head. His dark, saturnine orbs of eyes peered curiously at Vetra. "You claim astuteness in the thauma-arts? Where do you hark from?"

"Tolizia."

"Many magicians have come from that land—a stormy, moody place, faraway to the east. So who is the most renowned sorcerer of old from the 5th age of Tolizia?"

Vetra held up a hand. "Alas, lord, I am no bibliophile or history adept. I only know from the priests of the old tabernacle of Sot, who mumble prayers before candle-lit altars, that they laud Nerut of Tosthumus. He is spoken of in the apocrypha written on lambskin papyrus."

"You would be correct in that... And you subscribe to what teachings?"

"My views are syncretic, lord. I merely observe the world around me. I make deductions based on what my eyes and ears see."

Senesch nodded thoughtfully. "That is a wise response, mercenary. I see why Taranis holds you in high esteem."

"Can we cut the chatter?" Keren griped. "We have things to do." He waved an impatient hand. "My falcon has sprained a wing. She dove too fiercely upon Elgrex, my goshawk, and now is in pain."

"You and your birds can wait," Taranis said curtly. "I have called this meeting for various reasons. As you all know, the

Wizard's Exhibition is upcoming on the Eve of Valgon. The Time of the Whispering Winds. This year they will be held at Alantra."

"Yes, we know that, Archmagrix," the tall, thin man Voydred said with annoyance. "It is common knowledge. Do you wish to beat your breast about it? How we will win it with flying colors under your tutelage? I daresay we won't. We are too few. Our powers are too weak."

Taranis spat a mage's oath. "I hold the Eros Flame!" She jumped from her seat. "You are one of the last-living, old-school spellcasters, Voydred. Senesch is wise beyond his years. He has studied more tomes than can fill the Linderlore library. Keren is beastmaster of renown. He has traveled the far kingdoms and talked with the Weremarks of Kyldrie, the—"

"One jewel," interrupted Senesch, "and a few over-the-hill mages are not going to match the might of all the wizards of the Eight Kingdoms."

"I have to agree with that," Voydred said.

Keren gave his own grunt of acknowledgment. He stroked the feathers of his goshawk perched on his shoulder. "A traveling beastmaster or not, I find your vision overly ambitious, Taranis."

Senesch gave an affected sigh. "I'm not one for pomp and ceremony, Archmagrix. More important is another excursion to the ruins of Gotha, where our ex-apprentice Skirl discovered your talisman before he was excommunicated. The project is a worthy one. I think that is the only one I can fully support at this time."

Taranis sneered. "You're all a bunch of pusillanimous lack-wits. It seems you have all already given up before you have started."

"Nay, Archmagrix!" stormed Voydred. He slumped back in

his seat. "We are merely fatigued and practical."

Taranis stamped her foot. "I shall not be daunted. I mean us to be well represented at the exposé. It is an important event, a hallmark milestone, so it is for this reason I call these weekly gatherings. That we can share our resources and help encourage each other to strive for better, more puissant magic. The judges are the kings and queens of the realms—King Xilos of Mercia, Lord Ragnum of Lvendar, Queen Barbassa in Galashad, to name a few. If we win this exhibition, or at least score high enough, we can expect the royals' patronage in the exploration of our spellcraft dominance in the future. It is a boon which cannot be overestimated. We'll put Xalgossa back on the map! As an ancient seat of power, where she once was and where she belongs!" In her slender fingers, she twiddled the amulet around her neck such that its reflected light angled in each one of the mages' eyes. And yet it did not herald the same adulation or luster as it once had, judging by the amount of scowling and murmuring therein.

"A nice speech, cousin," Belgra intoned jeeringly. "What are your real motives? To seduce as many nobles as you can once you get your cheap ass in there?"

Taranis quirked an eyebrow. "You are as suspicious as a paladin badger. What eats you? Did your dainty day lilies die? Did the deer trample your precious begonias? Horse-weeds choke out your secret garden? I was chosen as Archmagrix, you were bypassed. All here know the fact. It is no secret you hold a grudge against me when your closet lover, the apprentice Skirl, turned cuckold and seduced me instead of you. I can understand your bitterness."

Belgra's face turned red. It was not as if she could deny what Taranis said.

Taranis gave her a patronizing smile. "Go ahead. Show us

what miracles of herb and plant you've discovered this week." She spoke not without three degrees of mockery.

Belgra smoothed out her dirt-stained gardener's apron still wrapped around her waist. "I have only this to share, cousin. 'Tis what I call the *Star Ruby*. Cultivated in my own 'secret' garden."

From her satchel, she withdrew an odd flower with drooping rosy head. "What looks a simple sunflower is one graced with mystique and mystery. Watch!" She blew a soft breath on its rosy petals. She murmured some words to it in an odd tongue while tapping away at the drooping head with a gray wand.

Instantly the flower began to bloom into a taller sunflower that came rustling out of her grip. The stem rose, the stalk extended, as if given fresh life by rain and sunlight. The petals opened in a wild rush. The central bud pulsed with a strange fervor, then came a humming sound and a murmur in the air as of a swarm of bees.

All looked around the hall, but there were no bees. From its effulgent, vital bulb emerged a magnificent silver-backed hummingbird which hovered for some time before the mages then rose higher to survey the hall.

Belgra's face glowed. The hummingbird dropped lower to linger before the nose of each mage, to greet them with formal courtesy.

Taranis swatted her visitor away. "Very pretty, cousin. But of what utility is such a toy-like oddity? A flower that births quaint birdlings? Pah!"

Belgra's face fell and her lip quivered. "Can't you see, cousin? 'Tis only the beginning. This bird demonstrates the transmutation of one species to another! It suggests a whole new branch of magic! If I can unlock the secret, I can..."

Taranis held up a hand. "Spare us your fantasies, Belgra. If you had produced a war-bred condor that could fire bolts of flame from its eyes, I would perhaps be a little more interested."

"Always scheming," Belgra hissed. "Always dreaming up new ways to harm people and maim. Any form of megalocracy to fuel your incessant power-mongering."

"Is that a new word, megalocracy?" She gave a mocking chuckle. "How can you claim that I am a 'warmonger' when I wield an amulet that casts only love and admiration in the viewer?"

"Because—" Belgra clicked her tongue "—it is something quite far from that."

"Let us not bicker," Keren said. "We are all friends here. United in a common goal."

"Of what?" Voydred grunted. "At times I begin to wonder."

Taranis gave a sullen shrug. "What can I say? Biggest wolf gets the choicest meat."

Senesch intervened. "The feat is unique, Belgra, and you are to be commended. Despite Taranis's criticism, it is an accomplishment to be written about in the spell tomes. In all my years of poring over magical scholarly works I have never heard of such a spell. While not earth-shattering, it shall surely turn a few heads at the exposé during the competition of wizards." He gave a brief pause and frowned. "I have had some revelations of my own to share among the gathering—"

But his words were cut off by a fluttering of wings. The hummingbird, which had floated too near Keren's goshawk, gave a frantic chirp. In its inbred feral instinct, the goshawk gave a shrill, savage screech. Up it flew to sink talons into the hummingbird, unheeding of Keren's shrill commands. Down jabbed the goshawk's beak in its side to tear bird flesh from its victim's defenseless hide.

Belgra gave a cry of dismay. "Stop your bird of prey, Keren! It is devouring my hummingbird!"

Keren muttered commands at the disobedient bird, to no avail. "It is too late." He shook a fist. "Your bird is good as dead."

With a whimsical gesture another sinister globe appeared in Taranis's glowing palms. She lobbed it on high where it engulfed the goshawk and its prey, encaging both in a transparent prison. The globe floated down to halt before all, eight feet in the air.

Taranis tilted her head back and gave an exultant cry. "Carved in living light, cousin! Framed like a picture. A gruesome snapshot of mother nature at work."

"Save him!" Belgra pleaded. Defeat loomed heavily on her pale face. She was unable to watch the ghastly sight and turned her head. Nor could she stand to listen to the savage squawking and carnage.

"There is no saving your bird, cousin. 'Tis the law of the jungle. Big fish eats little fish. As the goshawk flies, so it feeds." This Taranis spoke even as Keren's bird of prey tore Belgra's hummingbird to pieces.

"This spectacle gives me an idea," she mused. She rose up to her full height and cried, "Watch!"

Her arms lifted. They manifested a giant ball of blurry wonder. Swirling within the ball were the chaos of distant galaxies, forming and reforming. Magical clouds of dusts and planets swirling amid myriad stars.

The eyes of the mages stared up in wonder. The globe floated up, magically, miraculously to reform into something hideous, something unnatural.

"Picture it!" she brayed. "A strange magical plant gives

birth to new life. Feral falcon gets jealous. He attacks the bird, angry as it steals all the attention. Another scavenger flies to intercept, wanting a piece of the action itself, smiting the falcon. The jealous master of the falcon, resenting its death, manifests and unleashes a demon. The creators of both beasts, join the drama of their creations, just as the gods are wont to meddle in the drama of mortals. There ensues a full blown mage war!— Keren, me, Voydred and Belgra. We launch fire bombs and beasts at each another. There is an epic battle!—it showcases our talents. Only one survives. Can you see the artfulness, the beauty?"

There came blank stares.

"It strikes all the emotional archetypes of the human psyche!" she cried. "'Tis brilliant. Epic. We cannot fail!"

Voydred spoke after a time. "Aye, you are quite the macabre genius, but you are most definitely mad."

"Mad you say?" the sorceress rasped. "This is mad." The globe grew bigger, darker, pulsing with an eerie light. From within, the ghastly blueish ball morphed into a basilisk-like monster—half gargoyle, half bat in the likeness of Besemooth, Dal Sagoth's messenger carved in living stone in the nearby garden. And yet it was still in its birth, a youngling, not much larger than the goshawk.

"I too have been practicing my arts of transmutation. If you will not participate in my exhibition, then let us play pattycake in a drama right here!"

"What are you raving about?" Voydred cried in a hoarse voice. "The Hall of Mages is not a forum for summoning demons. 'Tis sacred grounds, for displays of benign magic and intellectual discussion."

"Don't you see?" Taranis implored. "This is the perfect tableaux to present at the exhibition. To showcase our talents and entertain the judges. Macabre and unpredictable! Unique! Twists of violence, jealousy and gore."

Senesch mumbled, "'Tis the mark of a diseased imagination." His lips crinkled in a grimace.

Voydred grunted his agreement.

Taranis gave a resentful jeer. "And you, Belgra, what think you?"

"I cannot abide by violence to animals. It smacks of the same cruelty you unleashed on Skirl shearing off his ear. Call off your spook, cousin! Whatever you are brewing."

"I might have guessed," Taranis murmured. The Archmagrix spat an old oath. "You are a bunch of sissies. Goody-goody simpletons pretending to be mighty magickers but beneath, nothing more than lambs. The stuff of weaklings. Even you, Voydred—I am disappointed, one who I thought entertained an ounce of backbone in his body. You would have us all presenting little hummingbird fantasies, whispering and humming sweet little rhymes in the judges' ears. Pah! This is my answer to that."

She repeated an old ancient evil spell that even confounded the ear of Voydred. She channeled the might of Dal Sagoth.

"Garshrak mi an hia globan!"

The beast within the globe swirled and grew to a monstrous size. It widened and bulged into a giant of what it formerly was, a bat-bird, like the sinister gargoyle in the garden court.

The mages drew back, strangled gasps catching in their throats. They leaped from their seats in horror.

CHRIS TURNER

Chapter 13

Even Voydred was slow to mutter his ancient incantation. Harsh, guttural vocables spilled from his lips to counter the monster that peered evilly down upon them, *"Agrak Nor Sensum Auditus!"*

But it did nothing to penetrate the nimbus of power surrounding the demon. The flux of word-bombs only clattered harmlessly against the shield of energy surrounding it.

In fear and surprise, Voydred lifted a bony hand to summon an even more fell puissance.

To no avail. The pulse clattered against the shield of the monster's armor and rebounded off to strike at the band of jewels surrounding the hall. Several gems fell clattering to the marble floor.

Taranis's magic channeled from the dark well of Dal Sagoth, reigned supreme.

In a raucous voice, the mage uttered an even more terrible spell that must blast the invader to bits.

Taranis lofted another of her grisly globes which blocked the flux, absorbed it and sent it showering into a thousand sparks.

Vetra stared on in morbid fascination. The demon flapped wings and sprang on the beastmaster who had cursed it with a hex of the elder beasts.

The man gave a bewildered cry and ran, shielding his head with his hands as it threatened to tear off his head. Voydred had failed. Upon seeing the impotence of the mage's word-magic, surely more powerful than his own, Keren the beastmaster must wonder, what chance had he?

For the first time in witness, the beastmaster assumed the form of one of his own minions, the goshawk. Lips a-murmur, eyes closed, he became one with the goshawk, though one more massive, the size of a hulking condor.

The transformation prompted a rapturous cry from Taranis. This movement of magical energy seemed all part of her plan, as if in the blink of an eye she saw her vision manifested—how her four fellow mages could be part of her mad impromptu stage play. Something darker too—them being used as props and pawns to play their roles from this day evermore. Not only in her fabulous drama which would win them the contest of the Mages, but at Dormoth.

Eyes dilated, her husky breath panting in almost sexual ecstasy, Taranis stood tall, like a female titan. She was black-clad, leather knit, a black-hearted demiurge, awesome, terrible, beautiful, all at once, and yet absolute in her power. Even without the real amulet ringing her neck, the power of Dal Sagoth radiated from her pores like hot steam from lava.

"A gift of Dal Sagoth!" she cried. "He sends his wishes."

The monster flapped around the spellstruck hall, diving upon the mages. From its vile beak jetted a noxious gray fluid, dousing them with generous sprays, fetid to the senses, even as the creature vented shrill chitters.

Vetra cursed. He ran forth, his blade swinging. The gleam of its silver hue attracted the demon. It dove. With an ungodly chitter, it swept upon his head. Vetra's blade twanged hard on its beak, hard as horn. And yet it was not horn. His blade bounced off it as if it were a mass of luminous energy rather than living tissue. He blocked only in the nick of time as the talons came clutching for his face.

The quick move saved his life. The bat reared up and screeched. Midnight black wings flapped as its left claw dangled from an ugly stump.

No blood flowed from such a wound, for this creature was

not of the three dimensional world; it was of the sepulchral mists of Dal Sagoth's crypts.

Nog ducked, dodging a fang…then flailing claws that would have gouged trenches in his back. But the swipe knocked off his helm and stripped him of his bandage.

In undisguised glee, Taranis clenched her fists and howled. From foot to foot she danced as she watched the delight of her creation. "Marvelous, marvelous! More, more! I must record these scripts! These can be modified for the exhibition to create a show of horrors!"

The Hall tingled with madness. The hair stood on end on Vetra's scalp. Keren flapped in close, to hover in opposition to the demon. His hooked beak clacked open, ready to sink into the bat's neck. Beady, burnt-umber eyes stared forth from an ugly, bulbed head. Wattled skin hung from his neck like a turkey's.

On a sudden whim, Taranis stayed her bat-minion which hovered ten feet in the air, glaring at them all.

"I am Archmagrix. I call to see who is loyal! All who are for me, come forth. Stand at my side!"

She held her arms aloft, her thick chestnut mane whipped back. Her long black-painted nails beckoned. "All those who are against me, stand over there." She twitched a jeweled finger to an eerie circle of light that had manifested some twenty feet distant.

Her chest heaved. Her fingers clenched.

Belgra was first to move. In utter defiance she stood in the circle of light. Senesch broke the spell and with a tired, aged scowl, doddered his way over to stand beside Belgra. She smiled grimly and put her arm around the old man's shoulders, her lips firmed.

Voydred made jerky steps toward Senesch, but then

stopped with an odd curl of lip. He seemed unable to look his friend and mentor in the eye. He muttered an incoherent word then moved quickly to stand at Taranis's side. "I stand by our leader. Twenty moons ago we elected her Archmagrix of our Circle. I honor that pledge."

Senesch snarled in disgust.

Taranis's teeth glinted in the candlelight. There came a nod of vindication and a feral glow radiating from her cheeks.

An uncomfortable silence fell over the gathering; an awkward standoff tainted the hall.

Keren who had now alighted on claw-feet somewhere in the middle of the hall, shimmered back to his human form. Dazed and starry-eyed, he croaked in a rusty voice, "I cannot stand against both Voydred and Taranis. I ally with the Archmagrix." On shaky feet he moved to stand on Taranis's other side, but stayed out of reach of her outspread arm, as if it were the touch of a viper.

Grindar moved like an automaton toward Taranis and stood in front of the group, his back to the mages, sword upheld. Now there were four.

All eyes turned to Vetra and Nog, who stood transfixed under the shadow of the hovering bat-beast and the glare of its burning eyes.

Nog drew Vetra aside, his swords gripped, for once thinking twice before making an impulsive move.

But Vetra had no counsel to give him. A dry sour taste lingered in his throat. A dangerous situation presented itself. One slip and they would both end up dead.

In a calm voice he addressed those in the hall, "We are new to Dormoth. We are not interested in getting caught in the middle of any mage wars. We come only to guard Dormoth's walls against thieves and intruders. We choose to stand on neutral ground."

Taranis's eyes narrowed; she smiled. "Very well, mercenary, you can play the part of the cautious man."

Then, as it had all appeared, all came to an end. On a casual flick of hand, the bat-beast shimmered and dissolved into a thousand motes and disappeared. The hall was plunged into silence. Belgra and Voydred's arms relaxed at their sides. Keren's eyes blazed with a timeless rapture and a lack of memory of the somnambulist, as if he were still in a trance of his own making. The sinister globe faded into nothingness and released the goshawk. The bird flew free to land on Keren's shoulder. But Belgra's hummingbird was no more, nothing but feathers and gristle in the belly of the goshawk.

Taranis's ruby lips parted in a jaunty leer. "Friends! Let us put aside our squabbles. This was only theater. A rehearsal for our big show at the exhibition. What do you think? Are we not stars? Are we not heroes?" She laughed aloud. "We will go down in history!"

Vetra gave a cynical grunt. He did not trust her. Nor did the other mages. He did not miss Belgra's silent sneer, or the twitch of doubt on Senesch's lips.

Snakes and curses! The intrigue among this brood of vipers was thick enough to cut with a knife. The machinations of these mages was little to his liking. They all seemed to bear some grudge against each other, except maybe the old man who seemed the wisest of them all.

Taranis's eyes narrowed. Long jeweled fingers strayed to her talisman, twirling its facets so its reflected light beamed into the eyes of each of her peers. But nothing seemed to happen, at least to any visible effect.

"Must you always shine that silly bauble in our eyes, Lady?" grunted Senesch in annoyance. "The thing's magic is weak. My guess, tainted. Every good mage worth his salt knows that true power does not come from objects—it comes from within."

Taranis looked on him in cold disfavor "Pretty words, Senesch. Old school rhetoric pales in face of real power."

The old mage's eyes flashed with discontent. "It seems that you alone were selected leader of this esteemed Order. You are strong, fearless, even adept in some of the arts, particularly the dark arts, but you harbor an arrogant cruelty and sinister cunning in your actions. It follows the very steps you take, the air you breathe."

"Are you following in the jealous footsteps of Belgra here?"

"No," the old man replied haughtily. "But do not forget that you used to be one of us not long ago. You were at our level it seems but yesterday before you achieved this exalted status as Archmagrix, to replace Elgress our leader who mysteriously disappeared. All of this suddenly happened after the Eros Flame was uncovered. Skirl and I dug it up, under the death-shroud of Sarkala. I wish to Dergath we'd never found it!"

Taranis laughed. "And yet you persist in digging up more trinkets in the hinterlands. Ere the caravan rides out to Gotha once more, you would jump on it as nimble as a goat. You are a hopeless addict, Senesch. Admit it. A hypocrite no less."

The loremaster looked away. His age-cracked lips muttered something unintelligible. "I see Dal Sagoth has given you a clever, forked tongue as well, Lady Taranis, always beguiling the ear and spinning endless deflections and counterarguments to hide your basic evil and lack of morality."

"Boo hoo."

"This bickering is useless," snarled Voydred. "Let us reconvene with clear heads."

"Silence!" The old mage's jaw worked. "There are words

long overdue that must be spoken. I denounce Taranis. I call for a new leader."

"Who are you to request such a thing?" Taranis jeered. "What do you know, old man? You spew lofty ideals about good and evil that are but whiffs of vapor in face of hard reality. You speak words that have no play in the real tenets of power and spellcraft, the power of Dal Sagoth. I hear only pretty maxims that cater to feeble minds gulled by idiots' compassion and the watchwords and parables of the fading past."

"Perhaps, but there is a higher order to things which you seem oblivious of, where those things I speak about carry foremost weight."

"And what's that?"

"It's beyond this forum and conversation," Senesch intoned. But his brow clouded and his lips pursed in silence.

Taranis loosed a mocking breath. "You cannot even name it, can you? It is as I thought. All talk and no substance." She turned on her heel. "This meeting is over." She sauntered out, her chin high, her hips a-sway.

The other mages watched her disappear and they departed in slow fashion to their own corners of Dormoth, dismayed by the cloud that had fallen over them and the awful potential of the magic they had just witnessed.

Grindar motioned Vetra and Nog along the adjoining corridor, now chased with shadows and the dim glow of guttering cressets.

Vetra's mood was dark. He set himself to musing. He and Nog needed to get this wretched jewel and quit this jackal's den before they were caught in the crossfires.

Only three hours remained till midnight. Skirl had better get his ass here quick-time.

Chapter 14

Skirl had been busy. He'd concocted some combination of false beard and mustache which he'd shaved from an unlucky sheep in the market. He'd smeared his face with some goose grease from the landlord and pasted on his new facial hair with a flourish. With a tattered slouch hat perched on his crown at a jaunty angle, a false stoop and feigned limp on a gimp leg, makeshift cane pressed in hand, he was all set to go.

Noon had passed and the mercenaries had not returned to the *Rat Peacock,* implying they'd made it into Dormoth, or'd perhaps gotten their throats cut. He'd find out soon enough. He hoped they had the resource to maneuver themselves into position at the rendezvous point near the Hall of Wands. Vetra was clever enough, but the other, Nog, the scar-faced brute... Skirl frowned. He had his doubts, though he thought the two had the potential to be fierce, if not capable.

The mission would not be an easy one. He hadn't described in great detail how perilous their task would be, or how dangerous the Archmagrix was, should she get wise to their ploy. That was their problem.

In his jerry-rigged disguise, he trod the nighted streets of Xalgossa to Dormoth, on a circuitous route through the dives and the distillery district. He kept to the main streets as much as he could. The cane would serve as a weapon against footpads should it be needed, though he would not count on it. He had other tricks up his sleeve.

Skirl's mind was a hive of ambitious and conflicting thoughts...

A sinking feeling crept over him. Was he a dilettante, like Keren had accused him of the other day?...trumpeting it before all at the conclave in the Hall of Mages? Words like 'washed up wannabe without talent' had come up.

No. He would never accept that. The mages were jealous of his abilities—abilities he once had. He had talent. He was going places.

Skirl calmed his nerves. He let the angry images of their mockeries subside. *Fools.* What were they but a bunch of codgers dabbling in weak witchcraft? All this paled in comparison to what could be, if he could tap into the power of the Eros stone.

A lot of ifs there, Skirlie…

No matter. He had bigger fish to fry. Greener pastures to graze.

As for the jewel, should he succeed in retrieving it, escape from this adder-ridden stronghold with his neck, he could never let it pass into the hands of a grubby market merchant or gem dealer. The jewel was priceless. He could never let his new allies know his true thoughts either. Better to use them as pawns in the overall scheme of things. He was a better guardian of the jewel, not Taranis or any of the other mages. When he had it in his grasp, there would be hell to pay.

He reached to touch his ear, or lack of one, and winced. The wound still throbbed like a devil. A fierce rage burned in his chest. He promised Taranis a reckoning more violent than the eight kingdoms had ever seen.

He took comfort in that thought as he plodded on with his fake limp, grimed cane and goose grease, down the cobblestone way.

The hour was near midnight and an awkward time to be calling at the gates of Dormoth. But no matter. He had great faith in his abilities as a dissembler.

He halted before the high gate. A single lamp burned from the spiked iron. Atop the south tower, all was dark, but from the west tower he could see a small torch wavering in an open, square window.

Skirl's lips curled in a grin.

"Who goes there!" came the guard's challenge.

Skirl put on his squeakiest, old man voice. "A half blind beggar, master watchman. One wanting crusts for his breakfast."

"Hardly a time for a breakfast, beggar! Go away. The hour is late. Dormoth is closed. Jungar and I are in a game of dice."

"Spare a few scraps of meat then? A bit of watered wine?"

"Begone, I say! The abbey and soup kitchen is down the way. Call on old lady Mildred to ladle you broths, not me. You'll find no pity here."

"Mind your manners, young grump! You do yourself no favors. I know people here. I have friends in high places. Like Keren, the birdwatcher. Where is the old coot? He's an old friend of mine."

"Sure he is," the guard jeered. He flashed his blade through the bars under Skirl's chin. "I said, begone, beggar. This is your last warning."

Skirl pushed the blade aside. "Peace, ruffian! Call on Keren, if you are in doubt. The beastmaster! Him and me, we go back a long ways. He'll vouch for me. Tell him his old friend Arkovitrix is here, to pull his beard and trade a spell or two. Remind him about the little mole on the left side of his buttocks, if he doesn't think it's me."

The guard paused, lips parted, as if fearing that this old man perhaps spoke the truth. Did he face a magician? With a grumble and a curse, he turned the key in the lock, mumbling under his breath. The gate jerked open a few inches to let the gaffer pass. "Keren's workshop is first on the right, past the Hall of Wands. But I'm sure you know that already, don't you?

Dally not, or I'll have you whipped!"

Skirl gave a cheeky salute. "Thank you, young whippersnapper, and I'll pass on your friendly regards too."

The guard pursed his lips. Even he paled at the prospect of Keren's wrath coming down on him.

Skirl hobbled swiftly across the courtyard, a cagey grin etched on his face.

Chapter 15

Five men awaited their orders in the bare, limestone guards' command post adjoining the barracks. Vetra and Nog were among them. Grindar gestured a rough hand at the first two stubble-chinned sentries. "West Tower duty for you. Yes, you, Dakin, don't look so surprised." His steely eyes settled on his two new recruits. "Get these two clowns on kitchen guard duty, patrolling the scullery staffs' quarters. It's very exciting down there, especially this time of night on a six hour stretch."

Vetra feigned a sigh of relief. "Anything away from heights, captain. Nog and I are a bit leery of high places, aren't we Nog?"

"Quite right, Vetra. Anything with parapets or lofty towers gets us queasy."

"Queasy of heights, you say?" Malice shone in Grindar's eye.

Vetra nodded.

Grindar jerked a thumb. "Get them to take the West tower then. You boys can start chipping away at your fears tonight."

Vetra put on a wild-eyed look.

Grindar held up a hand. "No buts! Who's going to show these mutts the ropes?"

"Garfu's your man," Dakin the red-bearded man with squint said, jerking a thumb at an ape-like figure with underslung jaw and lopsided morion. The man looked half asleep.

"Let Garfu alone," Grindar grunted. "He's paid his dues. Too many of them. I'd say it's like you're a bunch of old hens, chicken-pecking the one easiest to peck."

"Guess I will then, Sarge," a curly haired man said, polishing his plumed morion.

"Good man, Macdem. Tower's not too high, should these two babies fall and break their arms. You can relieve yourself at midnight. Call on Janos."

Vetra masked a grin. Better this than sneaking around the guards' barracks with these soldiers watching and ready to snitch on them.

Macdem made a gruff acknowledgment. Torch in hand, he led Vetra and Nog across the nighted courtyard to the west tower's lower door. He pulled open an oaken portal and beckoned them inside.

The landing was dark. Only a few spare weapons and gear hung on the wall: mace, dented helms, wicked looking polearms. Up the winding steps they tramped.

"I heard how you got the drop on our friend," Macdem said. "Danys looked a veritable mess. Would have loved to have been a fly on the wall, seen the look on Grindy's face when you busted him up."

Vetra gave a brief shrug. "It was over before it began." The echo of his voice gave way to the ghostly echo of boots on stone. The smell of dust and spider webs hung heavy in the air.

"My advice, keep your head down. Grindar's not the type to let down grudges. He's going to come after you."

"Thanks, we'll keep that in mind," Nog said.

The guard shook his head. "Surprised old Grindy even allowed you up here, instead of putting you down to clean the latrines." He gave a ribald laugh. "Must have a soft spot for outlanders."

Through the arrow slits, Vetra saw the murky glower of lamps from inns and the odd temple settling over the city. At another landing, Macdem led them out onto a high parapet, torch held in hand: nothing more than a narrow stone walkway where two men could walk abreast. Crenelations rose to waist height. The domes of the Mages' Halls loomed below. Commanding views could be seen of the surrounding area. Stars wheeled in the sky, the moon had not yet risen, lending a dark, humid feel to the air. Sound carried from a perch this high. A low hum of voices emanated from the city: drunken shouts, the high piping of musical instruments, the beat of a drum, the bawdy laugh of a tavern harlot maybe in a mud-hemmed kirtle hunting for a mark.

Torchlight shone from the main gate now barred for the evening. Vetra could hear muted laughter and jeers of the watchmen from this direction as they won and lost at dice.

Macdem pushed the torch under Vetra's nose. "Say, you don't seem too scared of heights?"

"It's not as bad as I thought at night."

Macdem gave a low grunt. "Not much to show you boys here. Just a lot of waiting around. You watch, make sure no skulkers come to breach the tower or over the parapets. In fact, if there're any movements at all, you yell first then beetle down to the courtyard with your swords ready. Now, it's harder to see anybody because there's no moon. Ordinarily no one can cross that open space without getting spotted. If you squint real hard you can see, Harfar, lean as a spring gopher, traipsing the parapet. Orders are he's not to keep a light. Makes him a sitting duck for archers. As I said, just a fearful lot of waiting around here. Maybe that was Grindar's way of punishing you." He gave another coarse laugh as if it were the funniest joke that evening. "Any of you fellows play dice? If so, I hope you're good at it. There's a lot of that goes on among us tower watch." He pulled out a sack of dice from his surcoat pocket and emptied four skew-faced stones in his hand. "We usually play double or nothing. Sigs and Sags. You play?"

Nog's brows rose in interest. "You play a lot?"

"As much as I can," he said proudly. He took off his helm. "What about you?" His beady eyes glinted, trained on Vetra.

Vetra shook his head. "I'm not a gambler."

"Pity. Well, keep your eye on the courtyard then, friend. While Lord Nog and I have a friendly game of Sigs and Sags, we'll swap duty in good time. Nice to have some company for a change."

Nog and the watchman settled in with gusto, squatting on their haunches, rattling their dice on the dusty parapet, jeering when they won and clutching ears when they lost.

Vetra smiled. This was almost too easy. Almost like clubbing a bunny.

The gong struck dully from the opposite tower. The moribund note echoed across the desolate courtyard. Fitting for the place, thought Vetra.

On Vetra's barest nod, Nog moved closer to his gambling mark.

His first punch came hard and heavy.

A quick mallet fist that clubbed the guard in the face, sending him toppling back. He gave a squawk, reached for his sword.

Vetra was already there, his blade tipped at the man's throat.

"Nothing personal, friend. Just business."

"Sure, just business."

While Vetra kept the man at bay, Nog tore strips from his breeches and bound his wrists and ankles.

"What are you two bullies up to? If it's thieving on your mind, you'll never get past the gate guards. Grindar'll skin you alive, cut your throats to ribbons—Hey, why you taking off my boots?"

Nog pulled off the guard's left boot, ripped off the sock

and grinned as he stuffed it in the man's mouth.

"Clean, and neat." Vetra stepped over and pushed the sweaty rag deeper into his mouth.

"He'll have a sore head for a day or two, I reckon." Nog scooped up the man's morion, looked at it, tried it on, found it too small and tossed it back on the slumped body.

"Let's not piss around, Nog," Vetra warned.

"If our friend's not at the appointed place?"

Vetra shrugged. "We'll just bust our way out of here. No worries. No use lingering around getting drawn and quartered." He nudged the slouched figure with his toe. "How long we have to sit here with our hands tied is another matter—"

"Wait!" Nog lifted his bulk, nudged Vetra in the ribs. "There's our man. Look! Visitor at the gates."

Vetra peered and caught a vague glimpse of a lean figure standing outside the iron pales.

"Here, pass me the torch, let's give our friend a signal." He waved it slowly for little while, then set it leaning up against the parapet. "Let's make like rabbits, Nog."

Nog glanced at their prisoner. "What if chatterbox tries to roll his way down the stairs and alert the guards?"

Vetra gave a mirthless grunt. "Let him if he wants to break his neck."

"Should we go down there and help our one-eared mage?"

Vetra studied the scene for a few moments then shook his head. "No need. Look, the gates are opening. Looks like Skirl managed to wheedle his way in. Incredible. Let's stick to plan."

"The torch?"

"We'll need it. Take it. How's your night vision?"

"Not good."

"Then I'll take it. Let's go."

* * *

Skirl passed from courtyard to portico under an archway then into a wide corridor flanked with ghostly statues and dimly lit by sconces. He paused. His fake beard and mustache itched like the devil. He pulled them off, cast them aside like one would used dishrags and wiped his face clean of the goose grease. His skin smelled rancid. No matter. Fifty paces to the Hall of Wands, another hundred to Taranis's quarters. An estimated 5 to 7 minutes skulking and eluding sentries, should nothing untoward occur.

He'd make no more than twenty steps past a darkened cross-corridor when a shadowy figure jumped out at him.

"The Hall is off limits for the night. Don't you know curfew's at 9?" He squinted in the sconce light and frowned. "Wait, I recognize you."

Skirl recognized Brezel, one of Grindar's roughboys, who had manhandled him on his way to the gallows the other afternoon. Skirl kept walking, hoping the problem would go away as he tried to come up with a plan.

"Hey, wait up, you skulker!" The guard caught up to Skirl and whacked him on the arm with the flat of his blade. "'Tis as I thought!...Skirl, the banished apprentice."

Skirl licked his lips and slowed to a halt. Catching his breath, he gave a conspiratorial wink. "Brezel...quiet down, come here. I have something to show you." He beckoned the man closer as if with an insider's tip. "You're a keen man, one with good senses and quick eyes. This is your lucky day."

"How's that?" The guard's suspicion grew. "What do you have to show me, a bloody ear?" He pushed his swordtip at Skirl's chest. Crooked teeth glinted in the sconce light.

Skirl pressed a hand deeper in his pocket. He withdrew a

coin, one of the misshapen shekels he'd won at the dart game back at the *Rat Peacock*. He flipped it in the air. "A rare coin of Dergath," he called. "I found it in the crypts at Gotha. 'Tis worth a king's ransom." He caught it in a quick palm then held it up.

The guard peered, squinting under the dim light. His hand reached for it. But Skirl flipped the coin in the air again before he could grab it and while the guard's eyes hungrily watched it somersault, he thrust his hand into the other pocket and flicked a yellowish dust in the man's eyes.

The guard staggered back, a shrill cry in his throat.

Skirl grabbed at the sword, snatched the weapon out of his grasp. He reversed the hilt and jammed the pommel in the guard's face. The metal smacked square on his brow. The guard gave a cursing cry.

Already blinded by salt dust, the man swung a wild fist and staggered forward. He flailed now, groping for Skirl's body.

Skirl jogged backward as fingers came clawing for his face.

The guard heard the scuff of Skirl's feet and roared, rage in his heart. Skirl was too close. He had no room to sidle away. The guard grappled him around his torso, clinging to him like a monkey.

Skirl tried to break free. He could not. He squirmed, desperately struggling to free his sword pinned under his armpit. His efforts were in vain. There came a grasping and heaving like a comical dance of monkeys and Skirl felt the air whoosh out of his lungs. His ribs started to crack. In a desperate panic, he wormed the sword up and jammed the tip under the man's chin. There came a gurgling as blood slopped onto Skirl's face.

The man's body relaxed. Skirl wrenched the blade free and arced it back for a strike. Fearing another assault, he swung with all his might and let blade bite deep into shoulder and neck striking bone. Brezel collapsed in a convulsive heap.

For long seconds, the apprentice stood there, his chest heaving. His blood pounded in his ears. He could hear his heart flap like a songbird chased by a hawk.

No sooner had he swallowed the lump in his throat when he felt his wits returning.

This was the first man he'd killed. A rusty gasp rustled past his lips. An empty feeling pressed in on him.

Being an apprentice, he was used to energetic movements of magical force and spirits. Now it was as if a disembodied entity, the life of Brezel, floated over his body and would demand a blood price at some later time when he desired it, calling from the grave.

He shook off the curse.

A nasty, dirty work.

Skirl stepped away. But not without a contemptuous look at Brezel's corpse. The bastard got what he deserved. That would teach him for dragging an innocent man to the gallows.

He grabbed the body by the heels and dragged it into a storage area off the hallway. He tore some fabric off the man's surcoat and hastily dabbed the blood off the stones, hoping the trail would not be noticed too soon.

With a fretful glance up the corridor, he scooped up the man's sword and hurried off down the hall.

Chapter 16

Vetra and Nog crept on stealthy feet under another archway and up the corridor that ran parallel to the inner court. On the rightmost wall, a giant sigil loomed, entwined with snakes heralding the emblem of the wizard circle—dragon and eagle.

Vetra motioned. "This is it."

A familiar figure limped out of the shadows bearing a blood-drenched weapon. He wore a blue robe and was gnashing his teeth. "What took you so long?"

Vetra glanced at the figure's weapon. "You been busy? We had some fancy footwork to do ourselves. Enduring Grindar's murderous swords and Taranis's intrigue. You could have warned us that auditions to the mage guard would be wrought with treachery and throat-cutting."

Skirl lifted his shoulders in a careless shrug. "I didn't want to discourage you."

"Pipe down," hissed Nog. "Where's this passage of yours anyways?"

"This way."

As one, the three crept on noiseless feet down the hallway. The mercenaries gripped their weapons with anticipation as they stole through the dimness. Vetra held the flickering torch; Nog dogged at his heels. Iron wall sconces barely lit the hallway's gloom. Vagrant drafts snuck in through small windows that opened high on the court side.

Skirl hissed a frustrated oath as he motioned to a figure up ahead. "Damn, there's a man guarding the door to Taranis's chamber. I expected no less. This hall loops around the back. It meets up on the other side behind the guard. I can distract him while you two creep around the back—"

Vetra pushed Skirl aside. Nog, grinning, followed on his heels.

Vetra strode up to the surprised guard.

"Hey, what are *you* doing here?" The sentry's blade moved to strike him down. "You can't come in here—"

Vetra blocked the steel that came flicking at his neck and twisted adder-quick to smash his elbow into the guard's face. Nog came sliding in and kneed the sentry in the groin and sent him to the flags.

Nog stepped over the inert body. He bunted the magician toward the door. "Inside."

Skirl dusted off his tattered robe and swallowed hard the knot in his throat. He pushed the door ever so slowly ajar. Vetra pulled the slack body inside. He cached it from sight behind a chest in the shadows.

The faintest murmur of voices reached their ears.

Across the dim-lit space a heavy door to an inner chamber was open a crack. From within, came the sound of a brief grunt of exertion. A man's. There followed a woman's soft moan then a husky sigh. Taranis. Now it was the man's turn to groan. Despondence? Fatigue? Duress? Vetra was at a loss.

Nog cast Vetra an impish grin. "Should we break up the party?"

Vetra shouldered him aside, warning him to silence. The two crept across the room to a shadowy iron portal where Skirl was beckoning them. Vetra had the crawling feeling that they were heading into a pit of vipers. But they'd come this far. To turn back now would be a waste…

He thrust the rogue thought from his mind.

As the sounds of pleasure escalated in cadence, the details of the room started to take shape. Rich tapestries on the walls. Dramatic, sweeping scenes—a demonic queen sitting on a throne, monsters on smaller thrones atop snow-peaked mountains, a prison below them with iron walls in the shape of a coffin. Skulls and swords intertwined. Dragons flying in the sky, breathing fire on the villages. Troll-haunted forests in the mix. A glut of cryptic runes and sigils interspersed throughout.

Before an iron-wrought mirror sat a heavy chair and scarred wooden desk bearing quill and stylus with ink and parchments crammed with crude symbology. A gold censer burned pungent incense, releasing a heady smoke, purplish in color. A pile of worn spellbooks lay stacked at the foot of the chair. Nothing Vetra could read, unless he was a rune-master or could decipher hundred-year old script. To the side sat an ancient iron-strapped chest, containing who knows what relics or magic talismans. The mirror looked as heavy as sin. Crude-carved gargoyles not dissimilar to Besemooth peered down from the top corners. What was a little reminder of Dal Sagoth in one's private space between friends?

Passing the desk, he caught a reflection of himself. One he did not like. A stalker, grim and sheeted in mail, tense as a tiger, with scowling face, a dark wanderer wondering what he was doing in a sluttish sorceress's den, one inch away from getting his throat slit. He wiped his lip and the crude thought away.

Nog scratched at his stubbled chin, nudged the mercenary's elbow. "This is getting tricky, Vetra. Even if we get this jewel, how are we ever going to get out of here?"

Vetra hissed back at him, "We'll figure it out, Nog, when the time comes."

"Not so loud." Skirl pressed finger to lips.

The heavy candelabra that dripped wax onto the desk's wood lit the space with a dim eerie glow, more of which came beyond the cracks of the open door twenty feet away, and from where more heated sex sounds drifted. Now a sexual battle. The man appeared to be losing. Vetra licked his lips. "Quick mage! Show us this passage," he hissed.

Skirl gave a grim-lipped nod, drew back the bolt, grimacing as it scraped.

With no more noise than weasels, the three slipped into the darkness and shut the door.

Chapter 17

The three plunderers navigated the stone stairwell on wary feet. Skirl led, Vetra stalked behind, his torch spitting from time to time. Nog took up the rear, a strained grimace on his face. The narrow way seemed to plunge down deep into the earth, perhaps to its very core. At times Nog nudged into Vetra, his boots seeming to slip on loose stone, and only reaching out a hand at the last minute to stop his weight from pitching into Vetra's.

"Watch it, fool!" Vetra growled. "Sending me face first to my doom isn't going to help us, is it?"

"Relax. You're wound too tight." Nog wet his lips. "Not used to all this stale air and stench. What is it?"

"Who knows? Dead rat? Stagnant pool? What does it matter?"

Vetra peered down at the steep, crumbling steps that dropped ever deeper into thick gloom. His unease grew. "What else is down here, Skirl?" he demanded.

"Nothing, mercenary, just gloom and must...maybe the odd spider."

"Spiders? You said nothing about spiders!" Vetra gripped the magician's shoulder with fingers like claws. He had had a frightening experience when he was a boy, trapped in his father's cellar full of webs and wolf spiders.

"Must I describe every creepy crawly? Beetles, mice, rats, bats. Goblins maybe?"

"You didn't tell us about spiders before you got us into this caper."

"Why should I?"

"How big are these spiders?" Vetra demanded.

Skirl drew fingers about three inches apart. "Maybe a bit

bigger than normal." He had underestimated the size by several inches. "Nothing we can't handle."

Vetra rubbed his jaw. His eyes darted to and fro at the walls of dank limestone as if expecting one to leap out. Sweat glistened on his brow.

Nog grinned, amused to see some chinks in Vetra's armor. He clapped his friend on the back. "Come on, boy, toughen it up. What we can't see, can't hurt us, can it?"

Vetra shook off Nog's hand. "How much longer, mage?" he griped at Skirl.

"Just down here. Look." The stairs had come to an abrupt end. At right angles to the stair ran a narrow passageway that cut crudely into the damp bedrock. Skirl ushered them down the rightmost branch which at first only allowed a man to walk single file but soon opened up to two then three abreast. He led them on unfailing feet for a fair distance where the smell of animal hide only worsened.

He slowed, a frown growing on his face. "Not far now," he mused. "Or is it?" He halted, head cocked, foot in midair like a hesitant hound.

Vetra cast the mage an impatient stare. "Look, it's either here or it isn't. You leading us on a wild goose chase?"

"Dergath's hexes, Vetra! Everything seems so different in this witchlike darkness."

Nog balled his fist and got Skirl stumbling forward quick enough. "Move it!"

"Wait. I remember!" Skirl hissed. "This block of fallen stone…it has an odd shape to it. The smell has changed too."

"What, from hideous to unbearable?" Nog said.

"Over here," Skirl motioned. "Past the stone grate, then on to the leaning gargoyle. I remember the way. I cached the Eros Flame in its mouth."

The mage plunged on with deft steps, his boots tramping on the flaked flagstones. The two mercenaries followed behind with dubious strides.

It was in those halting steps that their destinies would change forever.

For they came to what looked like a crosshatched stone barrier to the right, through whose six-inch gaps admitted glimpses into a cavernous space beyond.

Vetra paused. He frowned. There appeared to be movement in that black gap beyond. His lips parted while Nog snatched at Vetra's torch to get a better glimpse.

"What the—?" He peered between the stone blocks that formed a kind of crude but ancient barrier.

A massive reptilian shape sat crouched on all fours in the thick darkness. A thing with talon-like claws and scaly hide glistening like plate-like armor. The tail was eight feet long if it was an inch and snaked along the molder like a twisted trunk; the hooked claws scraped into the stone itself. A gigantic eye opened, large as a gong, and a pale saucer-like light gleamed in the torch's reflection.

Nog pushed his nose in closer, spellbound.

"Don't—" Skirl reached.

There came a skin-crawling rustle—of leathery wings then the ratchety movement of scaly flesh as a violent mass bounded out of the blackness. The great jaws snapped open and a torrent of fire came belching through the gap, whistling past Nog's face. The force sent the mercenary flying backward on his heels. He lay prostrate on the dank stone for some time, slapping at his singed hair. He cast off his helm, tamping at the once dark fringes that had caught fire. The tips of his fingers still tingled from where they'd touched his helm that had the devil's heat to it.

"Loins of Dergath's whores!"

Vetra hissed, bared his blade. He crouched, ready to spring at the thing should it burst through the wall. But he ducked to the side instead behind the protection of the flanking stone. He peered sideways at the grate, breath held.

"What other stygian horrors aren't you telling us about, mage?" he hissed. "Do the wizards hold dragons in these catacombs?"

"I—didn't—I d-don't—" Never did Skirl imagine such a creature existed down here.

"One of these wizards' pets, no doubt," Vetra spat.

"He's young, no more than a lizardling—" Skirl stammered "—if anyone can call a beast that lives a thousand years 'young'."

"I don't care how young he is," said Vetra. "Let's get to this gargoyle of yours…and try not to get crisp-fried in the meantime."

Nog picked up his smoking helm. He rubbed at his scalded ear.

Skirl gestured to his own ear or lack of one. "Looks like we're a pair now, eh Nog?" he quipped, trying to dull the stress with some humor.

"Good joke, mage. Now button up, unless you'd like some white teeth knocked out."

Skirl stared at the middlemost stone and crouched for a better look at the grate. A star-shaped runestone with four parts like some quasi diamond, glinted with an eerie light.

"I don't recall this rune on my last tour here," he mused. "Funny how things get muddled."

Recovering his wits, Nog reached out a hand, feeling he was protected by the protective stone, and made a funny face at the dragon that peered through the gap.

There came a roar and another gust of fiery breath that nearly scorched Nog's skin. The winged dragon, or whatever it was, moved fast as a greased eel and smashed its crusty head against the grate, threatening to bring down the very rock around them. The stone barely held.

Dust and rubble fell from above. Vetra arched arms to shield his head. The creature reared back, charged again, rocking the very foundation of the bedrock.

He and Nog wheeled away, grabbing Skirl at the waist and scrambled past the barrier and up the passage. The stone blocks still held but had shifted a few inches.

"Dergath's bane, we've roused a hellspawn!" Nog cried.

"Move!" Vetra bawled. He shoved Skirl forward up the passageway while the beast turned to thwack its tail now against the grate in regular rhythms.

"Find this jewel, mage!" Vetra cried.

Skirl scuttled ahead, nodding as if his head would fall off. He stumbled on tender feet while the flickering torch sent monstrous shadows leaping across the walls, showing ghostly pillars, stelae with carven figures and glyphs, slanted slabs and crumbled masonry.

Vetra gave a colorful curse.

They scrambled down a set of six broad, crumbling stairs into a vast forum of ancient columns. Around them reared fountains, altars and shrines amid sunken walkways. The only sound was their boots crunching on rubble with the echo of the dragon's freakish malice dwindling behind them. The ceiling soared above, lost in a cloud of darkness in what seemed the vague curve of a dome.

A broken hall of statues and pillars, Vetra mused, a temple or forum from ages past. The grim, staring faces of statues and their uplifted arms symbolized pagan rule, ritual, power, torture and enduring darkness.

Skirl drew them to a halt in order to recoup their bearings.

A crypt-like silence fell over the ancient ruins but for the distant thud of the dragon entombed in its stone prison. Indeed, a feeling of death hung over this eerie place like an ancient curse.

Vetra peeled back his lips in a strained grimace while Nog swallowed hard. "I hope this gargoyle thing of yours is nearby," he said.

Skirl pointed a shaky finger into the murks ahead. "It's this way."

Chapter 18

On shaky feet the three threaded their way across an expanse of rubble and broken stones fallen from the ceiling or flaked off the statues.

They stepped over two toppled columns crisscrossed in an eerie configuration at the entrance of what might have been a ruined courtyard. At once Vetra leapt back as the scuttle of a black shape, the size of a small rat but could have been a spider, nearly had him jumping out of his skin. "Dergath's shades, mage! Could you have picked a less perilous place for your jewel?"

Skirl made no comment.

When Vetra thought the mage was utterly lost and leading them in circles, he stopped short and gloated with triumph. "There! As I told you."

Vetra saw a disturbing bat-like statue shrouded in the gloom. Frozen in some frightening stony repose between crumbling slabs of rock that may have been altars, it loomed with a face carved of an obsidian leer. One of the bat-like ears was missing. The rest of the face was worn, hideous: a snub nose, toothy maw and outstretched claw-like digits.

Skirl crouched and withdrew a chestnut-sized shape from the gargoyle's mouth. An improbably large sapphire. At first it gleamed dully, but when Vetra lifted his torch, he saw that it radiated an unnatural lambent glow.

"Look how the flame swirls within!" Skirl hissed to himself.

Vetra saw it change from deep crimson to ultramarine then back again. It suddenly dawned on him the improbability of faking such a jewel with its play of light.

"I hired a master gemsmith to create a replica of the original jewel," Skirl explained. "To mimic its living fire! I paid the woman handsomely for it. By clever design she carved the flicker of light to appear as a moving flame. When anyone peers from a different angle, the stone changes color. Look! Reflection and refraction. It's intricate. Enough to fool the witch."

"Very interesting," Vetra mused. "Time's wasting. We need to get back past that dragon."

Nog muscled his way in. He snatched at the jewel. "Here, let me see it."

Skirl pulled the gem away in one jealous motion. "By no means! I am the keeper of the Eros stone. This is an object of power, unfit for layman's hands." He shoved it deep in his pocket.

Nog's face lit with a hostile grin. He advanced with menace.

"Cool your heels, Nog," said Vetra, laying a hand on his shoulder. "We've got what we came here for. Let's not squabble. We've got to get away from this loathsome place—"

A faint clink echoed from behind them. The jingle of armor, a slivering scrape of a sword being unsheathed.

"Dergath's wrath!" Nog hissed. "Can they have stumbled on us so soon?"

"Maybe," Skirl murmured. "With all the ruckus we stirred up with that youngling."

"No use going back that way," Vetra grunted. "Quickly! Let's push on. We can hide somewhere, ride out this storm then sneak back with the gem."

There didn't seem to be any other plan. Quick as rats they hurried deeper into the gloom. Vetra cursed the torchlight that would give them away if the guards saw it.

They mounted another set of broad steps and came out of the eerie ruins only to scramble deeper into more of the same. Vetra liked this turn of events little. Things were getting out of control. More molder, more crumble. Dergath! More grim looking statues and now an even more stagnant waft lingering in the air.

They hurried along a sunken pathway and mounted another set of steps.

The sound of bootfall echoed louder behind them. Vetra heard the murmur of men's voices somewhere back the way they'd come. His lips formed in an oath. "Douse the flame."

"We can't!" Nog rasped. "How are we to find our way back?"

"Better that we're not seen, Nog. Douse it."

Nog winced. He went to swat out the flame, but then shook his head vigorously. "No, Vetra. We do it the traditional way. We fight! What are we, pansy asses?"

Vetra gave a curt nod. "You're right, Nog. Let's head deeper into these ruins and find some higher ground. The torch we can use as a decoy."

Somewhere ahead of them, a dull plink sounded, like the drip of cool water cascading into a pool.

"What's that?" Nog rasped.

Vetra perked his ears. He moved ahead. He shone the light. His eyes discerned a rectangular pool of black water, about 50 feet long by 15 wide. A foot-high stone curbing framed its perimeter. They'd come to its long-side edge and, it seemed, the end of the cavern.

So, a dead end. A dank smell wafted from the waters. Across the pool, a barely-discernible bat-like statue as macabre as the one Taranis had cached in her summery garden, perched on a time-eaten pedestal. The effigy was reached by a ramp of broad, ancient steps. This statue was thrice Besemooth's height. The ruins continued across the water, but the sight prickled Vetra's scalp. What new chilling surprise would they discover in this eerie, creepy place?

"Just our luck," Vetra grunted. "A pool of sorts. A reservoir maybe? You've seen this before, Skirl?"

Skirl shook his head. "I remember a plink of water."

Nog reached down to slosh his hand in the water. "Care for a drink?"

"Not just now." Skirl lifted a hand. "Let's move on. This place is evil."

"I think we've come to the end of the line, Skirl," said Vetra.

Skirl's brow furrowed. He crouched to trace a finger along the crumbling ledge. "A cistern is my guess. Old beyond belief. See the cracks on the stone?" He pushed his nose closer. "The glyphs of winged creatures, faintly engraved. Look, mythical sea beasts too. My guess, Marizon the Second's reign when the great dragons flew—"

"Enough," Vetra snapped. "It does little good citing history—"

"Sh! Voices."

The clop of boots came louder.

Vetra stifled a curse. He knelt, poked his sword down in the inky black water. It did not touch bottom. Even when he pushed as far up to his shoulder.

He withdrew his blade and muttered sullenly. No chance to swim across this pond with their heavy gear.

He motioned them back behind the pillars that fronted the curbing.

Their pursuers had sighted them. Many of them. Shouts drifted across the gloomy rubble. Then the clap of boots came on stone and the flickering dance of torchlight on the walls and the time-eaten masonry.

Vetra counted eight figures, all with swords and maces

drawn, their teeth glinting in the uneven torchlight. A third of the Dormoth garrison, he guessed.

Eight in hauberks and helms came leaping and snarling out of a near-distant circle of crumbling columns.

Vetra bared his sword. They were all doomed unless they could take down these new foes. But how, trapped at the edge of this dark water?

Vetra leaned the torch up against a broken column and motioned Nog and Skirl to take cover. They spread out behind the broken columns. Skirl and Vetra flattened themselves behind ones about six feet apart; Nog crouched at the base of a column whose top half had been smashed off. Vetra clutched his hilt. In his mind's eye, he mentally counted the moments when he would leap out, uncoil his thews and rain bloody ruin on these vermin.

A familiar voice echoed out of the darkness. *Grindar.* "They're here. I can smell them. Spread out."

As the first helmed guard came within six feet of Vetra's hiding place, he lunged and chopped down on the man's helm. There came a grunt and clang of steel. His morion was dented but the wearer only dazed. Vetra swung his sword again and the edge ripped through the man's throat.

The man fell to his knees, gurgling, clutching at his neck.

He ran to the torch and thrust it in the mage's hand. "Quick! Guard the jewel! Stay behind us! If we fall, run!"

"You traitorous bastards!" Grindar spat.

He lifted his blade and Vetra parried as another man came sprinting in at him. Nog was five feet away, twin blades scissoring, crouched in his Thrakian war crouch.

The clash of steel rang loud in the dimness and sent strident echoes arcing about the once silent hall. Dusky echoes disturbed the spirits of this desolate place. Spirits better left in slumber.

Vetra moved back as another attacker came slashing in at him to replace the dead man.

To his side the water spread like a dark mantle of clouded glass. Uttering a coarse oath, he sped across the curbing even as it crumbled under his feet. It was only twelve inches above the forum's floor, yet a perilous path to take. From the corner of his eye he caught a glimpse of Skirl darting away from a man twice his size with plumed morion. How this mission had gone sour!

He turned and slashed at the stalker behind him, then ran on ahead. The guard gave pursuit, others behind him, seeing that Vetra had nowhere to go. Twenty feet down the curbing loomed a cold dank wall. Vetra turned with a snarl and bared his sword at his attacker.

The man lunged. His foot gave way as part of the crumbling shelf disintegrated. Teetering on his heels, his arms pinwheeled, and Vetra helped him along with a sudden kick. The man fell into the water with a cry thick in his throat, vanishing beneath the glassy surface, pulled down by the weight of his helm and mail.

There came a glooping from below. A viscous surge of lighter-colored liquid?

Blood?

Ripples broke the surface and with it a broader stench. Not what Vetra would expect from a single man plunging to his doom into stagnant waters of indeterminate depth.

From the ripples came a writhe of movement. Vetra's mouth sagged. A dark mass lifted...an octopus-like head. Except it wasn't an octopus—it had a frog-like face with salamander snout and mottled skin that might have been boils. Vetra did not want to stay and examine the fine details. A single eye burned from the wrack of a face, glaring like an evil moon at him.

Dergath. He leaped off the ledge, almost staggering to his own doom into a thicket of steel.

He parried blades as three mage guard hacked and slashed and were hot on his tail. They would have slain him then and there had not a strange, whistling tentacle flickered out from behind him. It whipped across his line of sight, curled about the snarling, cursing man in front of him. The obscene thing latched onto the man's ankle and pulled him down on his back. He slid across the molder like a possessed man as the tentacle wheeled him toward the waiting frog-like monster perched on the curbing. The man cried out, lashing at the tentacle, severing it nearly in half. Before he could lift himself, another coil whipped about his waist and lifted him high off the ground. It pulled him toward the waiting monster and the water.

A horrid gob-slobbery maw snapped open. The frog-like head reared and while the man dangled like a fish on a hook, its fanged teeth clipped off the man's leg, as would a boy in cruelty tear off a fly's wings. There came a horrid screech as an arm was snipped off next, gobbled whole.

The guards reeled back in horror.

"Get back!" Grindar bellowed.

Time seemed to slow. In the darkness of a dead hall, fangs of nightmare sank into flesh and Vetra's ordered world turned into one of nightmarish fantasy.

In a moment of inattention, Grindar's blade chopped down at his helm. Vetra reeled and twisted about as blackness threatened to engulf him. He shook off the daze of death, caught Grindar's next blow on his upheld blade. He did not relish fighting amid such horror and against such a foe as Grindar. Only too fresh in his memory was the opponent who had bested him in swordplay in Taranis's eerie garden.

"Die, thief!" Grindar cried.

Skirl stepped forth. "No!" he brayed. "It is you who will die." He brandished his jewel like a sinister beacon.

Grindar shrank back in the wake of the light that stung his eyes.

"Look me in the eye, you rogue! Behold your doom. Bow to your master!"

Grindar paused in the shadow of wrath before them. For a brief instant logic slid sideways. The magic held sway and the men of Grindar's company could lift no steel against the tentacles that whipped forward like snakes. In its sphere, Vetra himself felt his limbs heavy as if fettered.

Skirl stood sorcerer-like in the darkness. The Eros jewel lay lifted in his claw-like grip, a haunted look on his face. His ferret eyes gleamed; his limbs shook and he waved the pulsing gem like a fiend himself.

The mage seemed oddly oblivious to the monster lurking in the water not twelve yards away and the flicking tentacles that could seek his neck any moment, as if they were but small intrusions on his world. This bore testament to how deep and all-encompassing the power of the jewel was, when a man could not see danger when it treaded on his shadow.

"My fear lost me the jewel days ago!" he raved. "Now I will rive you limb from limb!"

A tentacle-arm whipped through the air and curled around his waist. The member whipped the mage three feet off the ground and sent the jewel slipping from his hand to land at Vetra's feet.

The spell was broken. Two of Grindar's men hacked at Vetra. Others came at him tooth and nail.

Nog surged forward, a savage cry on his lips. His twin blades sang melodies, cleaving flesh, chopping the waving tentacle in two before it could drag Skirl to his doom. The magician fell to the moldering stone, clawing, squirming, drenched in gore. From the severed member oozed a black, viscous fluid. Skirl skidded back, his feet kicking convulsively at the fetid loops that still quested his limbs. They were slackened now, but pulsed and jerked about mindlessly.

On the tentacle's tip piked a four fingered claw—of bone, horn or flesh, who knew—was this used for some crude form of navigation underwater or afoot, in some improbable way?

The monster's frog-like head reared up and leaned over the curbing, with hungry glassy orb eyeing easy pickings. The creature seemed oblivious to a few maimed tentacles. Black water dripped from its grotesque snout. The only saving grace was it appeared unable to venture beyond the well of its captivity. But the reach of its cursed tentacles was long.

Vetra thrust steel into an exposed leg of an attacker, prompting a scream. He blocked a strike, then another. In a moment of indecision, he crouched to snatch up the jewel.

An impulsive move.

The upturned jewel gleamed brightly in his eyes. It stymied his brain for a brief second. He felt a languid, dizzying rapture in his skull. No oversized toy marble was this, but some instrument of power. His fingers clasped its egg-like smoothness. It burned there with an unnatural warmth. Like Skirl, he fought its jealous grip, and he plunged it in his pocket.

"Vetra, behind you!" Nog cried.

He whirled in time to twist out of the way. A mace, swung by a big-boned, heavy-footed guard, angled for his neck.

Vetra jerked back. The spiked ball skidded hairs' breaths from his face and smashed against his helm just above the left ear. For a moment he saw stars, then his vision clouded and the world became a sea of dead calm.

CHRIS TURNER

Chapter 19

Nog and Skirl staggered off on a path parallel to the edge of the cistern, at right angles to the melee, trying to get as far away from the horror as possible. Behind them came the din of men's cries, the thwack of steel on flesh. All faded. Now only the muted slap of tentacles on stone as Grindar and his men fought to keep the frog monster at bay.

Ahead a wall of damp stone reared before them. But on the rock face of the giant cavern was etched a darker blot: a square-cut passage.

Down this murky tunnel they scrambled, plunging into shadowy mystery. Skirl led the way, his torch in hand. Nog lagged behind, watching their backs, making sure that no one followed them.

After several twists and turns they slumped down in exhaustion where the tunnel forked into two equally dark passages. Skirl's torchlight flickered. It cast uneasy shadows across the walls, but the fugitives could not be seen by anyone from the main tunnel entrance.

Nog stared about, not without some unease. The two black tunnels burrowed deeper into the rock at a steady downward grade. The walls looked hewn by giant hammers. Stranger, deeper scoriations marked the bare rock, as if hewn by giant claws.

Nog licked his lips. A sprawl of bones lay scattered at their feet: human, animal? He was past caring. They were parched and desiccated and old beyond belief.

He kicked at a broken femur and stared at the apprentice and heaved a heavy sigh. His last image of Vetra was his slack body being hauled away by hostile hands and a wall of guards threatening to leap after them if they pursued. The jewel was lost. There had been nothing he or Skirl could have done. They too would have been caught and dragged back to the sorceress Taranis.

Skirl muttered curses at the loss of the Eros Flame. "I had it in my hands, Nog!" A fresh claw mark lay imprinted across his left cheek where the frog-monster had lashed out with the end of its tentacle. "Then *poof,* a swamp thing comes out of nowhere and clips it off me."

"You're lucky not to be in its belly," Nog grunted. "What were you thinking back there, just standing gawking like a loon? How many times must Vetra and I save your miserable hide, mage?"

A hoarse murmur caught in Skirl's throat. "You don't have to keep mentioning it. But yes, I should be more careful, and be grateful. I owe you two my life."

"You owe us more than that," Nog said, teeth clenched. "Vetra's still back there! Because of that stinking jewel, he's as good as dead." His fists bunched, tightened on his sword.

"We've got our lives, Nog. That's the good side. I say we lay low for a bit and—"

"Let me think!" He waved off the mage's babble. Too many gaps in this story. He was addled and frustrated. He flashed another apprehensive look up the tunnel. "How can creatures live down here so deep sealed off from light and air?"

Skirl lifted his palms. "Who knows, Nog? How deep did the builders delve? How deep did their underwater channels run to connect to the cistern? That well is hundreds of years old. Did they know what they were digging into?"

"What about the dragon?" Nog rumbled. "What does it eat? How did it get here?"

Skirl spread his palms. "I have no answer for that. Nor the origin of these cursed ruins."

"What of Taranis?"

"What of her?" Skirl spat. "She's a witch, what more do you want?"

"How'd she get so powerful?"

"She comes from a long line of powerful mages, is all I know. And wealth. From Smrin in Lower Umbria. More than her cousin, Belgra, she had skill in thaumaturgy, taught her by her master, the Warlock of Tharax." The apprentice gritted his teeth. "If I had the jewel, I'd rive her limb from—"

"You'd do no such thing...shekels to peanuts you'd whimper like a cur and get your other ear chopped off too."

"You don't know the half of—"

"Fat lot of good that jewel did you back there!"

Skirl turned on Nog angrily. "You'd sell the Eros Flame for a whore's pleasure when we could have the power to—" Skirl bit his tongue, realizing what he'd just said.

Nog snarled and lifted him by the throat and slammed him up against the damp wall. "No more lies, you miserable trickster. You didn't know about the dragon, you didn't know about the water monster. What else haven't you told us?"

"You're threatening to crush my neck," Skirl croaked.

"Good. Now shut up and listen. I'm not going to sit back and let Vetra die at the hands of those apes and that ghoul-witch, Taranis. We have to get him out of their clutches then make like bunnies out of here. First, we have to make sure we don't run into more dragons or serpent monsters."

"A tall ticket, mercenary. We're holed up in a dark cave with nothing but a sword. Better we save our own hides," he said hoarsely.

Nog grunted and lifted Skirl higher. "There may be other exits or hidden escape tunnels out of this warren. Where?"

"I—I just discovered this place for the first time a few days ago," he gasped, "to h-hide the amulet in the gargoyle's mouth."

Nog shook his head in hopeless frustration. He clutched the mage's neck tighter. "You're not saying the right things, mage! Give me something, anything at all! Think harder!"

"I can't. It's hard to think—" he croaked "—when someone's crushing your Adam's Apple."

Nog relaxed his grip. "Better?"

"Not much," Skirl gurgled.

"You'll be the first to die, mage, if you don't tell me the truth."

"We'll get your friend Vetra," he gasped. "Just let me down! They're probably dragging him back up to Taranis's chambers."

"No kidding." Nog let the mage fall to the ground where he slumped in a heap, massaging his throat. The mercenary paced back and forth, murderous hands clenched behind his back.

He picked up the fallen torch and flashed it in Skirl's face. "Take this." He hauled Skirl to his feet and thrust the torch in his hand. "Lead the way, pretty boy. If you steer us into any traps, you'll be the first to die." He bunted the apprentice back up the passage where the lingering darkness only waxed deeper. "Part of me thinks you'd be happy to see me gone. No tears either if Vetra got his throat cut."

Skirl stumbled on marionette feet, refusing to answer the unasked question. Several empty, muddled curses hung on his lips.

They mounted the set of broad steps they'd passed earlier then came at last to the passageway that housed the dragon.

Nog saw four figures moving quickly down the darkened passageway, less terrified now that the dragon had quieted down. They were all that remained of Grindar's guards: two muscling Vetra's loose bulk along the passageway, gripping heels and shoulders, another taking up the rear while Grindar led with a torch.

Nog gripped his blade and made motions to press on, but Skirl held him back. He made a cryptic signal across his neck indicating to hold off and wait.

From behind the stone grate came a rattling gurgle ending in a snuffling roar. The dragon.

Nog heard one of the guards mutter, "That's a mighty big rat back there."

Grindar motioned his sword. "No rats, soldier. Move along. There are devils in these murks you'd rather not know about."

The guard lagged. He uttered a nervous laugh. Grindar sheathed his sword and smacked the man a heavy wallop with a massive hand. "You heard me, fool! Move out!"

The three shuffled off past the grate. The stench of unwashed dragon was fiercer than ever. The guards trod down the crumbling way, muttering and grumbling.

Nog and Skirl followed at a more leisurely pace. They lagged behind on weasel feet as the company made their way to the steep stair that angled up into the gloom back to Taranis's chambers. Nog cocked an ear, listening for danger. Only the echoey tramp of men's bootfall, their grunts and heaves as they bore their heavy load.

Now there was only one left. Nog forced a grin and nudged Skirl forward. A single sentry had been left to guard the crooked stairs. The man bore a single torch. He whipped back his sword in a trembling hand when he saw Nog approaching out of the gloom like a wandering vagrant with steel in his hands.

"Back, I say!" the man cried.

Nog blinked and laughed. He advanced with slow, easy steps, a funny, cattish grin carved on his grime-streaked face. "Nice day for a head-stomping, isn't it, mate?"

Chapter 20

Vetra came to. His head throbbed to a splitting headache and a thick sour taste welled in his mouth. His left shoulder ached to the pulse of ten drums. A dozen bruises plagued the rest of his body.

A soft but familiar glow lit his surroundings: of dim-lit candelabra that rose above him. To his side, the gothic mirror on the wall and the stack of spellbooks toppled beside him, wafting a faint, musty scent. Hands gripped his wrists and ankles, pinching into flesh; crude, unsmiling men whose breath smelled of ale.

He groaned as the memory of past events flooded back to him.

"Sick of lugging this brute," snorted a familiar voice.

"Leave him here." One of the two red-coated guards let Vetra's bulk fall unceremoniously to the floor.

"Here he is, Lady," Grindar said, "as you wished."

Taranis's cat-like form stood over him, her legs braced, arms folded on her chest. "So...we have a traitor and a spy in our midst. Where's his peer, the one with the ox-like face?"

Grindar frowned but did not answer.

Vetra rubbed the back of his neck. He shifted to a crouching position. His helm was dented. Two sword tips immediately flicked down at his throat. "Stay where you are, scum."

Vetra grimaced, but complied, still groggy.

"He was clutching this," Grindar growled. He held in his open palm the sapphire they'd plucked from the gargoyle. The real Eros Flame emitted a sullen radiance.

Taranis's eyes blazed. Her trembling hand snatched at it and her flawless face pinched with madness and fury.

"A thief! You stole the stone and tried to replace it with this fake!" She ripped the bauble from her throat. "How you got it off my neck and its leather cord, I can never guess. Maybe you are a magician like me. Yet I detect no magic about you."

Vetra remained stone-faced. Anything he said would incriminate him. Nog and Skirl must have either been slain by Grindar's men, or gotten pulled down by the frog monster. Slim chance they had somehow escaped into the warrens of the ruins below.

"I don't know how you got in here or what you and that other impostor's game is, but when I find out, you will all roast."

"There's nothing to tell, Lady," said Vetra in his most convincing voice, struck with a sudden ploy. "One of the guards planted the gem on me, perhaps even your star, Grindar. Look for your traitor among your own conspirators. You said yourself, your own organization required more security."

For a moment Taranis's eyes flashed with spite. Then she mumbled a curse and stared hard at Grindar. "That may be the case, but you are still up to no good here, creeping around the crypts."

Steel flashed in men's hands and Grindar started toward Vetra.

"Hold, Grindar!" Taranis stormed. "I'd have the truth, before anyone's slain!"

Grindar halted in midstep. The man was seething to the bone, a lurid oath on his tongue. "This man is a liar, Lady! I'll kill him myself! I knew on first sight of Macdem trussed at his post atop the West Tower that he and his sidekick from Thrakia were blackguards. I came scouring the compound for them. It took every ounce of my resolve not to slit this weasel's throat when we caught him below. But I heeded your instructions and brought him as he is to you."

"Very wise and good that you did, Grindar, else you would be the one with his throat slit. Others are down there. His treacherous friend is missing. I want to know where they are. I want to know how he got this in his paws—" she shook the gem. "But first, how did his ox-eyed friend escape?"

"My lady," Grindar said delicately, "some horror came up from the water. We don't know what it was, some mutant from an elder time."

Taranis's face registered incomprehension. "What do you mean?"

"From the filthy stagnant pool at the edge of the ruins of Old Sagoth. 'Twas on us before we could apprehend the others."

"Fools! You woke the guardian?"

"We…I mean—this rogue, he was responsible!" Grindar shafted an angry finger at Vetra.

"How can he be responsible?"

"Gisil, one of the men he was fighting—the rogue kicked him into the pool and Gisil never resurfaced."

"What? Where are the rest of you?"

Grindar licked his lips. "We are all who are left."

"You're an incompetent ninny and fool!" Her gaze shifted sideways upon Vetra, a new awareness dawning in her. "And you—a meddler, almost as bad as that Skirl skulker I banished from Dormoth."

"Speaking of which, Lady—we saw the apprentice down there. How he got his clutches on the jewel I could never—"

"Skirl? Down there in the crypts?" She gave an incredulous bellow of hate.

Grindar nodded. He bit his lips, as if afraid of saying more.

"Now it begins to make more sense," she cried. "Find

them! On the double!"

"But Lady, the mercenary, he will—"

"He will cause me no trouble." She held forth the jewel. "With this gem, no man or creature can stand before me. Go now! Find me these infidels, Grindar. Before I have Dal Sagoth blast your brain to mush."

She clapped her hands and from her palms came a burst of sinister energy: a blue ball which came vaulting at their feet, sending blue fumes up which blinded their eyes and stung their noses.

They coughed, swatting at the vapor while Grindar kicked his two men toward the iron portal.

Grindar followed after them.

No sooner had the three disappeared beyond the black gap when two new figures strode into Taranis's chambers, swatting at the smoke themselves. Each man bore sleepy, slitted eyes, mussed-up hair, and scowls on their faces.

Voydred halted and hissed, "What is all this infernal din and booming coming from below?" His loose black cowl draped around a cadaverous face, robe swishing about his ankles. "Hades, but the foundation of the Hall of Mages must crumble asunder!"

Lugubrious, square-shouldered Keren supported his peer's complaint and voiced a querulous oath, clearly peeved at being woken from his slumber.

Voydred, hawk-nosed and gangly, stared menacingly at Vetra, as if wondering, and guessing correctly, what the rogue was doing here in Taranis's private chambers.

"Calm your fears, Voydred. 'Tis nothing. A few thaumaturgical glitches. Nothing more. Everything is under control."

"What do you mean, 'thaumaturgical glitches'? Why are

your grim men skulking down into the forbidden passage?" He lifted a bony hand. "I warn you, Taranis. I've heard it is a secret passage leading to the crypts below the stronghold, where you keep secret things. You have kept it long out of the topic of conversation at the Mage's conclave."

Vetra spoke in a harsh and gravely rasp. "Lord, if it pleases you, it is a quagmire of ruins and statues down there. Some beast is entombed, quite likely a dragon. The thudding you heard was its horned head and tail banging against the stone."

The color ebbed from Voydred's face. "A dragon, you say?" His beady eyes glinted in disbelief.

"There is nothing down there, Voydred," assured Taranis. "Only must and murks. Mice and stenches. This man is a weaver of fables. He is ripe for punishment. I fear we have been struck by an earthquake. A savage one. I tried to counter it with my magic, but failed. It has luckily passed."

"Earthquake?" he laughed. "That is the most ridiculous thing I've ever heard." He nudged his companion in the ribs. "Come on, Keren! Let us see this 'dragon' for ourselves." He strode past the magic mirror toward the portal. His hand reached for the iron grip.

Taranis held forth the jewel in a cupped palm. "Halt!" The ruby light shone forth: a vivid gleam that reflected in both sets of eyes.

Keren sneered. "Must you keep wasting our time with that silly bauble of yours, Taranis? It is tiresome. It has no power to—"

But suddenly his jaw hung slack and his eyes stared glassily. Voydred's hand likewise slumped at his side, as if he had been rendered passive by its sinister shine. Robbed of his senses and wits as if they had been switched off.

Taranis's ruby lips twisted in a ruthless grin. "You two will go to your workplaces and await further instructions. Please, carry on as before. Nothing is untoward. All is under control. There is no disturbance. Dormoth is safe, and secure." She said the words in a wheedling tone, as if toying with a pair of pet cats.

Keren twitched at his rust-colored beard as if fighting a powerful spell. His face relaxed. Then he and Voydred both nodded as one.

Vetra stared aghast, lips curling in disgust. These two fops were the pride and might of Dormoth? Really? The two had basked in the magical essence and now both gazed at her spellbound, in almost boyish adulation. Taranis's luscious curves and magnetic presence held an ultimate mesmeric clutch over them.

Like automatons, they shambled on duck feet to the door and disappeared, closing the door softly behind them.

CHRIS TURNER

Chapter 21

Taranis cast Vetra a most sulfurous glare which gradually, as the moments passed, gave way to a look of grudging admiration. She cooed, a sinister and insolent sound. "As for you…"

She dimmed the candles and set another incense stick burning in the censer. She closed, but did not bolt the heavy, corroded portal from which dank odors crept, leaving the two alone in the quasi gloom.

"Let us move to more comfortable quarters," she suggested. She led him by the hand unresisting to the open door of her inner chamber where Vetra caught a glimpse of a low altar and candelabrum by a satin-sheeted bed. He did not like the look of the obtrusive effigy jutting out from the wall. A half elk, half bat monstrosity overlooking the bed. He gestured to the grotesque figure with glaring eyes and a bestial snout. "Should I make a guess as to what that is?"

"That is Yeasaba," she intoned. "Dal Sagoth in different form. He is the great god who watches over me and comforts me, in times of trouble."

A saturnine smirk played over Vetra's lips. "Are you in the habit of keeping quaint bibelots as this in your bedchambers, or do you like to stare up at freaks in the heat of passion?"

Her lips quirked, but otherwise she made no reply.

"Well, are we to play patty cake here in this pretty room? You seem to be in the habit of inviting strange men into your bedchamber."

She gave a gruff laugh. "Is it your wish, mercenary, or just a nervous witticism? Perhaps something more exotic's on your mind, something in which your trained sensibilities forbid you to indulge?"

Vetra narrowed his eyes. He in turn offered no reply. The instinct of the Tolizian warrior told him to ignore her wiles. Not a tavern wench she. Yet his blood burned at the sight of her. She was like a hell cat pulsing with sexual mystery. He was bound like all the men before him by the lure of the seductive female. What was worse, he was not used to sultry, seductive, bewitching women.

"Not tonight, I have a headache," he muttered. "Your bully boys have given me too many raps on the skull."

The pulsing, hypnotic power of the love jewel in her fist had put him in a dreamy torpor as an overall dizziness pressed at the edges of his throbbing head. He felt as if he were drifting at sea, awash in foam-crested waves.

She pulled a small glass vial from her bodice and popped the cork off and shoved it under his nose. "Here, rogue. Sniff this."

He reeled back from the sharp odor. Camphor? Something stronger yet? He felt like retching and yet…his head seemed to clear. It had stopped its infernal pounding. Now a delicious, warm numbness replaced the throb in his skull. His senses swam, as if trying to slip away from him like a fleeting dream.

He looked back longingly at his blade leaning up against the chest by the mirror not ten feet away.

She opened her gown and his eyes traveled to the gleaming line of fresh-oiled woman: the sly, sullen slant of jaw, the dusk-chestnut hair, tangled and sun-streaked, the daring sweep of thatch below the flat, smooth belly and the rounded hips. Was she goddess or demoness? His awakened senses wondered.

It would only take a quick leap, a sudden twist of strong hands to strangle the she-fiend where she stood.

But something stayed his hand, perhaps a primitive survival instinct. Any murderous intent on his part would have him slain.

He had no doubt the witch would blast him with her sinister globes of power where he stood.

Another means must suffice. He had a gloomy premonition this would not be to his liking.

Vetra shook his head, fighting the spell. He drew back from the door three steps into the main chamber and thought to steer her energies in other directions. "This beast you keep down there, is it then a pet you wish to keep secret?"

As she languidly refastened her gown, she exhaled a sharp breath. "Yes, Drako, the apple of my eye. Do you like him?"

"He almost singed Nog's beard and fried us to crisps."

She gave a breathy chuckle. "I had Grindar build a stone grate with the help of some workmen we brought up to Dormoth. The egg had hatched and I needed some pen to contain the youngling. He arranged to have their throats cut so they could not speak of what they saw, or the rare beast encaged. I have leverage against Grindar. A lock of his hair, a fingernail, an old boot. With such items I can cast a powerful spell on him under Dal Sagoth's direction. Should Grindar ever grow loose of tongue or turn against me...his soul would be blasted to such fires of hell that he'd wish he'd never been born."

Vetra licked his lips. "Convenient. As is the place to hold the dragon."

"'Twas an old cathedral or temple of some kind, left unfinished somewhere in the mists of time. Bare walls. No masonry. The reek is abominable down there, I know, but it must needs be worse, if the creature were not one of the more intelligent species. A natural well—a crevice that opens up underneath his chambers—drops to a swift underwater stream. The creature is smart—smart enough to lift tail and defecate there and let the feces be carried off by the current rather than foul his own bed."

"Clever beast."

She nodded. A flush rose in her tanned features. "I have Grindar sneak baskets of meat into my conservatory unbeknownst to the others. Even my fell purpose he does not suspect. Only that I keep a dark creature for my own amusements, and experiments. Which is not far off from the truth.

"I fed Drako deer, hares, scraps of bones and sinew from the many abattoirs that I patronize. All the time I hoped I could win him over. I must have been mad! Easier to win the moon. And yet, I succeeded somewhat. The dragon could easily have taken me and crunched me in his jaws—or fried my body to crisps with his red hot breath. But when the jewel came into my possession, I shone its dusky light into his feral eyes and I have awoken a trust in the beast, a fierce love for me that no animal in the world has ever known for its master. So much so that he will fight for me to the death if I wish it."

"You are an army unto yourself then."

"The chamber is sealed. Only an entrance from above, which I have had filled with earthworks and garden shrubbery planted overtop the ceiling to hide its existence. I can always dig the earth up and let the dragon fly free."

"You would loose the dragon?"

"A wise woman never reveals her secrets, haven't you learned that? Now what to do with you?" Her long-lashed eyes looked at him lazily, playfully, seductively, as if she had every intent to milk the moment for all it was worth. "You saw my dragon, Drako, then? Or did you only hear him?"

"Both, if you call that scaly creature a dragon."

"He is not just any creature. He is young, a Kyldrie, one of the old ones, a breed thought extinct." She circled him, eyeing him lasciviously from head to toe. "You're too fine a specimen to maim or kill. Nobody must know my secret. Do you understand, mercenary?"

He did, but he chose not to acknowledge her.

"My guardian and mentor, loremaster Tharax, entrusted me with a secret. While middling in age when Senesch was young, he watched the thing for a generation, carried the egg singlehandedly from the wastes of the north... from the Haunt of Kyldrie where came the dragons and creatures of nightmare, and the marshals, the Dragon Lords of old. They all died centuries ago. Only legend and myth remain. Of tombs and ancient resting places where the dragons lie—and the odd egg.

"But enough for now. I seem to be boring you and there're far more interesting things we could be doing ere the night is through, lover."

Her lower lip curled and her eyes glinted mysteriously. "Seeing as you're so obsessed with this jewel, I think you'll be the first to taste its power on this new moon of love. It strikes in an hour, an auspicious alignment of stellar bodies. Are you ready?"

Vetra held up both hands. "Let's talk some more."

"The time for talk is over! The Eros amulet will uncover all!"

She held forth the jewel in front of Vetra's eyes. Before he could react, its throbbing light awoke some inner fire within him. Like a sunbeam striking off a lake's surface that blinds the viewer, the sultry rays seemed to pulse with a spectral energy and dance off his brain, like a thing alive, threatening to pull him with it, like a cascade of molten lava flowing out of a fissure.

He tried to turn his head away but couldn't. For a while he

seemed frozen, one step away from becoming her plaything.

Flashes of quicksilver crackled at the border of his senses. The pulsing light was penetrating the deepest core of his soul. Its power and rhythmic movement threatened to make him a helpless automaton to her breathy suggestions.

She did not miss the look of desire in his eyes. A lust so fierce, however masked...for her figure, her heat, her mystery, induced by the erotic spell of the jewel and the sultry setting. Her slim body twisted languidly, her arms arched behind her back, her hips moved with a lazy undulation and the lithe ease of panther.

She leaned in, slipped an olive-skinned arm about his muscled shoulders. Her sleek half-naked flank pressed against his thigh. The jasmine perfume of her dove-tailed hair flamed in his nostrils.

Despite the jewel's mesmeric pull striking at the heart of his resolve, a part of Vetra yet remained aloof and witness to the eerie thaumaturgy at play. He managed to keep a tiny essence of himself intact. But this was only a small victory. When she gestured and stared at him with seductive eye, he felt in his chest battering ramp thumps that beat against his ribcage and sent him into overwhelming passion for this woman. She with the perfectly coved hair, the slinky hips and the full breasts pressing through the tight fabric of her mage's gown. Every fiber of his being wanted to rush over and tear off her clothes, pull this goddess down and ravage her. Vetra started forward on ox-like legs while a lascivious roar rumbled in his throat.

"Very good, mercenary," she taunted.

She slapped him as he bulled forward, a withering blow across his left cheek, then she stood back and watched him freeze like a statue. Vetra, the schoolboy, marionette in a parody of frozen pantomime.

"All in good time, mercenary. I will enjoy you at my leisure. Pleasures beyond your puny imagination. Even you, the simple mind you are, will get a taste of real ecstasy. But through every erotic moment, 'tis you who will be the slave and I the master."

By the hand she led Vetra past the wide, oaken double-door to her side chambers where she had taken many men to her bed.

There, dwelled a small boudoir with high queen-sized bed with elegant satin sheets. Leafy alpadacus plants rose in all four corners of the room, giving a waft of eucalyptus scent to rival many a tropical island. A small fountain bubbled to the side where clear waters fed a small pool and small reddish-gold fish swam, which looked like goldfish but could have been piranhas for all the teeth on their snub-noses. A pungent incense drifted from the altar to the side. Faint purplish fumes, a sickly sweet odor enough to make Vetra's senses swim.

The magic continued to work its way and the jewel latched ever tighter in her fist.

She pulled him down into the bed, kicked off what little remained of the black gown around her luscious hips and Vetra's breath caught in his throat at the sensual beauty of her, her lush figure, her animal vitality, her fulsome flesh pulsing with a radiance that was divine as much as it was evil.

"You are only one of a long line of lovers, mercenary. I take them all to my bed. To test their mettle. Be honored, Vetravincus of the flashing sword! Doff your war gear and make love to me as you have never made love to a woman before!"

And like an obedient serf, Vetra kicked off his clothes and clung to her. Part of him resisted the overpowering, yielding flesh, the red-hot heat of her tanned skin, but her luscious sensuality was more than his willpower could master. Indeed, each clutch of oiled limb, thrust of naked hip, moist tongue licking on hot skin and quivering flesh achieved new heights of ecstasy and meaning in the dusky light of the oil lamp beneath the bestial effigy. And even as her vixenish heat blasted his skull with bursts of pleasure, he felt as if he were entwined with a serpent.

Chapter 22

The only thing more powerful than Taranis's Sagothian magic was the Eros stone itself, which lay clasped in her fist as she straddled Vetra, riding him like an exotic mare, oiled and naked.

In the heat of the moment, amid moans of sultry abandon and slap of flesh on flesh, none noticed the skulking figure sliding like an uninvited shadow at the door.

Creeping up from the dungeon crypts of Old Sagoth, Skirl made three quick strides to rip the jewel from the sorceress's grasp.

Taranis jerked aside; the spell was broken. Her sensuous loins slipped from Vetra's spent body and her gray-green eyes blazed with disbelief and hatred.

"You filthy traitor!" She spread palms wide to launch a death globe.

But Nog grabbed her wrists and the globe went caroming off the wall. He dragged her off the bed, ogling her olive-toned nakedness and curved perfection and the thick black bush shrouding the wet loins.

"What a pleasant surprise," he muttered.

"You're all dead! You hear? Dead!" She lashed left and right like a fiend in his grip.

Skirl wielded the stone in a trembling fist, not yet registering the fact that the power of the gods were now in his fledgling's fist. "Back, witch! I will use this bauble to rend you asunder. Make no move, if you value your skin!" The apprentice looked a vision of fury, though haggard, unkempt and wound tight as a demented clock.

Vetra raised his bulk to a half sitting position, blinking dazedly. Groggily he shook his head.

Nog gave his own head a shake of jealous amazement. "I see you've been dipping your wick mighty hard, Vetra boy. While we've been out fighting an army of hostiles—"

"I'll gladly switch places with you," grumbled Vetra. He staggered off the bed. His lean muscles rippled, poised in all his well-spiked phallic majesty. It seemed the sorceress had waved certain exotic incenses under his nose prior to their lovemaking, thus prolonging his tumescence.

Nog drank in the sight of the gleaming witch, licking his chops…from her sweat-glistening thighs to the dark nipples on her ample breasts, her slender waist, busty hips, rounded buttocks and oiled and gleaming hide.

Skirl seemed immune to the sorceress's allure. He seemed to be fighting some dark part of himself. He'd already had enough of the wench. The mere sight of her repulsed him.

Though the shimmer and gleam of her voluptuous body dangled on a thread within his reach.

Taranis shifted and shafted the apprentice a cruel smile. "Yes, Skirl, you remember our twining in this bed, don't you?"

Vetra struggled to wrench himself from his stupor. With jerky motions, he donned his leather jerkin and black boots, trance-like. He searched for his sword, recalled it was leaning against the wall in the other room. He went to fetch it, paused there on stiff legs and shot fast the bolt to the cursed door that led to the bowels of Old Sagoth beneath the Mages' Hall.

He came back to see Taranis in all her gleaming glory, sweat-laced and magisterial, advancing on Skirl.

Skirl shrank back. "I said, back, witch!" he cried while Nog leered. "Your power is dim without this carnival prize." He clutched the cursed gem tighter as if fearing it would bite him.

Vetra grabbed the magician's arm. "Better not, mage. There's no time. The guards'll be here soon."

Taranis jeered, "Aye, mage, you know not how to wield it."

"Says who?"

"Says me. You're a better bookworm than mage."

He rounded on her hotly. "I found the exact location of the sorceress's tomb." He shook the gem in an angry hand. "You'd have been fumbling around for ten years if I hadn't pinpointed the exact location of the secret tunnel to Sarkala's mortuary chamber. The jewel lay there on her breast, her body parched and mummified, a thousand years dead."

"'Tis all true, it was there, eight moons ago on the expedition to Mmos we found the Eros Flame, thanks to your hard work and diligent digging, apprentice Skirl. But so what? Only I can wield the stone's power. It has been habituated to my use. 'Tis you who yield to me, the head sorceress of Dormoth."

Vetra snarled, "Ignore her. She's up to her old tricks. How did you get past Grindar?"

Nog gave a cheeky grin. "We disposed of the sentry left to watch the bottom of the stairs. When we heard Grindar and his ghouls clopping down the stairs we dragged the body over into the passage with the dragon for more fun, then hid. From there it was easy to make our way when they passed. Here we find you bedding this she-panther, not in a torture chamber."

Taranis noted all information with a cat-like gleam in her eyes.

Vetra stirred, seeing the witch's devious gaze, one sizing them up as a cat does mice. "Enough! Let us be away from this witch. The more time I spend here in this abominable crib with her and her leering statue, my soul sickens."

Nog stood rooted, staring lustily at her voluptuous, naked flesh.

"Wake up, Nog!" Vetra rapped his knuckles on his helm. It

took all of Vetra's prodding to snap him out of his infatuation. Even without the jewel, the woman's mesmeric power was formidable.

"You will burn!" she cried after them.

Nog motioned carelessly. "We can't leave this vixen running free."

Vetra scowled. He reached for the dresser, flung her garments on the floor. Tearing strips of cloth from one of her gowns, he bound her arms and ankles while Nog stuffed a gag in her mouth. To her sullen dismay, they tied her securely to the bedpost. They shut the door, retraced their steps back to the hall.

Empty, but for the sound of boots and men's murmurs echoing up the hallway.

"Follow my lead," muttered Vetra. "If anyone asks, we're on our way to the main gate, on a mission from Taranis herself."

Nog cracked wide a grin.

They took heel and ran down the hallway.

At the first archway, Vetra halted. A pair of lighted censers wavered to drafts of cool air wafting from the blackness opening on the court. Freedom was close, but it would have to be prodded delicately with stealth and guile.

They scrambled through the archway out into the court, grateful for fresh air and the star-filled sky. Vetra's mind raced. He could hear the rustle of men near the gate, as if divining that something was up. To get out of here may not be so simple...

He hustled them along the portico and winter palms to where a pedestal stood with a bronze gong hung from a chain. He snatched the mallet and beat it against the gong. "To arms, men! To arms," he cried. "Hearken, Taranis is waylaid! She is in her inner chamber. Treason is afoot, men!"

A guard came running, a bewildered look on his face. "What do you mean 'waylaid'?"

"Someone has ravaged the Archmagrix," Vetra said breathlessly. He gestured back toward the Hall of Mages while Skirl tipped his face away from the man to avoid recognition.

Vetra shook a fist. "From her lips I heard her utter the word 'Grindar'. She has banished the rogue while he fled off shamed of his deed. Heed not anything he says. They are all lies! Some men are helping her now. I have come to summon the town watch. Grindar must be caught!"

"What? This is an outrage!" The guard went to scurry off but Vetra grabbed his arm. "Take this mallet, man! Beat the gong. Warn others of the outrages."

The man gripped the handle and took up the task, nodding, in a feverish sweat.

Vetra chuckled, grinning maliciously as he moved off with the others.

He turned to Nog. "Let us flee this hive. It'll be a swarm of bees before long. They will be out for our blood."

He peered back toward the hall and caught a brief glimpse of Belgra disappearing through an archway in a flash of white robe. Senesch trailed behind her with a cane.

Torches were ablaze in the covered colonnades abreast the Hall of Mages. The sound of men's shouts echoed amid the slithering of blades from sheaths while the gong rang incessantly.

Where were the other mages? Likely huddled in their workshops like obedient puppies.

Vetra did not mind. With a satisfied grin, he booted it with his partners in crime across the nighted court, past the shadowy well toward the iron-piked gate, heedless of any guards they met.

They came to a breathless halt before the watchpost, limned in amber light gleaming down from oil lamps on the gate.

The gatepost sentry leered at them through his wooden wicket. "Where are you three monkeys going to? Can't you hear the gong? No one enters or leaves. Taranis's orders."

"We were told to summon the town guard!" Vetra grunted. "Why do you hesitate, man? Hurry! The Archmagrix will have your head for not letting us out. Grindar has defiled the Archmagrix. We were told to summon the town guard."

"This is irregular. I have had no such orders. And why the three of you when only one need go?"

"Do you doubt your orders, captain?" Vetra rasped.

It wasn't working. The ruse was going sour. Vetra peered into the shadowed street beyond the iron bars and thought to try a gambit. "Hoy, thieves!" he cried. "Blackguards!"

"What? Where?" The guard strained his eyes into the murk but Vetra slammed him hard in the face.

The guard toppled over and fell in a heap on the flagstones.

Nog yanked the chain from around his neck and snatched up his key ring. They unlocked the gate and he and Vetra pulled wide the iron grille.

"Slick," grumbled Skirl as they scrambled out.

"What I wouldn't give for a Tolizian war horse right now," groused Vetra.

"No matter, the *Pauper's Cauldron* is down the way," Nog said. "We can hide our noses in some brews. The sight of that sultry vixen has whetted my—"

"Pick up your feet, fool. There'll be no *Pauper's Cauldron* or *Rat Peacock*. Less ramble and more speed, old man. Run! Run!"

Chapter 23

A faint glow grew in the east over the towers of the royal palace. The clatter of distant carts had already intruded on the passing night: merchants keen on delivering wares to market before the bustle started. Long runners were also on the road: caravans, teamsters, horse-pulled wains. It was to these that Vetra and his two companions looked.

They'd walked for several miles, steering clear of the dives, alehouses and main roads where they thought the Dormoth guards might be looking for them. They stood now before the stone bridge leading out of the city over the canal heading east to Alantra. It had been agreed upon by the three that heading south and east was their best bet as far as fencing the jewel was concerned. Between Smrin to the west and Alantra to the east, Alantra had won out.

They saw the first of many wains clatter by: laden with hay, geese, farmers' cheese, eggs wrapped in straw for protection. Heavier vehicles too with bulky cargoes—metalworks fresh from the smithies.

Wolfsha, the half wolf, had sniffed out their trail and caught up with them. Maybe her bloodhound's nose had tracked them as far back as the cobbled road at Dormoth. Perhaps she still remembered the noble service Vetra had done for her, saving her life from the murderous wolf-baiter. More likely she was just lonely and remembered Vetra for the affection he'd given her.

"We're getting nowhere," Nog said. He flapped his hands down at his side, discouraged by the many fruitless attempts to get a cart to stop for them.

Vetra stepped into the middle of the road with his hand raised, his other hand pushed down on the pommel of his sword at his hip. His red surcoat swirled in the breeze as he pretended to be a member of the city guard.

The next cart driver ground to a halt, scowling into his salt-and-pepper beard. "What do you devils want? Can't you see I'm busy? Move aside!"

Vetra rambled over to the driver's bench to stand two feet away. He patted the nearest gray mare and squinted up at the surly man who was muttering between his teeth. "You heading to Alantra?"

"What of it?" The man drew a knife. Wolfsha growled.

"You have ample space in the back of your covered wain, I see. We'd like to hop a ride with you east."

"And witches like to fly to the moon," he said. "You can go on 'liking' all you want, friend." He looked them up and down. "Don't see anything in it for me."

Vetra gave a carefree shrug. "At the very least, we can offer protection."

"Protection from what? Your wolf?"

"No, Wolfsha'll keep guard of your wain from footpads. Our swords'll also lend a hand."

He hissed a soft staccato sound through his teeth. "What's to say you don't cut my throat somewhere on the road half way to Alantra, then ride off into the wild blue yonder with my goods?"

"We could have already done that," Nog said cheerfully. "What's so special about half way to Alantra?"

A steely grin spread over the fat man's lips. "Okay, well, hop in then, rogues. Dergath curse you if you betray me. If anything happens to my cart on the road, by Lingara's elder beard you'll pay for it in spades. You're running from something, I can smell it in your breaths, on your breeks, not counting your bloody and disheveled looks. Sure as my name's

Marath, I hope my good deed doesn't bite me in the ass."

Nog chuckled. "Unless you keep yapping about it, why should it, old man?"

The cartman mumbled, black front tooth showing in the fugitive morning light. He flicked the reins and the twin mares jolted off, barely giving Nog and Vetra time to jump in the back. They caught Skirl by the arms and hauled him in. Likewise, Wolfsha leaped up in after the mage. They covered themselves under some dusty burlap tarps next to the sacks of flour and baskets of chicken eggs protected in straw. Wolfsha happily snuggled herself in beside them.

The steady clop of hooves came and went on the dusty cobbles. The squat weathered slate-brick apartments gave way to rolling countryside then fields of corn and harvested stacks of wheat. Hidden in the covered wain under tarps, the fugitives caught occasional glimpses of the passing scenery: wisps of gray smoke curling from the flaked chimney of a single-story stone farmhouse, the ruffle of wings of a crow perched on a dead elm, the trudge of foot-wayfarers, goats, geese, lowing oxen, the jingle of tinkers' wagons as they were pulled by donkeys. The occasional clatter of imperial wagons as they too pushed by bearing men and arms.

Skirl peeked up from his dusty tarp and again appeared gloomy. "Taranis will come after us. The Eros Flame—is too valuable."

"Dergath, man!" Vetra cursed. "All this sneaking about and killing, for something that is supposed to make people love each other?"

"The magic was corrupted ages ago," he sighed. "Like everything else in this wicked world. So many good things turn black and treacherous, like the flesh of a ripe apple—at least when too many people get their fingers into them."

"I don't know," said Nog, "I hear some of the women at the *Bounding Boar* in Alantra aren't too shabby. Maybe we can use this black magic, see how many dames I can bag."

Skirl rolled his eyes and gave a dismal grunt. "Such minds of limited capacity in our company, Vetra. Where do you get them?"

A gleaming blade flashed against the apprentice's throat. "Are we going to go through this exercise again, Skirly? You have a death wish?"

"Knock it off, you two," Vetra rumbled. "This journey's long enough—"

"Okay, everybody out!" a voice bawled from up front.

The wagon juddered to a halt. Vetra peered out to see they were at the dusty crossroads of a main junction heading to Tarnlake.

"This is the last stop," the cartdriver warned. "I head north to deliver my eggs…pick up some hens then it's back to the city for me before nightfall. This is where we part ways." He uttered the words with some relief.

Skirl jumped out and made a gracious bow. "We thank you, cartmaster. Your kindness in escorting us thus far has been only too timely."

The man gave a brusque shrug. "Extra weight slowed us down. Tired Bessy out more than she needed."

Skirl nodded in sympathy. "The mare looks worn."

Before the man rattled off with a jolt, he brought the Eros jewel out and its ruby-rich rays caught the farmer's attention.

"Beautiful isn't it? How would you like that piece of glitter to adorn your wife's neck?" Skirl gave an easy grin.

"I—" The cartman's pale eyes mooned.

"Alantra is not far," Skirl said brightly. "'Tis but a hop and skip down the main road. I'm sure you'd like to ride with us to Alantra, wouldn't you? Gaze at the pretty jewel?"

The cartmaster seemed ready to utter a disparaging comment but then his jowly cheeks slackened, his eyes glazed over and his lips parted. "I suppose I could visit my brother in Alantra. Try my luck at the famous market there. Did you know it's the largest market in the northern kingdoms?"

Skirl clapped his hands. "A marvelous idea, cartmaster." He lifted the jewel higher with an impish grin on his face. Nog and Vetra had wandered over to stare wryly.

"The jewel? Would you offer it in exchange?" he gulped.

Skirl beamed.

His face was flushed rosy red. "It would be my honor to escort you," he stammered. "How silly of me not to suggest it in the first place. Hop in the back!"

Nog, unable to restrain a snigger, murmured, "Pawning our lodestone so early?"

"No." Skirl tucked the jewel back in his robe. "Our friend the cartmonger'll not get it. You saw him. He'll have forgotten the gem by morning. He's putty in our hands. A jay. He'll do anything I tell him."

Vetra scowled, not liking the power of this jewel, or the one wielding it.

The cart rattled forward before Wolfsha and the three were barely back in their usual places. For extra security, Vetra and Nog turned their surcoats inside out so the dragon and eagle emblem of Dormoth would not be visible to anyone peering in the back.

"A bit much," said Vetra after a time. "You didn't have to go that far, did you, Skirl?"

"You heard him," said the apprentice, "he wishes to visit his brother."

"Yeah, sure," Vetra snorted, "go 80 miles out of his way? I don't think so."

Skirl gave a whimsical shrug. "Marath may fare better in Alantra than Xalgossa, for all we know. What's a little venture out in the country anyways? Not going to hurt anyone."

Vetra gestured bleakly. "That jewel is evil and you know it. You're becoming a menace."

"And a fabulous con artist," Nog added.

Skirl tipped his head in smiling acknowledgment.

Vetra inspected the apprentice through slitted eyes. Not for the first time did he have doubts about this venture. "This jewel, magician...it seems to be more trouble than it's worth. How did you say it came into your hands? What makes it so powerful?"

Skirl fingered the jewel in his pocket out of habit. "'Tis said the priestess Sarkala infused the stone with her life essence a thousand years ago. Embedded into the very fabric of its glow is a magic most puissant, most elemental—a stunning sapphire dug from the rugged mines in Kyldrie. The ones bordering Vinland where the dragons once flew. The Legend of the Eros Stone is an old one, known by only a few people. Mostly scholars. Her dying wish was that the jewel be placed at the head of her shrine so that all could remember the charitable deeds done throughout her lifetime. Not for her glory, but that the common citizen could follow her example, practice good will, respect the freedom of everyone in the lands and give more than receive. When she died, such was her power that she could get all who gazed upon the stone to love her and revere her good will and legacy. A rare being in the black-hearted world of today, full of war, strife and hate."

"It seems like an old wives' tale," said Nog.

"It may be. But you have not heard the rest. There were

those who were jealous of Sarkala's lingering memory and her renown and her power after death. Those of the crown hired villains of the night to steal the stone and desecrate her shrine. They came in the dark before dawn to pillage and tear apart her shrine and make off with the jewel. They failed. Some bite of lightning singed their hands when they tried. The unwarranted vandalism only angered the people and they rebuilt her shrine. Even though the jewel now had many notches and scratches on it, its inner flame burned with a fire brighter than ever. The hews of the vandals' blades could harm not its beguiling facets.

"They were depraved, and though they defiled it—slapped mud, rotten fruit and offal on her temple, the red flame burned ever brighter than before.

The ruling class who came after, grew ever bitter and conspired to hire a dark magician to curse the jewel and lay a spell on Sarkala's shrine. The sorceress they hired was Arcana.

"'I will do even better,'" she boasted. "'I will taint the jewel with such hexes that it brings an equal amount of darkness to those who gaze upon its contours.'" Skirl, seeing he had a captive audience, assumed the guise of storyteller of grand and animated gestures.

"The king rubbed his hands in glee. He handed over five bags of silver and gold to the evil witch.

"Arcana rived and blasted the jewel with spells from the underworld. The undying flame flickered. It was replaced with bursts of green and blue. But only at odd times. No matter how hard she tried, the sorceress could not quench the flame utterly. Such was Sarkala's power beyond death. For brief moments all that could be seen was the flame turned to blue, as it signaled that the unfettered power of good, once free-flowing and eternal, was no longer pure. The jewel, though still powerful, was tainted now.

"After a dark age, Xalgossa was razed to the ground and King Minos's head hoisted on a pike. The skeletons of towers and temples and market forums fell into ruin. But it was said that Sarkala's mummified body was spirited away to a mortuary temple, and the jewel placed at her breast. It was this very same legend which inspired me to seek the jewel and the underground temple of Gotha where the sorceress lay and retrieve the talisman. Which I did. I believed that if it existed, chances are, in the mists of time long passed, it had not been grave-robbed."

Vetra blinked as if lost in an ancient world. "An interesting story, mage. So real…and yet, I could almost feel the cool stone of her tomb and hear the coos of the citizens as her fane was desecrated."

Skirl held up the jewel for them to see. Vetra gaped. He could feel its warm and ancient power seep into his bones. It filled the confined space around him, even as the cart jolted over potholes. A familiar dizziness once more swam in his head, and with it a tremor of unease.

Wolfsha gazed at the jewel too, cocked her head from side to side as if it were not of this earth. She gave herself to whining.

Nog scoffed. "I don't know, Vetra, I've heard a lot of talk. Seen a bunch of pretentious people dressed in robes and costumes posturing as sorcerers. Even seen a halfwit cartman goggle and moon and offer to drive us to Alantra. But witnessed little proof of its magic."

"You still don't believe, mercenary?" Skirl cried aghast. He pushed it closer to Wolfsha's snout. "Watch as I—"

Vetra slapped his wrist away. "Keep the jewel away from her. I don't like its light shining at the dog…it disturbs her."

Skirl clicked his tongue. "The wolfling loves it. Look, it's a love jewel."

"It's a sinister relic. Probably better off burnt. Or thrown in a deep pit."

"You're harsh, Vetra. You're talking about the thing that's going to make us rich."

"Speaking of which," Nog said. "What's the plan? Do we pawn it at the market at Alantra as soon as we get there?"

Vetra gave a moody scowl. "It's as good a plan as any."

Skirl bared his teeth. For a moment it was as if he found the idea repulsive. Then, catching himself, he gave an affected sigh. "I guess it falls on my shoulders to be the stone bearer."

"See that you don't lose it, apprentice, or misuse it," Vetra muttered.

Nog laughed. "Misuse it? How can it be misused? Give me this jewel and I'll teach some of those young tavern maids a thing or two about the art of love."

"If you're such a stud," Skirl said, "why do you need a prop?"

"You make a good point. Let's give it to Vetra. Looks as if he needs help in the charm department."

"You forget who lay with Taranis," Vetra growled.

Nog's lips curled in half jealousy. "What I wouldn't have given to have been in her bed back there. Dergath's apes! What was it like laying with that vixen?"

"Let's just say I'd trade places with you any day."

"You can't be serious?" Nog cried.

Vetra's face was dark.

Nog leaned back in the straw, his face a mask of puzzlement.

* * *

The night that Skirl and Nog had invaded her chamber, Taranis had wept in rage and frustration. The freakish twist of fortunes had cast her into a cauldron of misery. That the skulkers had bound and gagged her was imprinted on her mind forever. Shame and humiliation burned in her soul. When Grindar and his men had finally clambered in to cut her loose, she had sworn the thieves all would die in agony and had sworn the guards to silence, on pain of death.

Now she fell to her knees on the hard cold stone floor and dug her nails into her palms, so hard they drew blood. She gazed with hatred upon the sinister idol that she had worshiped for years—Yeasaba, the dreaded one, the grotesque half bat, half elk that would wither the heart of the most hardened dark priest of Umbria.

"Why have you deserted me, O Great One?" she wailed.

A voice came from the bowels of her mind, of pain, torture, a long dank well of ebon depths ringing in her hollow skull.

"Deserted you I did not, dark child. Look to the crescent blood moon on a starry night in the June sky. This setback was but a test. An obstacle only. To test your loyalty to me, your faith in the creed of Sagoth..."

Taranis cried, "A test? A setback? But they have stolen the jewel from me, Lord! From me, the Archmagrix of the Circle. The audacity! The impudence! The brazen insolence. They will all die in lakes of their own blood, O darkest One!"

And with violence in her heart Taranis moved to shatter the dark effigy hanging above her bed to a thousand pieces.

But with the next message given unto her by her dark lord through her mind's eye, Taranis's hateful sneer turned to a croak of laughter, then a leer of sheer anticipation.

Chapter 24

By nightfall the fugitives'd made the hill station of Ravenknoll: a small village surrounded by high hills on both sides north and south. Noted only for the mighty stone heads of kings with ravens' beaks that lined the overlooking ridge and marked the ancient borderlands of the north with the bird-kings of old. The cobbled road continued into the plains, on to Alantra in Lvendar some 30 miles distant.

The cartmaster rented a room at the *Boarmaster's Rest* while Vetra and the others were content to stretch out in the back of the wain to pass the night in the hay and protect the cartdriver's goods. The canopy had certainly shielded them from any prying eyes that day.

While the cartmaster fed the mares and watered them at the troughs set out by the inn's stable, Vetra visited the taproom with Nog and Skirl to see about some food and ale. The weathered gray oak door, Vetra noticed, sported a husky hill boar's stuffed head nailed to it. A bit of local color to welcome the passing stranger...

Inside the inn was dim, warm and cozy. The three were afforded the usual odd stares expected for a couple of rough-looking mercenaries in mail and a blue-robed mage with a bloodied bandage tied slantwise on his head. They sat at a table apart where they chewed their mutton stew in silence. After downing some watered ale, they repaired to the wagon to maintain anonymity. It was agreed upon that Nog and Vetra would alternate on watch while the others slept: Vetra had still not rejected the idea that some form of the Mage Guard would be on their tails before long.

By noon they passed through the great gate leading into

Alantra city. Under the piked walls adorned with ceremonial gargoyles they clattered along the main thoroughfare to the tune of bustling thousands. Archers bearing the yellow eagle of Lvendar on their jerkins ranged the parapets of the high stone walls. Two massive bulls' heads flanked the gates and dwindled behind them. The bulls' round, staring glazed-eyes were plated in pure silver, large as gongs.

The cart creaked to a halt a stone's throw from the market and the old man's voice bellowed back at them. "An uneventful journey, friends! Good luck to you. Nice to have your swords at my back. I hope your enterprise fares well."

"Likewise, cartmaster," Vetra rumbled as he came hopping down with Wolfsha.

"About that jewel now…" The cartmaster frowned, his black eyes glittering.

Skirl skipped out and approached him on nimble feet. "I release you from all holds, bond and obligations."

"What do you mean? Can you not give me the jewel—?"

"Alas, the bauble is an heirloom," he explained, "a family treasure. A memento that must stay in my possession."

"You—" He gave a gulping cry. Then frowned. "A pity. May I see the gem at least one last time?"

Skirl reluctantly withdrew it. The scarlet radiance had the man blinking and sweating, his face lit in a bright, red flush. A last longing look back and the cartmaster gave a wistful sigh and an acquiescent nod.

Had Skirl cast a spell on him? Vetra patted Wolfsha. She circled at his heels looking for treats. "We appreciate the ride, cartmaster," he said gruffly, handing him a small coin. "Do you know any gem dealers in the area?"

"Gem dealers?" He frowned. "Not really. Try the market. You can ask around." He clicked his tongue, flicked the reins and the cart jolted into the milling crowd toward the afternoon market.

The companions took their leave and wandered in an opposite direction, away from the hubbub toward one of the soaring temples fronted with a sandstone sphinx. Vetra noticed that the cartman, upon a quick look back, had tarried and sat in his seat staring back at them. When he saw them peer his way, he shook his head and frowned, then whipped his cart forward with a slap of reins.

Vetra cast a shrewd glance at Skirl. "What was that bit about ties and obligations and whatnot?"

Skirl shrugged. "The Eros stone magnifies the emotional link between wielder and receiver. I merely released the cartmaster of the spell. His memory'll come round, in about a half hour. Maybe he'll feel a tad angry, maybe bitter, no big loss. We'll be long gone."

"More than a tad angry, I think," Vetra muttered.

"We're at the last of our coins," Nog said. "Only enough for a room for one night."

Vetra peered up at the sun as it dipped behind clouds drifting in from the east. It was already late in the afternoon. Maybe rain coming? "Let's follow the old man's advice. Get the word on who's good to sell rubies to. Worse comes to worse, we'll rent a room at one of the dives and pawn it off in the morning."

He strode among the crowd under the shadow of a forty-foot high temple. The sheer face of the smooth-polished blocks were carved with the faces of kings and martyrs, sages and half-human gods with horned heads and half goatish bodies. Vetra kept thinking, so many deities to worship, how could a man decide which to put his faith on? So many diverse kingdoms and people. He kept the apprentice well in sight of him.

Alantra! Most populous of the cities of the northern kingdoms. The crossroads to Mercia, Umbria, Sahir and Tolizia. To the south, Behundria and Galashad. The city of a hundred gods... if not the Temple mecca of all the kingdoms, predated only by Old Gyzia, 120 miles south. They'd crossed the border into Lvendar back at Ravenknoll. There was little need for tolls or tariffs here; Lvendar and Umbria were firm allies. The volume of traffic and goods made it impractical.

Past the temple district, the market was astir with the usual honking geese, clattering carts, roving merchants and peasants. Everyone afoot in one mad jumble of humanity.

The three waded their way through people, animals, carts, merchandise and noise, Vetra noting that festival time was upon the city. Ritual and pomp were the rules rather than exceptions. From far and wide, mendicants, holy men, fakirs, soothsayers and pilgrims had come to pay homage to the pantheon of gods that ruled in this city, or more accurately, the eight kingdoms. The most aggressive were the merchants, eager to sell their tawdry trinkets, homages to Dergath, Azath, Morgot and Aramis, and such stuff. Jade figurines hung from hawkers' racks of staring eyed priests, prophets and alleged holy relics of toe-bones of saints.

Nog muscled his way through the throng, stepping on toes, elbowing touts and hawkers out of the way. Proselytizers and shoe-shiners received no better treatment. Urchins ran in packs, pawing at thighs and waists for coins.

The slender, pale gray-blue slate minarets of the Temple of Lingara reared up in the sky, overlooking amber-colored cupolas where holy men came out to ring their bells. Others came out to shake castanets and belt out prayers in singsong voices to the city. It seemed, this was a competing game among the diverse factions. There came higher and shriller calls and entreaties. Solemn-faced priests moved as one on quiet feet through the crowded streets, their loose white robes trailing at ankles, arms crossed over their chests, hands tucked in voluminous sleeves. Hoods draped their shaven heads. Some of these holy men ran ahead, beating gongs and announcing the presence of the third coming of their god, be it Lingara or Azath. The pilgrims and votaries alike swooned in their wake like swaying cobras.

Vetra stuck close to the spellcaster on the chance that some vulturous cutpurse might try to rifle his robe and snatch their priceless jewel. In their favor, Skirl, garbed in his ragged, torn and muddied apprentice's robe, looked about as wealthy as the next beggar in the gutter. The thick bandage plastered to his left ear gave him the look of a leper.

Grinning, Vetra stuck close to the apprentice, nevertheless, his dark eyes were ever roving like a hawk's.

A grizzle-haired woman intruded herself between the Vetra and Skirl and thrust one of her cheap, soapstone figurines from her basket into Vetra's hand: a mermaid with crown, tiara and trident-staff.

"Only four bits and quarter shill for one, good pilgrims! The festival of Tiara is on. You'll need a figurine to get past the monitors at the Lingara temple to receive your blessing from the virgin!"

"That is good to know, lady, and thank you for the information," Vetra said. He pushed the trinket aside. "Perhaps on the way back. We're visitors here, looking for a dealer in gems. Do you know one?"

"Gems?" She frowned, showed a mouth full of missing teeth. She jerked a shoulder back to where they'd come. "Most well known gemsmith I know would be Zlandar. As for reputable—I don't think there's such a thing in this city." She laughed and flashed him another toothy grin. "Still, Zlandar's your man, if you're looking for gems…"

Vetra nodded and motioned the others to the place the woman had indicated.

Chapter 25

They traipsed on to a less busy district of shops and taverns set in neat, polished-brick rows. Vetra set his feet toward what looked a respectable establishment with old brown brick and ivy, and ornate iron grilling set in stylish swirls, with fairies and birds laced over the dark-tinted casement. A placard was posted on high, *'Zlandar's Fine Gems'*. The lettering was archaic, perhaps lending an air of respectability to the place.

Nog grunted his impatience. While Wolfsha sat obediently at the steps, her ears ruffled, Vetra pushed through the heavy door into a squarish room with high ceiling inlaid with dark, lacquered wood. Cases of necklaces, rings and bracelets stood under glass in the center aisle.

The gemsmith looked at them with shrewd eyes across the counter—a hunched man with stooped shoulders, hooked nose and heavy gray-brows. It seemed the gears in his practiced brain were already working to size them up. But nothing could be more difficult than to assess this motley group.

Vetra approached, pushing Skirl forward. He motioned the apprentice to lay down his jewel.

"Hoy, sir!" said Skirl. "We are in the business of scouting out the sale of a family heirloom."

The man blinked and for a second seemed to gasp at the size and beauty of the Eros Flame. "Where did you get such a jewel?"

"I recently acquired it from my aunt. Our family is wishing to divide the coins of whatever it is worth." Skirl motioned to Vetra. "This is my brother, Valar, and my brother's friend, Nojen."

The gem dealer lifted the Eros stone in a trembling hand and gazed at its faceted wonder for some time. His bespectacled eyes stared, turning it over in his gnarled fingers. He seemed entranced at its living color, the crimson of blood sage or dahlia and the mesmerizing flame wrapped deep within its contours.

"A fascinating specimen," he coughed. "Let me scrutinize it in more detail in the back. I have magnifiers in my workshop, and salts and solutions that can test its authenticity. I'll quote you a price in a trice, gentlemen." He turned with salamander quickness and went to take the gem, but Vetra laid out a hand and gripped his thin wrist. "No, gem-monger, the bauble stays with us."

The gem-dealer scowled. "As you wish." With a droop of shoulders he wet his lips. "Very well, but I must consult my indices at the very least. Wait here." With a cluck of annoyance, he shuffled into the back room on heavy feet.

Nog grew bored after a time and circled the shop, poking his nose into every nook and cranny he could find, which wasn't many. Albeit, the dealer was gone for an inordinately long time and Vetra began to get suspicious. He suddenly got cold feet about this, recalling the shrewd look of the gem dealer, and he muttered, "Let's go!" He grabbed up the stone and stuffed it in Skirl's pocket.

"We just got here," Nog protested.

Vetra nudged Skirl to the door. Nog followed, shaking his head in bewilderment.

Sure enough, out on the street under the graying sky, Vetra saw the hunchback of a gem-dealer at a far corner where the roads crossed, whispering to a trio of bravos. They had knives stuffed in their belts, bandannas and hoods on head partially obscuring their young, rough-looking faces.

So, the dealer had skipped out the back to inform his network of thugs. Likely they planned to waylay them in the shop or on the street. It mattered little, so long as the jeweler got the gem.

Vetra steered Nog and Skirl down a side street and urged them to haste.

While Wolfsha took off ahead to chase a scruffy cat that had slunk out of a worm-eaten basket, Vetra swore under his breath. "Seems as if old Taranis's got a watch out for the jewel. Even as far as Alantra? Dergath! That conniving wench has a long reach."

"She does." Skirl seemed oblivious to the botched sale, only breathed a sigh of audible relief, a reaction which Vetra found puzzling. But then it dawned on him. Skirl was already getting cold feet about selling; he was far too attached to the gem. In no hurry was he to see it change hands.

His inner voice advised him that things were sliding into dicey territory. "The day's getting old, friends. I fear we'll have to wait another day to fence the jewel. Time to start looking for lodging."

"As long as you're paying, chief." Nog grinned. "I'm fresh out of—"

He did not finish that sentence. A ripple of movement came from ahead. Three hooded shapes leapt out of a darkened doorway. Vetra had been slow in drawing his blade. One of the bravos from earlier hobnobbing with the gem dealer got his mitts on Skirl and smacked him down on the dirty cobbles. The cutpurse snatched the Eros Flame out of his pocket and took off in a run up the alley while his other two accomplices squared off against Nog and Vetra, blocking the way. They kept the mercenaries busy with eight-inch knives and knotted clubs.

Wolfsha had heard the smack of fist and leaped at the fleeing footpad with a growl. She caught the man's bare arm clutching the jewel. He gave an anguished cry. The sapphire clattered to the cobbles while he sagged, trying to shake the wolfling off his arm. Wolfsha released her grip and he ran clutching at his mangled wrist, howling, leaving a blood trail behind him.

The two other cutpurses were less sure of themselves after that cockup.

Vetra parried a sweep of steel as a wicked poniard with curved tip flicked at his throat. He reversed his motion and smashed down hard on the knife arm of his attacker, knocking the blade out of his grip.

In the same breath his mallet fist came angling up to the man's face and sent him crashing to the street. Nog did a twist, ducked a swing of club and plunged a half yard of steel into the other rogue's guts. He doubled over, unable to stop his entrails from spilling out.

Wolfsha had snapped up the jewel and came dropping it at Skirl's feet.

Skirl knelt down and hugged her with joy. "You are a treasure, little one!"

The wolfling drank deeply of the crimson beams emanating from the jewel.

Vetra rubbed his jaw and debated whether he should kill the man worming his way in the dust. The thief was on his belly, murmuring, pleading, ready to rise in a crouch and flee.

In all practicality it was not wise to let any more of them report back to their masters. With an unsympathetic grunt, he licked his blade out at the man's throat. The man rolled in a gurgling heap and died.

Nog kicked at the blood-stained corpse. "I've a mind to go back there and demand restitution from that treacherous gem hound, Vetra."

"Forget it. He's probably surrounded himself with street toughs. Let's unload the jewel somewhere else, get our money and save playing enforcer for another day."

Skirl nodded vigorously.

Vetra mused, "I have a feeling we'll have similar dealings trying to pawn this bauble through formal channels. The black market may be our only option. Let's find a room and regroup."

With a troubled stride, he took them to the temple district, the *Habar* it was called, where transient men lodged on the cheap, men on the run, men in layover or seeking their fortunes south and east.

They found a seedy room close to the Lingara temple. The muezzins bawled prayers from atop their amber-tipped minarets in loud voices on the hour. A minor inconvenience for the comparatively low price of the room, thought Vetra. Little better than a squalid dive, like the last one at the *Rat Peacock*. But that was the least of their problems. Every hour they spent dawdling in this town, the greater their chances of getting their throats cut.

Once again, Wolfsha gave a soft whine and trusted her luck to the streets. Where she went none knew. Probably she scoured the back alleys hunting for scraps of food.

"Not liking this chase and bait stuff, Vetra," Nog muttered. "We need to unload this jewel as quickly as possible. Nothing but trouble."

"You don't have to convince me, Nog."

Skirl gave a mournful bray. "It's powerful, you fools! We can't just pawn it off on anybody. I'm thinking it deserves better, that we're getting ourselves into trouble unloading it on any dumb schmuck claiming to deal gems."

"And why's that?" Vetra leaned in with some menace. "What of our agreement?"

Skirl thrust his chin out in an aggressive manner. "Agreements can be modified. We need to think this through some more."

Think this through some more. Vetra's fist knotted. Skirl was starting to get on his nerves, and a little too big for his britches. Whether the gem dealer was just plain greedy or murderous, or had been on the watch for an infamous jewel, was irrelevant. Had he to guess, he'd say a bit of all.

With a mirthless grin, he brought the cool edge of his blade next to the apprentice's good ear. "I'm through pissing around, mage. Nog's right. We need to get rid of this thing. We need to find a buyer quickly who's not bought off by the establishment. Sell it, get our equal shares, then we go our separate ways."

"As you wish, swordsman. Don't get so uppity."

Vetra gritted his teeth. "I'll be getting more uppity as the hours go by. Hades balls! You forget who's been saving your ass all these times!"

"And you forget that you're already under the sway of that miserable witch and this gem. You've lain with her, Vetra; she's shone the stone in your face. Somewhere you're still hers, somewhere she will hunt you down. You want to just let this jewel—the relic that has a piece of your soul—pass to any fly-by-night crook who can get their hands on it?"

Vetra frowned. The mage had a point. A shadowy pall descended over his spirit. He snatched the jewel out of the magician's grasp. "I think I'll keep this wraithstone in my possession for a while until we sort this mess out."

He rubbed his red-rimmed eyes. He was bone tired. His back ached.

While Skirl glowered, he unclasped his helm, kicked off his boots and lay on the lumpy cot, eyes growing heavy. Within minutes he was asleep, the stress of the last days catching him up. Nor had he recovered from his taxing hoedown with the sorceress.

While he lay lost in dreams of dragons breathing fire and seductive witches waving jewels, Nog slipped away to the taproom, keen on trying his luck at dice and maybe score some silver bits and extra drinks.

Chapter 26

Vetra awoke to find Skirl gone. And when he patted his side, he found the jewel missing.

"Dergath's tits! Damn to hell that apprentice and his conniving treachery!"

Nog was snoring, nose upturned, lips parted, slack mouth and larynx making ratchety sounds. Vetra came over and kicked him awake.

Nog blinked, wiped at his cheeks.

"Wakey, wakey, sleeping beauty. Our pigeon's flown the coop. With our gem."

"What? Little pissant. I'll whip his damn ass." He wiped his lips, grimaced at the sour taste in his mouth, doubtless the sour ale he'd drunk last night. "Agh, my head hurts."

"We'll walk it off. You drink too much."

"Who doesn't?"

"We have to find this scoundrel."

"What, in a city with thousands?"

"We've a lot invested in that trickster and his little talisman."

Nog gave his head a rueful shake. "True, but he'll be long gone, Vetra. Alantra's a big place."

Vetra rubbed his temples. He remembered the delight Skirl'd had playing darts at the *Rat Peacock*, conning the gamesters with his wind magic. He nodded with a cool grin. "Our apprentice'll be playing mage for a while, Nog. As much as he can, he'll milk the opportunity while he's got the chance. I know his mind. Let's make some inquiries at the local dives, some of the ale houses. Shekels to peanuts we'll find our mage there."

"You want to waste time on that?"

"One day, Nog. It's all I'm asking. It isn't going to kill us. At worse, you get drunk, scout out some of those sluts of the night you relish, then if we come up a bust, we part ways."

"Okay. You're a blunt man, Vetra, but deal." They shook on it and he pulled at his beard. "Why does life have to be so damn difficult?"

It was well into the evening after scouting out various dives that the mercenaries found their quarry at an ale house, graced with the evocative name, *Birdnest*, a hop, skip and a jog from the Temple of the Sphinx.

Skirl was laughing, spilling ale on himself at the bar stand, a jack of grog in one hand, the Eros Flame clutched in the other. A busty redhead was swinging off an arm.

Nog grinned. He marched over to Skirl's side and pushed aside the redhead and grabbed his ear. He gave it a savage twist.

"Ow! What's the idea of this?" Skirl cried.

Nog pulled his head down to the oak slab. "Thinking to leave us so soon, Skirlie?"

"By no means! I was just thirsty, came in for a swig."

"A swig, at what, six in the morning? Wasn't that when you last left us?"

"One thing led to another. I met Wenda here."

"I'm sure you did."

Nog looked the wench up and down. He liked what he saw. He licked his lips and released Skirl, smoothed his beard and tipped his helm in a convivial manner. "Perhaps I'll dally here, Vetra. You go off with our fink here and let him know about the birds and the bees."

Vetra growled. "Forget it, Nog. Taranis and her henchmen're going to be on us soon. There're probably already here. There're spies and informers everywhere in this town. Probably already got the word out. Remember what happened back at the gem dealer's?"

Nog frowned. "True."

Vetra'd no sooner uttered the words when a ruckus erupted at the door. A giant of a man stomped in, throwing another muscly figure out of the way. The man who was tossed fell as if he were a sack of potatoes, assumedly the bouncer. From the muttering, it appeared the giant had a history of violence and was banned from the bar.

From behind strode a short, goatish man with an oiled, tapered beard. He wore a peaked red cap tucked on a jaunty angle that contrasted oddly with his pale gold smock. The homunculus peered around with large brown eyes of whimsical interest. The towering ape-like figure beside him was four heads taller and had arms that hung down past his rumpled black cloak to knee. A child's simper was carved on the brutish face.

Vetra frowned. Really? Rings graced the brute's nose, sleeveless cape hung to calf, iron-studded bands ringed his hairy forearms, good for clubbing a man or gouging out his eye.

"Skirl!" called the waspish mouse of a man. His voice had a high ring to it, bordering on a warbling shriek. "Skirl? Is there anyone named Skirl in this hovel?"

The apprentice flourished. "'Tis I." He hopped forth. "Who asks? One of my fans?" The apprentice's head was addled with drink and Vetra rolled his eyes.

"Nay," the small wizardish man answered. "'Tis Farbar, prestidigitator and overseer of the Alantra Consortium." He studied the drunken Skirl with a narrow-eyed dislike. "Borknad here and I wish to have words with you. You harbor a forbidden relic, if not a dangerous one, which has come to our attention."

"Oh?"

"The gem is sought by Archmagrix Taranis of the Mages'

Council in Xalgossa, our not-too-distant neighbors. We are friends with those in the guild, and thus, are sympathetic to their needs. In fact, we've formed an alliance. Going back as far as the *Hundred Years* when magic was forbidden and Umbria and Lvendar were ruled by the sorcerer-kings, Drail and Smail. In fact, I am a personal friend of the spellcaster Voydred. Perhaps you have heard of him? Yes, I see the name has caused a stir in your faces." He tapped his chin. "We would study this jewel ourselves before returning it to the Black Mage and his master, the Archmagrix Taranis, as is standard procedure."

"I can't help you there, sorry friend." Skirl gave a dismissive shake of his head. "Try the *Painted Dog* next door. There are jackals and thieves by the basketful."

The man stamped his foot. "I am not interested in the *Painted Dog* or any other dive. I am interested in—" and here he blinked "—but ho! I see you clutch the gem in question. Like a beacon of radiance it glows. Do not try to hide it! Bring it forth, knave, for all to see! It shines like a woman's greedy eyes!"

"This?" Skirl held the Eros jewel up high for all to see. "'Tis a heirloom, of sentimental value. Isn't that right, Vetra? Is that so odd?"

"Give it to me!" the wizard cried.

"By no means! I discovered it in the ruins of Gotha nigh a hundred leagues from here."

"Mayhaps, but such things are not for the hands of laymen." The wizard's eyes gleamed a jackalish hue.

"I'm no layman," Skirl roared. "I'm a venerated apprentice of the Order of Xalgossa!"

"Perhaps at one time you were, but I hear you have been demoted, excommunicated in fact. From my vantage, I see a scruffy stripling barely out of his teens. One with a chip on his shoulder the size of Stonetroll Mountain."

Skirl grew red in the face. He was about to commit to a foolish deed when Vetra stepped in. "He's with us, wizard. Take your ape and begone." He knuckled his fist and gripped the hilt of his sword. Nog stepped in beside him, cracking his knuckles. The mercenary wore a huge grin on his scarred face.

The wizard studied them with both curiosity and amusement. "A curious mix of bodyguard and brawn for a lowly apprentice. Two bully-boys for one stripling? Ha, ho. It is irregular, even unorthodox. My...and an insolent stripling at that." His luminous eyes wandered back to his apish cohort at his side. "Borknad! Would you do the honors?"

The giant's lips split in a leer, showing yellow teeth. There was a red lolling tongue under an unpleasant cork of a nose. "Yes, my lord." He lumbered forth, a full head over Nog and reached a brawny fist under his black cloak to snatch at a club. The giant's shadow fell over Nog. Nog tugged at his nose, as if wondering what he'd gotten himself into. A wicked club of gnarled wood, all whorls and walnut, came singing down to lay waste to his skull. Nog leaped back at the appropriate moment to scamper to the safety of a table of ale jacks.

Vetra's sword sang out in a dangerous arc. But the wizard flicked a hand and sent him flying back with a push of his Moosh magic.

Nog launched a punch. The ape-giant caught the fist...even as Nog was trying to hook a sword tip into his eyes.

The giant picked Nog up and twirled him about like a toy. Then with a bellowed grunt, he released him and Nog's bulk came hurtling into a table halfway across the room.

Coins, drink and dice went crashing to the floor. Men were on their feet, cursing, knives in their hands.

Vetra picked himself up, shaking the daze out of his skull. The wizard had written him off and now kitty-cornered Skirl who was flailing away with fists, flinging curses. Farbar snatched at the Eros Flame. There came a schoolboy tug of war between wizard and apprentice.

While the giant stalked forth to finish off Nog, Vetra sprinted forward. But the wizard caught the fleeting movement and pale knuckles lifted and another Moosh pulse came sailing at Vetra's chest.

Vetra ducked, blade raised. The pulse, or whatever it was, caromed off his gleaming steel and struck a nearby patron in the chest, felling him instantly.

Dergath's balls! This murderous bastard is playing to kill.

"Down!" Vetra called. The patrons fell to the straw-strewn floor or fled.

Nog's bull's roar rose above the din. He smashed helm-first into the giant's waist before the ape could get his hands around his head. He jabbed a blade into the giant's thigh then plunged another into his calf. Easier to stab an oak trunk. Skirl managed to evade the wizard's clutch, thanks to Vetra's deflection and took heel. The apprentice was out the door, Eros jewel clutched in hand, the fuming wizard at his heels.

In five quick steps Vetra pounced and kicked the legs out from under Farbar. Vetra's heel came down and knocked loose some teeth. The wizard groaned and slumped down senseless, a trickle of blood oozing from his mouth.

Nog and Vetra turned their joint attention to the giant who had become doubly-enraged at the sight of his unconscious master.

"Master," he crooned like a baby, clutching at his leg wounds.

Vetra sneered. He strode in behind him and cut his sword into the giant's hamstrings.

The ape collapsed on one knee, bellowing like a bull. Nog

hit him from the side. Together they hammered him down until he cowered.

Nog jammed his sword into the ape's gut. There came a final wheeze of bloody froth then he fell silent. Nog glared around the astonished crowd. He snatched a mug from a table and chugged it back, spilling warm ale over his beard. He grimaced and spat it out. "This beer is swill, innkeeper! You put more water than ale. Makes for cat piss." He trudged forward, wiped the blood off his sword on the giant's cloak. Vetra gave the unconscious wizard a boot in the ribs and they both made for the door.

Grumbles and groans echoed behind them as the innkeeper and his regulars gathered up the ruin of the taproom amid the broken bodies.

Vetra and Nog took to the nighted streets.

"There!" Vetra grunted, lifting an angry hand toward the Temple of the Sphinx. The shadow of a fleeting figure was moving across a deeper background of darkness. Massive stone sphinx-paws flanked both sides of the temple entrance; a lion-like head reared overtop. Nog and Vetra hurried across the near-deserted square and up the broad steps before Skirl could duck past the iron-bound double doors of the temple.

Skirl shrilled, "Hands off me!"

"Going somewhere?" Nog rasped.

"I just went out for a walk, got caught up in the night life at the tavern and you persecute me."

"Sure, we know," said Vetra.

"Skirly, Skirly, little birdie," Nog rhymed. "Little birdie likes to flee."

They dragged him off the steps back down into the street.

"Hey, be careful!" Skirl called. "You're pinching my arm!"

"It's a cruel world, isn't it, Skirl?" Vetra grinned.

Nog flexed his aching muscles. A spasm of pain rippled across his face. "Old Borknad did a number on my back, Vet, when he lifted me onto that table." He massaged his neck that had been wrenched in the giant's clutch.

"You'll live," Vetra grumbled. He glared at Skirl. "I should have left you back there for that gray ape to work over."

The apprentice licked his lips. He was sober enough to realize how lucky he'd been to escape with the jewel without getting his neck broken...

Chapter 27

For the past two days Grindar and his men had scoured the ale houses and inns looking for the thieves, but they'd come up with nothing. Only a beggar's garbled story about three figures matching their description heading east on the road to Alantra.

Dal Sagoth's sepulchral hints had prompted Taranis to cram her brain with many, many dark spells for the days ahead. On swift feet, she descended the stairs to visit the dragon below in his den. She threw the runestones before the sphinx-like paws and looked at the angle of their configurations and the symbols they drew in the dusky candlelight. She put a finger to her lip and hissed. Was the time right?

Yes. Her dark master had spoken true, as he always did.

She hurried back to her chamber with a look of satisfaction on her face to pore over her ancient spellbooks.

Not two hours later, Belgra swept into her chambers with an angry step. There was a flutter of fabric about her white-robed ankles that made her appear almost whimsical in light of what she was about to attempt. Her mood was bitter. The conservatory had degraded into sloth the past few days since Taranis's metamorphosis, and yet her resentment was dampened by the pungent smells of the exotic incense that drifted in the air.

"What have you done to Keren and Voydred?" she demanded.

The black-leathered Taranis lounged languorously on her divan, engrossed in a forbidden book of runes written by the Old Ones. She blinked in easy complacence as she sipped a strange tonic of ruby fluid from an ancient goblet.

Belgra went on, "They are like lovesick puppies. They move

about on game legs. Slow as turtles, nodding and grinning. They cannot function, or put two sentences together. They come no more to the Hall of Mages or the Hall of Winds to instruct the apprentices. They just grin and nod like foolish children in their workshops. The apprentices are beside themselves. They languish. They learn no more new spells or useful skills. Dergath's hounds, but our own beastmaster and spellcaster have become zombies! The only ones sensible in this dark tomb of Dormoth are Senesch and me, in my opinion. You've spellbound everyone else."

Taranis gave a slow nod. Her smile was as sultry as midsummer heat. "It is that, cousin. You speak truth. Nothing that those two didn't want in the first place. Languorous little puppies—bent on amusing the whim of an alluring woman."

Belgra stood arms akimbo. "I'm not your slave or puppet. I'll never yield."

There was a pause in Taranis's breath. Languid amusement showed in her eyes, then an insolent lift of brows that Belgra did not like, that mirrored eyes as cold as obsidian.

"Your skills as a herbalist are all nice, cousin, but of little importance in the overall scheme of things. I think you have too high a regard for yourself. You think you are above the other mages. I think you will be subverted like the rest. I have just waited for the appropriate time." She gave a husky chuckle disturbing to Belgra's ear. "You come unbidden into my lair. Do you not know what you are inviting?"

"What are you talking about? Is that a threat?"

The Sagothian queen rose and sashayed forth to caress her cousin's shoulder with a sensual energy. "Pretty little thing. Belgra Skywatcher... I can use you, pet, as a love child. Whenever I need to subvert these petty kings or princes like righteous Ragnum or the barbarous lord of Mercia. Even the licentious rogue of Lower Umbria, our silly neighboring count, comes to mind. There is much wealth in the hills north of here. To be exploited and plundered—mines, minerals, wood and resources—if we can ever gain control of those territories, and make Umbria whole again." She gave a sharp exhalation. "We cannot with Nelfban, that silly count on the throne. He is a useful puppet, but a worse statesman. I have not enough manpower to manage all these petty officials and tracts of land. One day I will."

"You are nothing more than an evil slut, cousin."

Taranis sneered. "And so will you be, cousin. You cannot hide behind your uppish sanctimony and good-for-all airs forever. You despise me, yes, but deep in your black heart you secretly desire the same privileges as what I command, a long line of men to service your body and suckle you in bed."

Belgra's cheeks flamed and she looked away. Her lips pursed. A dark part of her knew Taranis spoke truth.

With a twirl of the false amulet, Taranis shone the light in Belgra's eyes. She said some strange words in an ancient tongue and a relaxed, almost listless languor came over her cousin. Licking her lips like a cat, Taranis led her fellow sorceress into the eerie back room that housed the queen-size bed and its pure satin cover, over which the sinister, leering head of the elk-bat idol Yeasaba, surveyed her boudoir.

Taranis stepped forth, limbs a-quiver as with a sudden expectant motion, she ripped the robe from her younger cousin's bosom.

Belgra flinched, but did not resist. Taranis exhaled a husky breath and stripped her naked and herded her onto the soft bed where the two clasped each other in heated embrace.

Belgra caressed and suckled her older cousin with a passion born of the memory of the Eros Flame that lingered in her brain. Their pleasures knew no bounds. The imprint of the stone's power lay so entrenched in Belgra's mind that she became obeisant to Taranis's every suggestion. Every touch of flesh was a memory so implanted in her psyche that even with the false jewel dangling around her neck, its shine could evoke the same response of erotic pleasure and madness. Such was the extent of Taranis's drunken power and current of emotion and sexual heat bordering on brutal lust, that she cared not whether she lay with a woman or a man, stranger or kin. She did not care if there was any right or wrong to any of it, only that she could slake her unlimited hunger for pleasures of the night here and now.

Taranis and Belgra assumed positions of ardor which culminated in domination for Taranis, submission for Belgra. Long through the night there came twin moldings of body, thrusts of hip, arches of back, entangled joinings of loins and breasts in manner and frequency undocumented... accompanied by the sounds of erotic stimulation so earthy and bare to blast the mind of a mortal.

The sensual frolic progressed to orgiastic abandon, until the dark alabaster of the leering, omniscient eyes of the cruel god Yeasaba, or more accurately, Dal Sagoth, glinted with movement, now a thing channeled from the nether spheres, a silent, greedy voyeur of the love play of mortals born of the tainted magic of the Eros Flame.

Chapter 28

Nog eyed Skirl with lingering distrust. "What now? We've got the jewel, bagged our feckless apprentice but half the city and its sorcerers will be out looking for us."

Vetra's features firmed in their characteristic moody cast. Because of the apprentice's foolishness they'd been tracked by the sorcerers' network as far as Alantra. So? Worse things had happened.

And yet, Vetra gritted his teeth. This could not be good. They had little time to act. The impulsive Skirl was a liability, also an asset. Another false move on his part and he'd slit his throat personally. Every voice in his head told him to seize the jewel and flee on his own, but he needed Nog. Better to keep a close watch on their wayward magician too, rather than have him running free, causing havoc.

"I say we head south," Nog suggested. "To Lausern or Dragonskull, away from Mercia and this priests' scumhole."

"Problem is, that's exactly what they expect," Vetra muttered.

"You want to venture north, closer to Mercia?"

"I have a friend of the family lives north of there, Nog, goes by the name, Vrigin. He owns and operates a vineyard. He can take us in. We can lay low there for a while at his estate before we head south."

"What about the jewel?"

"What of it?"

"Shouldn't we—"

"Better we wait till the heat dies down. It'll be easier to unload."

Skirl twisted visibly in his tattered robe. "You're both talking nonsense. I've outlined the danger to you, Vetra."

"Never mind your pretty head about dangers, Skirl."

"But the jewel—"

"To hell with the jewel!" He was sick to death of it. He couldn't care if the damn thing self-destructed. But a ray of hope sparked in his heart, and he secretly grinned, struck by a sudden idea. If all went well, the jewel would burn, and he would reap the rewards from it. He would be rich, and he'd rid himself of this canker on the lands, and a sorceress's magic binding him.

He would not breathe a word of such plan to Nog. Let him blab off at the mouth while drunk on ale or in the arms of some sleazy tavern wench and his plan would be foiled.

"The way is clear," he intoned. "Let's get moving. The night is still young and we have many leagues to make."

"What?" Nog croaked. "It's midnight for Dergath's sake!"

Skirl gave a hoarse groan. "My brain's reeling from that wizard's mooshing and the inn's ale."

"That pisswater?" Nog jeered.

"Onward, you louse!" Vetra gave Skirl a rough shove. They headed up the flagstoned way with Wolfsha trotting happily at their heels.

The gates of Alantra were always open except in times of war. The trio passed under the stone archway, with the steady gaze of the stone bulls upon their backs.

They had little to fear from footpads at this hour. Their surcoats and murderous looks and swords gave them a look of authority. Light was the problem. It was pitch black. No stars showed and only the ghost of moonlight behind thick cloud was to guide their passage. With dogged steps, they followed the cobblestone way where it touched the weeds. They passed the odd cart with glimmering lantern mounted out front, but these conveyances mostly steered clear of them, distrustful of wayfarers at this hour.

At Farwin's Junction the sun was just peeking over the city of Alantra at their backs. They'd trudged all night; feet and muscles ached. Skirl had eventually stopped his whining, courtesy of Nog's frequent slaps.

Wolfsha seemed happier. She'd grown since they'd found her in the market, taken on more protective layers and more devotion. Prancing about on graceful paws, she ran up ahead and came bounding back with her tongue lolling. Her dark pelt was glossier than ever, her blue-black shadow tracing dancing shapes in the dawn's glimmering light.

By midmorning they'd flagged down a hay wain on its way north to Aspenmoor, a hamlet known for its farriers and smiths. They caught a few hours of sleep in the back of the cart despite the bumps and jolts of the road. Many fields of oats and barley and apple orchards passed and the rickety cart ground to a halt near Vrigin's country estate a few hundred yards off the main way.

Fall was in the air and dry leaves rustled in the lonely court that fronted the house and vineyard. They let themselves in past the wooden gate. No more than half way across the flagstones they'd stepped when a middle-aged man with the beginnings of gray in his short-cropped hair, looked up, fumbling for his blade and shouted a challenge. He'd been trimming the first of the grape vines to the side of the house. But his pruning looked haphazard, as if his mind were elsewhere. In the background came the baa of a sheep.

"At ease, Vrigin," Vetra called out. "Do you not recognize an old friend?"

For a second the man squinted, then his eyes lit with recognition. "Vetravincus? Dergath's ghosts! Can it be? You've grown. Uglier and stockier. Gaunter of face."

"I'll take that as a compliment," Vetra said. He gestured to his companions with a grin. "This is Nog, a swordsman ugly as me, and Skirl, a magician of repute."

"I am Vrigin, good sirs." He tossed aside his shears. He held out a hand. "Welcome to my abode, *Vinemoor.* Come gentlemen, inside!" He clapped his hands. "There is drink, good wine from my vineyards and meat and bread. We have much news to catch up on. My home is yours."

The travelers accepted Vrigin's hospitality; they stepped into his impressive atrium overlooking the vineyard.

He clapped Vetra on the back. "What brings you to these parts, friend? When you went off east, I thought you were gone for good."

Vetra's mouth quirked. "It was in my heart not to return, Vrigin—but I did. And you, how much land do you now hold? Looks as if you've done quite well for yourself since you moved." He gazed about the rich furnishings, the massive fireplace and its stone hearth, the stone-cut walls and their rich, wine-colored wood paneling.

"I have, Vetra. Fifty acres—" the man's expression darkened. "My heart is heavy though. Tatla, my only daughter, has gone missing. Snatched, I fear, right out from under my nose. You may remember her from your younger days? A fair maid with light brown hair, amber eyes, not small, not large. A fine girl. Though now she's all grown up and quite a beautiful woman. Three other girls were taken too. The youngest, choicest maidens of the region. Who knows where they have gotten to?" His lower lip quivered.

"This is sorry news, Vrigin."

"There have been several abductions of late. Have you not heard?"

"I've been in Alantra for but two days," Vetra said gruffly.

"My guess, it's a local gang who call themselves the Ravenclaws," Vrigin spat. "They ship them to various cities: Masern, Soho, Syrn, Lausern. I fear your own sister has been taken too."

A startled breath caught in Vetra's throat. "What? Minas?"

"Did you not know?"

"I have been east for a long time," Vetra said in a hollow voice.

"A month ago, snatched from her village Tarnwold, a few hour's ride north of here. She and Tatla were friends. Three other maids were taken from various hamlets around the region by these cursed, murderous bandits. By no coincidence either. All the fairest of the fair."

Vetra licked his lips. His heart thudded in his chest. He felt as if part him had been ripped out. He croaked in a hoarse whisper, "Minas settled here three years ago. When I was away, she ran off from the family riding school. No more relishing the fate my father set up for her than I did. But how—?"

The vintner shook his head. "In the dark of night, she was snatched from her bed, like the others. I fear for their lives, Vetra. Their souls."

Vetra hung his head. Clutching at his temples, he choked back his grief. "This changes things."

"And you? What brought you here?"

"We were on our way south—in transit—seeking respite from trouble that has come down on our heads at Xalgossa."

"Ever the wanderer and disruptor, eh Vetra?" he said. "Always stirring the bees out of their hives." His lame attempt at humor was shortlived. The smile quickly faded, replaced with a hollow-cheeked sigh.

Vetra pictured Minas in his mind's eye: a tall, sensitive girl, slender as a willow, graceful, elegant with blue eyes and a simple grace she'd inherited from his mother. Where he had been dark and stern like his father, often moody, brutal and volatile, she had been his opposite.

Now she was gone. Likely sold to some cheap lecherous lord for a handful of shekels at the slave markets. Vetra's fingers curled into claws.

A deep sorrow struck him. "The local sheriffs?" he croaked.

Vrigin gave a wolfish bark. "What do those ringworms care of a few maids gone missing? This is backwater country, Vetra. To them the villagers are like serfs, poor downtrodden cattle, to be exploited. We live richly in the country compared to most folk in the city, but to the lords of the capital, we are but chattel."

Vetra knew this to be true. His mood was bitter.

In light of Minas's capture, the Eros Flame became less important. If anything, it could be used as a stepping stone to acquire funds to launch an expedition to track down her oppressors.

"They carry the pennon of the raven with a red skull behind it," Vrigin said sullenly. "Merciless killers. Plunderers. Ravishers. They've been growing in numbers since Mercia pushed fighting men across the Lvendarian border. Launching skirmishes against her southern and western neighbors. A mix of Mercian outlaws and rogue mercenaries consorting for fun and richer spoils. More freedom than their tyrannical masters could give them."

Vetra rubbed his jaw. He recalled the golden triangle of hills bordering Umbria and Lvendar. A no man's land and maze of canyons, gullies and caves ideal for thieves. Lvendar and Mercia formed its eastern tip. "Clever," Vetra mused. "They have easy access to the borders of all three territories. Vulnerable if not defenseless villages are the only settlements on the hinterlands."

"The royals turn a blind eye. What is it to them if a few farmers' daughters get nabbed and sold into a distant seraglio? As long as the number is within reason to evade notice of the general citizenry. Young boys are taken too for sick pleasures. Older ones sold into slavery, the mines, rough labor or worse. 'Tis a lucrative trade."

"'Tis a vultures' world," Nog rumbled.

Vrigin gave a grim nod. "To make matters worse, war brews. There's talk of a Mercian invasion on our northern borders. Already raiders have crossed into our territory to push southwards. My fear is they're but forty miles away from where we stand."

Nog licked his lips.

"Lord Ragnum launches horsemen by the hundreds to lend aid to those from Alantra as we speak."

"What? This is fresh news." Vetra's face darkened. He recalled the wagonloads of soldiers passing by in the temple district and those on the east-west road on their trip to Alantra. It seemed his hasty plan to push north had not been a wise one. And yet, if he hadn't, he'd never have learned this grave news of his sister.

Shifting from foot to foot, Skirl clutched the Eros Flame in his pocket. "We will use the Eros stone to help your daughter, Vrigin. Also to help Vetra's sister, if we can. The gem's power is ancient and profound. It fills men's hearts with love." He lifted it with a fierce determination and the man's eyes for a brief moment were set blazing.

"Thank you, friend. But what can a mere jewel do?"

"Much!"

"Put it away, Skirl," Vetra said quietly. "It is no toy to comfort distressed men."

"If you find Tatla, you will find Minas," Vrigin said. "I am not asking much, old friend. If you are heading that way anyways, to escape the law or some other demon that harries your heels, I only ask you to keep your eyes and ears open. If you can find these rogues, discover who they are, where have they taken her, perhaps I can petition for her freedom, at the very worst bribe the lord or lords, or whoever has taken possession of her."

"I will do my best, Vrigin. I owe you for the help you gave me and my father in times of trouble when I was young. Though I can promise nothing."

"Your honesty is enough, Vetra. You're a good man. A trustworthy one." He tipped his head. "If you can get her back, there's 100 gold pieces in it for you. It's all the wealth I have." He left and returned with a small, dusty sack. "I'm an old man, beyond my fighting years. Twenty in advance for expenses." He plopped the sack of jingling coins down on the table.

Vetra murmured. He took up the coins. "I'll not fail you, Vrigin. I'll return with good news or bad either way."

Vrigin nodded. He left by a side door to fetch supplies for their journey. Vetra and his two companions wandered out into the courtyard which was made even emptier with the man's sorrow. Leaden skies crowded down on them. The first cracks in the clouds showed rain.

Nog took him aside. "Look, I can understand your grief for your sister, Vetra…but our necks are already on the line without running such risk."

"I owe the man, Nog," he explained. "He was like a second father to me when I was growing up."

Nog shrugged, resigned to Vetra's moods.

Skirl had been contemplating the words spoken and his mind fell to churning. "I can defeat these slavers, Vetra. With the jewel in my grasp, nothing can stop us. Once we return Vrigin his daughter we will use the jewel to defeat Taranis," he rasped. "You, Nog and others will be my prime bodyguard."

Vetra blinked, not sure whether he had heard the apprentice correctly.

"Listen to me, Vetra! I can defeat this vile witch. The one who holds power over you—and me too, for I have lain with her. You've nothing to lose by joining me in my quest."

"Except our silly heads, boy," Nog grunted. "Still, these sorcerous freaks have rubbed me the wrong way. When have I ever turned down a challenge, eh Vetra?"

"You can do as you wish, Nog. I only go north to set Vrigin's soul at ease, then to find my sister if I can. Like Skirl's mother, Minas has been taken by slavers, perhaps these same filthy traffickers who nabbed Tatla. I have no love for these Mercians. They strike secret deals with the slavers, that is my belief. They are a warlike people who push their empire ever south, east and west to create misery for the rest of the world."

"So. What's your plan, Vetra?"

"To look for Tatla. To find my sister, if there's hope."

"A tall ticket. The trail is cold. Even if you could find which harem she was at, a few men against an army'll achieve nothing."

"It doesn't matter, Nog. I must try. My conscience will never leave me in peace if I abandon her."

Nog grunted. It was something he could understand. "You realize we must pass through war territory, if what Vrigin says is true? Mercia's king is at war again with Lvendar's. Not a pretty scene."

"These cursed lands are always at war, Nog! Jealous kings, petty monarchs, pitching feuds against one another. Peasants and mercenaries used as pawns to fight their endless wars and to shed their blood. It will never end. It's gone on for centuries."

Vrigin returned, carrying two horse saddles.

"I can give you horses. I have two to spare. Come." He led them beyond the courtyard to the pasture where three fine mares grazed. They came drifting over, heads bobbing, their manes swishing. Two black mares, one chestnut. Vrigin fed them oats from a shaky hand through the fence.

They passed through the gate and Vetra stroked the mane of the youngest black mare, a mettlesome animal, self-willed and proud. Nog and Skirl picked the larger chestnut-hair with a quick, prancing step and a milky white eye.

After outfitting the mounts they filled their saddlebags with what food Vrigin could spare: stone ground bread, strips of dried venison, bladders of water. Within the hour they rode off at an easy canter. Wolfsha tagged easily at their heels. The three took to the dirt road north, with the wolfling happy to be out in the fresh air, frolicking at will away from the stink of the cities and her cruel masters.

They wound ever north through rolling country, the potholed road muddy in places, at times heavily hemmed by copses of young hemlock and alders that showed a mauve color this time of year. They saw mostly orchards and vineyards like Vrigin's, maybe not as lush or well-maintained.

The leaves of aspen had yellowed from their summer green and a fresh wind pushed at their backs, warm and soothing.

The ground became steadily hillier. With an omenish cast, an old rook with a gaunt beak flapped down from a high perch to squawk at them for invading his territory.

"This is lonely country," Vetra murmured. He rode in silence beside Nog. "I can see why my sister Minas chose it. It reminds me of home."

"'Tis not my choice of homeland," Nog muttered. "Give me the seaside any day."

They passed through the village of Smildren and halted to water their horses at a communal trough. The villagers gave Wolfsha wary looks. They seemed spooked by the wolfish look of her loping in plain sight. But they relaxed when Vetra stroked her and let it be known that she was a pet. The three kept their ears open for news. Riders had been sighted, with the devil in their hearts. They flew a black pennon much like Vrigin had described.

Vetra urged his party on with grim fatalism. Toward the village of Tarnwold where Minas had been taken was but an hour's ride away.

"This is insane, Vetra," Nog murmured. "We cannot stand against a band of raiders with only three."

Vetra stared moodily at the thin track ahead that wound through the silent lands. "If we can locate their hideout, perhaps we can find a way to surprise them. The advantage of stealth and speed is on our side."

Nog gave a stony grunt. "A small one at that, Vetra. You're too much of an optimist."

As bad luck would have it, a small group of riders, bandits, blackguards, whatever they were, had spotted their company from a distance, and now spurred across the open fields to confront the fresh prey on the road.

Vetra gave a sullen curse. He wished to Dergath he'd not been so impulsive. The burning rage he'd felt at Minas's abduction had addled his wits and stoked his need for swift justice.

"We can't outrun them," he muttered. "But perhaps we can outfox them."

"How?"

"Stay your ground, Nog. Follow my lead." He gripped the hilt of his sword. He rode on to meet the band. To his squinting eyes they looked to be about eight.

"Are you crazy?" Nog cried. Shaking his head, he rode on after him.

Vetra only turned his head to peer back at Nog, his face lit with ghoulish vengeance.

On fleeting paws Wolfsha shot off at their heels with a growl in her throat. The hair bristled on the back of her neck; her high-peaked black wolfish ears piked straight up.

Vetra weighed their odds. The outlaws knew the territory, they did not. He and Nog were strangers to the land, riding double on unfamiliar horses. If there were bowmen among the riders…Vetra did not wish to finish that thought. Either way, he vowed that he'd not sell his blood cheaply. The thought of his sister reigned foremost on his mind.

Chapter 29

As the horses came pounding in on unshod hooves, there came the sound of wild whoops and men's yells. Vetra saw their mounts were strong and fit, and of fine quality. Thoroughbreds, if he knew anything about horses. Nostrils flaring, the beasts were much used to the long runs of the outlaw, the sudden quick spurts of charging a quarry or escaping the law.

They clattered to a sudden halt before the vigilantes, circling them, snorting loudly. Their lean flanks were lathered with sweat. The mounted men spread out around them, in an ever tightening circle to prevent their escape or sudden flash of violence.

A mixture of rascals and roughnecks, Vetra surmised. Living in the rough in the hills and on the blood and spoils of honest folk. Eight rag-bearded outlaws, two with slit noses, one with ear bangles, all bearing scars of battle. Men with nothing to lose, only the wild wind in their hair, the pulse of malice in their hearts. Blood-stained leathers clad their backs, cruel blades armed their fists. Black hearts in their breasts bent on thieving and murdering, dark fire in their eyes to carry them through the day. Fine steel lay strapped at their hips. Two carried maces and bossed shields. None wore armor, only tough leather jerkins and matching bowl helms topped with two-inch steel tips.

One bowman rode in their company, a lean, hatchet-faced rogue with a round black shield strapped to the back of his saddle. A pennon stood piked at the horse's rear, marked with the emblem of the raven's beak over a human skull. The crossbow tip pointed down, aimed at a spot in front of Vetra's horse should it be needed.

The leader of the pack flicked eyes off their torn surcoats and frowned. A tall rangy man with scarred cheeks, steely gaze and a draping, gray cape who said, "You some kind of high lord's guard?"

"We fought as part of the Xalgossian Mages' Order," Vetra answered.

The man wetted his lips. "You're a long way from Xalgossa, if that's what you call home. Running from something?"

"Maybe we like the country air," Nog replied carelessly.

The leader did not like the quip. He tugged at his brown beard, the man they called hetman, and crowed, "So, a trio of wayfarers on a lonely road?"

Vetra ignored the remark. "Have you seen a young woman? Young, fair, daughter of the vintner."

"Maybe we have, maybe be haven't," the man crooned. "What's it to you?"

"She was snatched several nights ago, by men looking much like you."

"Fancy that." He leaned on an elbow tucked at his saddlebow, his mouth partially open as if catching flies. "A maiden taken. What are you going to do about it?"

"We mean to get her back."

The leader stared in disbelief at him. "You heard that, men? You and what army, chief? That pipsqueak in the blue robe yonder with the bandage over his head? Looks as if he couldn't fight his way out a gunny sack. And your ugly bully with the crooked teeth and ox smile? Couple of beat-up rats if I ever saw any."

A low growl rumbled in Wolfsha's throat. She backed up, took two steps forward and snarled at the rider, spooking his gray stallion. His horse reared.

"She doesn't like you," Vetra said, smiling.

"And I don't like her," the man rasped. He got his mount under control and gave a small jerk of head.

His mate at his side, a heavy-set man perched on a sleek roan, lifted blade and heeled forward to slash steel down at Vetra' skull.

Vetra parried. He flicked blade off the descending steel and set it flickering up in a reverse thrust to send the man reeling off his saddle.

There came a flurry of horseflesh moving in and about and a thicket of swords flashing around Vetra's head.

A horse reared. Men grunted in anger. A crossbow lifted. Vetra felt a bolt whiz inches from his ribs to thunk into a man's saddlebow behind him.

The thrown man came sprinting in at him, sneer on his lips, trying to hack him off his horse.

Vetra cut down at him. Wolfsha leapt, sank teeth into the man's sword arm, sending him screaming back in a fog of pain. She dodged another rider's blade and leaped up, caught the mounted man with her teeth, playing a vicious tug of war with his leathered leg. The man's sword came slashing down on her and slit a three-inch gap along her back. She wheeled, yelping, spinning in circles. Her spine was laid bare. A great spurt of blood soaked her thick black fur.

In some quixotic act, Skirl jumped down from his place behind Nog and scrambled toward the crippled dog, lifting the Eros Flame high. "Stay back, bullies! One glimpse of this gem and it will blast your skulls wide open. 'Tis riven with ancient powers! Look deep into its contours!"

For a moment, the riders sat stunned on their saddles. One lean rogue with black eye patch, unaffected by the spell and only half registering the magical light, spurred forward and smacked the jewel out of Skirl's grasp with his shield.

Swords came flickering in at Skirl. He dodged. Vetra reined in, drawing his horse in a wide loop and blocked the first savage blow that came at Skirl. Arms swung. Swords clanged. Blades hungered for flesh. Vetra's mail absorbed the excess sword strikes, his sword parried the rest. His agile ability to twist in his saddle out of harm's way was his savior. Nog swung in to shield him, swearing as the blows came hard and heavy while Skirl scrambled to snatch up the Eros Flame from the bloodstained grass. An unhorsed rider kicked the mage in the chest, sending him flying, the wind knocked out of him.

There came a flurry of steel. Vetra dodged and drove murderous blows into his flailing assailants. But he felt a mace graze his helm and knock him off his saddle.

He was up on his feet in time, shaking the blood out of his eyes. He was breathing husky gasps. He leapt aside before the horses' hooves could trample him. He bellowed a war cry, parried four sword thrusts whistling over his head. He struck, blocked another strike that would have taken off half his face. Nog scrambled in at his side, unhorsed. The two fought side-by-side, spitting and cursing. They were hemmed in by a pack of enemies. Of the eight outlaws only six remained.

Vetra turned in time to send a spiked ball of a mace skidding off his blade. He slashed a mighty backhand that took off the bandit's sword arm at the elbow. The man screamed. Vetra twisted in to plunge cold steel into his gullet.

The spilling of blood had brought a communal rage upon the outlaws. A storm of bodies fell on Vetra and dragged him down. Nog was next.

A shouted command rose up over the din. The hetman's. It had been their blades that had hewn Wolfsha. They expected it to be theirs to dispatch Vetra and Nog. But it was the man's voice that had their blades halting their course of death. He sat back on his horse with a brooding look of distaste. Up till this moment he'd let his cutthroats do all the hackwork. Now with two men dead and one without an arm he was not so cocky.

He leapt off his mount and stared down at the bloodcaked corpses. "Peace, brothers." He made a savage flourish and slew the man with the severed arm where he lay on the ground. He marched over to Vetra who struggled in the grip of three captors. The hetman lifted his blade for a killing blow, but his face relaxed. His eyes took on a tranquil quality. "You're quite the sword meister, aren't you, rogue?" His lips curled in amazement. "A rebel? A scrapper?" He laughed, spread arms wide as if beseeching his fellows. "Look here, rascals! In this man's dark heart lives the true spirit of the outlaw! See? A killer, reaver, a braveheart among rogues, a courageous soul. I praise you, swordsman, even though I hate you for slaying Mest and Duar. Two of my finest men. No, I'll not kill you. I may have need of you... But as for these other mongrels..." His eyes lingered on Nog and stared at Skirl as he fingered his blade.

From the side came a flash of cold steel. The hetman whirled and blocked the murderous downswing of one his men that meant to put an end to Vetra's life. The hetman lifted a knee and kicked the man back, an oily-haired raider, with a rumbled curse. "You defy me, Jarno? Trolls' heads! You miserable skulker! Back! You forget who's the leader of this rascals' band. Brule of the Ravenclaws!" He gave a mighty ululation that had the air tingling with menace.

The four other riders stared with vicious contempt. Sour leers crept over their leathery faces. Malice and expectation played in each black heart while white-knuckled fists strained at their sword-hilts to kill and avenge their clansman. They loved the random law of the outlaw, these rogues—the blood, death, and fickle swing of power. Tension crackled in the air, thick enough to be cut with a knife. Indeed the fate of the clan hung on a spindly thread.

The man Jarno gripped his sword. He took two steps toward the hetman with a murderous gleam in his eyes.

The hetman sprang back on his heels and parried Jarno's first strike. He called out in a throaty drawl, "We're all blood brothers here, aren't we, Ravenclaws? Say it! Say it!"

The others raised a muttered cheer. Two lifted swords and moved to fend off Jarno.

Jarno dipped back and his sword arm fell, his lips moving in mutters of disgust. The spring-coiled event had turned in the hetman's favor, as it always did. To a rogue, one crafty as an adder.

The hetman's brooding gaze fell on Vetra. "You gallop up, draw swords against thrice your numbers, knowing full well you would lose, and sit there smug as a bug. Why?" He squinted at the mercenary in puzzlement as if he'd never seen such a brazen display of foolishness.

Vetra allowed himself a tense chuckle. He licked his bloody lip. "You only live once, reaver. Better to die courageously and have lived valorously than survive a week with one's tail tucked between his legs, wishing he'd tried this or that."

"Pretty words for one who's already half step in the grave."

The hetman stooped to snatch up the glittering jewel lying in the bloody grass. He squinted at it with curiosity, then he tossed it to an ugly hound-faced man with a sloping brow, jutting mouth and hangdog look.

"Take it, Igir. The bauble'll adorn your neck. You like pretty things, don't you?" He laughed, a coarse guffaw. "That, or sell it. I could care less. Probably a fake anyway."

The skew-jowled man grinned. For a moment he tested the stone with his teeth as if for authenticity like some gimcrack jeweler.

"Their weapons are of good quality," said another, the

ragbearded man with the squinty eye and eye patch. He bent to gather Vetra's and Nog's blood-stained blades.

"We'll take them for our own then, Halfhan."

The man smiled. "I think I'll take this ox-faced rogue's beard cutters." He hefted Nog's short swords. "They have a sleek, murderous feel to them which I like."

"All the power to you. The world's your oyster. So long as you keep these knitting needles to yourself, away from my new pups, you hear? That goes for all of you slew-faced rascals." He glared at Jarno and the rest of them.

There were grumbles and a few muttered curses. Jarno seemed content to claim Vetra's sword for his own.

The hetman made a curt gesture. "This here dark hair's got some piss and vinegar in him. I think he'll do fine at our game of Ranks. What say you? Bind 'em, boys. Hoist 'em up on their horses!"

The raiders left Wolfsha where she lay bleeding out. Vetra, biting back his dismay, shook his head in sorrow and anger.

The dark fringe of trees ringing the north was where the dirt road meandered. But they did not take it. To the west across green plains they rode, toward low grassy hills which rose with faint gray-blue rocky outcrops. Further beyond lay bare crags, wind-carved and skull-domed, crow-haunted and mysterious peaks that delineated the range separating Lvendar from Umbria.

Thither the raiders whipped their mounts and Vetra felt himself jerked forward, wrists bound on his own mare while Nog and Skirl trailed behind, hog-tied on theirs.

They left in a flurry of hooves, back the way they had come. Vetra shook the blood out his eyes that dripped down from the slit on his brow. A fierce fire burned in his coal-dark eyes. He promised to make every one of these cutthroats pay in buckets, choking on their own blood.

Chapter 30

Down below the Hall of Mages on the narrow passage that led to the ruins of Old Sagoth, Taranis held a candle in hand. Her fingers pressed an engraved rune on the center-top block above her head. She whispered ancient words.

The lower blocks shifted. With a grating screech, the centermost ones slid almost effortlessly aside.

She ducked under the mantle of darkness into the deeper blackness within—the lair of the dragon. She strode with confidence toward a moving shape, a shadow darker than dark, unheeding of the fearsome reek of the thing's scaly hide, that of young dragon.

A slither and scrape of scales echoed off the towering stone walls and she glimpsed armored plates, of tail and belly as massive as a small whale, as an enormous shape reared before her, a bastion of sinew and strength. The lizardish head rose twice her height in the cavernous murk. A drip-drop of water fell from unseen heights to splash on the beast's glistening back. The giant claws scraped the wet stone underneath its bulk in its quest for freedom.

"You have the rut of lust of a young buck on you," she murmured. "Good. But good luck in finding a mate in this unhappy world, Drako. All your kind are gone. Poor dragon! You have only me. And in truth, only a face which a mother could love. For who else could love such a beast as you, nurtured from an egg that birthed you to dragonhood?"

The dragon, as if understanding her words, opened its huge jaws and returned a foul breath, showing rows of serrated teeth. From each fang dripped foul thick drool. The creature loosed a fledgling roar as if to char the sorceress. But the slim, black-clad Taranis did not flinch. Nor did the dragon exert further energy to fry her. The love jewel had seen to that. The Eros Flame had worked its magic on this demonic beast, even though the real jewel was not in the sorceress's possession. Only the fake one, collared about her neck. The memory of the moons of programming and subtle, soft words spoken in ancient tongues and the shining of its eldritch magic into the huge, lamplit eyes, had bedazzled the dragon. Even the sight of the fake Eros stone was enough to stimulate a response in the beast of renewed devotion. Such was the gem's power, and such was Taranis's confidence in its lingering hold. She cared little whether she wielded the original or a replica.

Taranis gave a wolfish laugh. She was the dragon's master and she thought to herself how she could exploit this fast-growing minion. The might of beasts and men were hers to command! It only remained for her to secure the real Eros Flame, and dominion over the eight kingdoms…and Drako was her ticket to this goal.

"We will ride, young dragon!" she roared. "Ride! To the ends of the earth where the sunset has no cease. We will conquer the eight kingdoms. We will send the proud and petty kings back on their heels!"

The dragon rumbled. Fire huffed from its huge maw, claws pawed at the rubble, digging trenches into the moldered stone.

Budding horns curled from its ridged brow and yellow eyes peered forth from dim slits.

Taranis set down her candle on the dank stone and lifted hands above her head: in a U-shape that wielded some thaumaturgical significance.

From her palms lofted blue-gray orbs into the sepulchral darkness.

The orbs bit into the ceiling, at a particular spot, and sent hefty chunks of earth and rock falling down into the narrow chasm below where an underwater stream flowed.

The dragon watched in curious fascination. A stray hope grew in its febrile brain. Indeed, a fearful intelligence lurked behind those eyes that was much in sync with the sorceress's ambition.

On quick feet Taranis fled up the steep stairs back into her chambers; then out into the corridor that ran past the Hall of Mages. She came to the garden which housed the eerie bat-statue, Besemooth, messenger to Dal Sagoth. For here was a spot she'd marked days ago directly above the fresh tunnel she'd just bored. A narrow space only separated the dragon from freedom. With lip curled in delight, she launched more of the sinister orbs upon the heavy flagstones at her feet, blasting them and laying bare a cone of darkness that connected the two tunnels. Here the two shafts met, releasing with it dank airs from Drako's den of Old Sagoth.

The dragon wormed his long, flexible body up through the conduit as a rodent squeezes through spaces many times smaller than itself. Greedily his five-inch talons clutched at the rock.

The furor had alerted the Dormoth guards and now a troop of them came clattering down the corridor abreast the Hall of Mages with shields and swords.

Eight stood in unison, gaping in terror at the hide of the ponderous dragon that lifted above their heads on wings of crusty sinew to hover there like some bat of the underworld.

"Slay it, men!" a doughty man-at-arms cried. He waved his sword and came in bent-kneed at the monster.

Only he and another dared come that close to the dragon.

Mace and sword licked out, as if to sting the winged devil's crusty hide. Fresh from the nether depths, the dragon was in no mood to be re-confined and it bared its scissored teeth and blew a raging fan of fire, charring the two men where they stood.

The other guards recoiled in horror.

Taranis stepped out of the shadows, warding them back. "Fools! You would oppose this juggernaut of the earth? Stay back, or be singed!"

They cowered back, swords and mace gripped in trembling fists.

More figures arrived: Belgra and Senesch. They stopped short to glare at the beast thus summoned from the murks by Taranis. Its black mass hovered, horned head tipped in a menacing direction their way. Voydred and Keren too had now come shuffling down the hall with the captain Grindar, to gaze on the mythic beast.

"Stay back, you fools!" she ordered Voydred and Keren, who particularly had shambled close to the dragon like a pair of zombies.

She lifted arms and the dragon landed on its clawed feet and clattered toward her as would a pet hound.

"Rise, you dumplings!" she cried. Her eyes blazed at Voydred and Keren. "Be warriors! Fight for me. Fetch me my jewel!"

She approached and muttered arcane words in their ears. Tracing the forbidden sign of an arcane rune on their brows, she then snapped her fingers and hissed a final word, 'Erunk!'

Voydred and Keren seemed to rise inches higher, like knights of Umbria. No more the automatons of the past but transformed of mind and spirit. They shook their heads and gave vengeful cries and vowed to serve Taranis unto death.

"Good!" Taranis cried. "Now Voydred, you will take a steed and search for the traitors who took the jewel. Keren, you are my eyes and ears." She gestured with a jeweled finger.

Keren gave a quick acknowledgment and his body blurred and shimmered into the form of a giant condor, a bird of majesty.

His outspread wings flapped, his gray beak opened and dim slitted eyes blinked as the bird took flight northward.

Voydred took himself to the stables and mounted the fastest steed. He sat with ramrod-straight back, his fierce gaze straight ahead as he spurred the black stallion through the gates of Dormoth. Grindar and a dozen mage guards likewise took horse and clattered after him down the torchlight cobbles.

Taranis's glittering eyes fell on Senesch and Belgra at last. "You two will remain here and guard Dormoth in my absence."

They rose to object.

"Silence!" She held up a preempting hand.

"Rise, Drako, rise!" she crooned at her dragon. She climbed on its back. "Follow the bird, Keren. Whoever finds it first, Voydred or the beastmaster, we will be there to claim it."

The dragon lifted its crusty wings and soared into the darkening sky. Senesch and Belgra watched with growing dismay as the laughing sorceress clung to its scaly back with a clenched grip on the budding horns, then disappeared, a dark blur crossing the moon, like an omen out of the lost chronicles of Sahir.

Chapter 31

The outlaws' horses cantered across the green fields and angled upward until they were lost in the hills. Brule led them down secret ways and wild-goat paths that twisted among scrub and bush.

Two of his men dismounted to lift a screen of foliage, cleverly disguised to conceal what would appear to be an overgrown trail. They put it back up as soon as the riders passed then remounted their steeds and fell in behind the grim cavalcade.

After a time they came to a narrow horse trail only wide enough for two mounts abreast. In double file they trotted in silence. Pools of water puddled in the deep ruts of hooves, testament to the recent rains. Bare stone slopes rose high above them on either side. Verily this was the wild hill country of ibex and bighorn sheep.

The trail opened onto a small clearing backed by another protective hill. Smoke rose from the embers of a stone-circled fire pit. A rude shelter stood off to the right, a stockade of sorts, about thirty feet square. Human figures were contained within. The crude pen was crafted of tight-knit wooden stakes, sharpened at the ends. The farthest edge was flush against a sheer wall of rock. A dozen young women huddled within that Vetra could see, in various states of distress.

A massive guard dog came bounding up to greet the hetman. It was all wide drooping jowl, corked snout, bat-like ears and shade-gray fur. He reached into his saddlebag, threw down a hank of beef. Ravenous teeth gnawed the morsel— some breed of a half mastiff—which was gone in seconds. The dog surveyed the new arrivals with distrust. Under hooded eyes, it took a proprietary piss at their horses' hooves then trotted back to guard the padlocked gate of the women's stockade. Its teeth were bared.

"How do you like my beauties?" the hetman gloated at Vetra.

Vetra saw the maids were lean and mud-streaked from teens upward. Wild, desperate looks showed in their eyes which peered from behind the wooden bars. Hands of those who sat in the dirt were clenched with arms wrapped tightly around knees; others clung to the fence with fingers bunched like claws. All had hollow, pinched and tear-stained faces. The odd moan or forlorn whimper came from the group, pleading for mercy.

But no mercy would come from Brule and his black-hearted rogues.

Somewhere Tatla was among these wretches, Vetra thought. Minas, he noted, was nowhere to be seen.

His keen eyes took in the rest of the gang's hideaway. A sheltered lee on three sides by steep grassy slopes pocked with rounded outcrops and boulders. Above climbed stony hilltops, piked with aspen from where noisy ravens squawked. Some vultures circled oddly farther afield.

The black mouth of a cave gaped in the hillside dead ahead: a cavern eight feet high. The hillside to the left gave way to a narrow footpath flanked by sheer rock 40 feet high. This path ended in a heavy door drawn with a bolt and seemed some trapdoor to doom. Blue-gray stone arched overhead many more feet.

The place was quiet but for the low moan of wind and the shuffle of the listless women in their pen. The clearing would be difficult to attack from above. Indeed, as difficult to escape from. The only way out was the way in—through the narrow pass of rutted track.

The lonely encampment appeared to be deserted but for

the penned women and the vicious dog, pissing on everything it came across, including the corners of the stockade much to the women's dismay.

The riders dismounted, forced the prisoners off their mounts then sat them before the embers. The hetman milled about with his men, muttering, deciding what best to do with them. Riders in groups of eight or more arrived, bringing in fresh spoils. Two new women were thrust into the stockade to add to the dispirited souls huddled within. The numbers of the outlaws swelled to forty now.

Two of the ragbeards lingered to ogle their new prizes, muttering crude jests and making insinuating gestures with hands and tongues, one even gripping the stakes to get a closer look.

The hetman came loping over and slapped the first man with the flat of his blade. "Get away from there, you cur! Any ideas of night play or deflowering and Malfar'll make short work of you."

The hulking half-mastiff, hearing its name, came trotting over to raise its hackles and growl, sensing the displeasure of its master.

"Our buyers'll give us half and less for dames with any hint of virginity spoiled. Go to a whore's tavern in Alantra and get your pleasures there, if you feel an itch."

They grumbled and slunk away. Brule returned to the fire pit where his indifferent gaze swung back to Vetra and Nog.

From snatches of conversation, Vetra divined that a slave agent from faraway Guiritia was due to arrive on the morrow to negotiate the purchase of up to six women.

His fists knotted. A keen rage curdled his blood. Maybe this was the same scum who'd spirited off Minas?

"What about them?" Brule's lieutenant inquired, jerking a

thumb.

"They'll fight in the pit," Brule said.

Halfhan's squinty eyes gleamed. "And the jewel?"

"Pawn it somewhere," Brule intoned in a bored voice. "In the cities, as I suggested to Igir." He waved a brusque hand.

"Yes, hetman."

Skirl gave an agitated yelp and struggled to his feet. "You can't pawn it!" he shrilled.

"And why not? Who is this popinjay?"

"An insolent pup, sir," Halfhan said. "Calls himself an 'apprentice'."

"An apprentice? He'll be apprentice to my ass, cleaning it out with his tongue if he yaps any more." The hetman gave a signal and Skirl was smacked down into his ungraceful squat again. "He'll fight with the others, Halfhan. No, wait." The man's lips curled in a baleful grin. "Let Igir have him. He has need of pretty boys, doesn't he?"

Halfhan laughed.

Skirl's eyes bulged. "No, you can't! This is inhuman malice!"

The hetman turned his back on Skirl as would a lord his lowly slave.

"Put these other two mongrels in the hatch for now."

Jarno, Igir and two outlaws seized Vetra and dragged him and Nog to the mouth of the cave.

With a grim and restless glower, Vetra strained against the hemp that bound his wrists. But he and Nog were pushed mercilessly into the murk. Behind them the sun sank behind the hills.

The hetman gave a sphinx-like smile, stirred by the prospect of some fresh sport.

Vetra caught a glimpse of a natural cave of high rounded

walls smoothed by the rush of mighty rivers eons ago. The outlaws' living quarters? Primitive but serviceable.

Pools of shadows lurked everywhere. In the spider-webbed nooks, the ratlike crannies, around the pillars of rock that may have been stalagmites at one time, hung a feeling of longtime decay. Oil lamps burned from crevices in the walls, emitting a dim orange light. An odd, musky smell hung in the air—of old rags and frayed garments that should have been long discarded. That and unwashed bodies. Vetra saw tunnels and crawlspaces where rough-and-tumble men could sleep.

Igir dragged them to a low wooden door set into the rightmost wall of dark rock. One of the foul-mouthed rogues got it creaking open before they were thrust inside into the murk. A small rank cubbyhole greeted them: with the smell of mice droppings and bats. The crack under the door let in just enough light that Vetra could barely make out Nog's hard-chiseled face. It was etched in a vindictive grin.

"Well, we're going to have to bust out of this place somehow, Vetra. Wonder what's happened to our mage?"

"Don't know, Nog, probably warming Igir's bed."

The other laughed but then seemed to cringe at the precariousness of their situation. Vetra could hear him shuffle restlessly in the dark.

Those poor women.

He thought of Minas and the terrors she'd face, trapped, desperate, without hope. Used like a breeding mare by shallow, lascivious men. It made his blood boil and he paced the confines, exploring every nook and crack with his fingers. Nothing. Only sheer rock. Cold, damp, unyielding. The door was three-inch oak and strapped with iron. It was already getting stuffy in here. How much air had they used up? It seemed not much leaked through the small cracks under the door and around its edges.

"It'll be sealed tight, Vetra. Forget it."

Vetra gave a sulfurous curse. "We can't just sit here and be used as entertainment, Nog. They're going to barter off those girls."

"What can we do? We're like two rats caught in the hold of a sinking ship. Are we going to gnaw our way out of here?"

"We have to come up with a plan. Think!" Vetra smacked a fist in his palm.

But no plan was forthcoming. Vetra sank back on his heels. Even if they could surprise creepster Igir or any of the guards, there was small chance they'd win free of this motley horde with no weapons at their disposal. They were but two, unarmed and vastly outnumbered.

Time ticked by.

At last Nog's murmur intruded on Vetra's gloomy speculations. "Wolfsha…she was a good companion, Vetra. She didn't deserve what they did to her."

Vetra gave a gruff acknowledgment. An old memory flashed in his mind: of her running up ahead while he and Nog prowled the streets of Alantra, then she'd nip back, tongue lolling. "She helped save our skins, Nog. That's always going to be our memory of her." He recalled Wolfsha's glossy pelt, her happy bark, the sharp whiteness of her teeth, the ones she'd sunk into the street thugs without a second thought. He exhaled a bitter sigh.

"A life for a life," Nog murmured. "You saved her, she saved you."

"I think she saved our skins a lot more than we saved hers."

Nog's rusty exhalation echoed as grim confirmation. In it lurked a guilty overtone.

"Her courage reminds me of a story, Vetra," Nog said.

"When I was a young buck, haunting the wharfs of Kablin, I made friends with an old dog, a sheephound or some cross of white retriever. I was looking for work, or trouble, I don't know what. The hound only had one eye. Sailors and stevvies used to call him, 'Old Cyclops'. For laughs and kicks. One of his canines was yellow, the other black. He was half lame. But he could fight. By Dergath, he could fight! He could hold his own among the other mutts that prowled the docks looking for scraps. They left him alone.

"One day a new dog came to town. Came off a black-tarred ship sailing up from Syrn. It flew the black flag of the Vassal Privateers with a witch and skulls. A mean Hortooth Hill Hound with a touch of the Bearhusky in him. The buccaneer, Chivano—Roost, they called him—captured the dog and put in to port. He was a notorious pirate who sailed as far as the Mystery Isles and Guiritia. Been running spice and gold and silver and whatever else he could get his hands onto from all the carracks he'd sunk and sent to hell in the Vassal Sea. Him and his crew of sea dogs had sailed the Vassal before I was an itch in my pappy's pants. Past Baspu, past Mt. Palyr, as far as the Gray Lands. He came in like a sea lord, causing trouble in the town with his mates. They smelled of tar and sweat and blood, some with missing teeth or an ear. They swaggered about the inns, practically took them over. The innkeepers were forced to keep them busy with whores and free ale. There was no law there in Kablin, only the town watch, which was afraid to walk the streets at night down at the wharfs. But I'm getting off topic. I was working the fish nets just out of my teens, cleaning and gutting the catch of the day, setting billhooks and mending and repairing nets, but ended up getting mixed up in a fair deal of privateering myself before it was all over. But that's another story.

"This black giant of a dog whipped the other street dogs and sent them all running. Last to face him was Old Cyclops. He just stood there among the piles of fish scraps the sailors'd tossed out, munching his meat as if nothing were untoward, as if he could care less about any new upstart dog in the neighborhood. Only a sullen stare on his snouty face and a low growl in his throat matted with dirty yellow fur. The black hellhound charged. Near sent Old Cyclops five feet back. They rolled and snapped in such a flurry of fur, teeth and claws, I thought Cyclops was doomed.

"But he was a smart dog. After a time he lay as if dead, pretending to be beat, licked like a torn rat. While the other slavered over him and bit into his bloody fur, took a chunk out of an ear, as wild dogs would do, he didn't move a muscle. The bigger, meaner dog grew bored with such weak prey under him and he looked away, and in that time Cyclops leaped up, spry as a gazelle, sank those yellow teeth into the other brute's throat. He hung on for dear life, like a rattlesnake. Took some mettle and courage to do that, Vetra. I witnessed it all myself. The other dog couldn't break free. He collapsed and bled out. Old Cyclops lifted himself off the limp dog and staggered off as if it were just another day in the streets. Damnedest thing I ever did see.

"When old Chivano found out, half drunk from sousing at the *Whistling Sandpiper*, he near tore up the town, looking for the mangy yellow mongrel that people called Cyclops. I hid the old battlehound in the room I'd been renting on the cheap in the slum district south of the docks. I knew Chivano, the skulduggerer. He'd slit Cyclops ear to ear when he found him. I grew fond of that dog. His courage and cleverness moved me. And so, with a young man's idealism, I planned at night to stow us aboard on a carrack that set sail the next morning."

"So did you?"

"I did, and I tell you, Vetra. I never came back to Thrakia for eight long years! Managed to weasel my way aboard as one of the crew. The sights I saw... The daunting 100-foot stone palaces at Iskuldir, the golden domes, the cupolas of the Shemir, the wild beauty of their dark-eyed women. The wild, haunting fastness of the Isle of Baspu and its petrified forest. The colorful and exotic fruits and spices of the faraway markets. From Graemon in Guiritia to Kirnland. Mouth-watering olives and figs the size of apples. Three-humped camels carrying ingots of gold across the sands from faraway kingdoms. Coconuts the size of gourds. The roll of the sea, the emerald wake, the ever-changing moods of her waters and skies, from tempest to midsummer squall to calm blue. Hairy fights on the seas with only scimitar and cutlass...

"I'm telling you this story, Vetra, because I think life leads us down strange paths. Whether we're sitting in shackles in a dungeon like this one, or we're up to our eyeballs in sorcerers, outlaws, dragons and hellhounds, something tells me we got a lot of Wolfsha-ing and Old Cyclops-ing to do. If we're going to get out of this pisshole and send these bastards to Dergath, we'd better do it fast!"

Vetra gave an explosive grunt of rekindled vigor. "I like your spirit, Nog! You say some dumb-ass things at times but some wise jewels pop up. When I met you in the market, I thought you might have been one of those blowhard grifters, but I'm glad we crossed paths, even if it was under a dark moon. Even if we may not live past this night."

Nog gave a rumbling laugh. "Let's make a pact then, Vetra!" he rasped. "We fight back-to-back to the end. Whatever surprise they spring on us with this Ranks nonsense, we protect each other, watch each other's back...When the time comes, we kill. We take down as many of these mangy rats and butt-wads while we draw breath."

Vetra's lips curled in a murderous sneer. "Deal!"

They both clasped hands like brothers…and thus marked the fellowship and seal of bare-knuckled camaraderie that was to change history.

Chapter 32

Igir had gained special privileges being longtime goods-peddler and watchman; he was granted a small chamber to himself, a pot of silver and a maid. The chamber, barely fifteen feet square, was adequate for his needs. Only the hetman and Halfhan enjoyed chambers as large.

It was in here, in a nook off the great cavern that housed the black-hearted outlaws, that Skirl had been shuttled and was now confined in a small, iron-barred cage. Here he crouched disconsolately in the dim lamplight. It was a space not dissimilar in configuration to Vetra's, but one with light and the feel of living beings in it.

A brass-bound chest sat beside his cage. A few weapons were tacked to the wall behind him: mace, sword and shield, before which sat a wooden chair and a wolf-skin rug before a small hearth in which a tiny fire could be lit and meat roasted if the master of the house should desire it.

Another figure crouched in a cage of similar size to Skirl's about six feet away. A young boy from the look of him, with long ruffled black hair. The desolate lad squatted and stared zombie-like as if escaped into a world of his own.

All this was extraneous to Skirl's focus. His burning eyes rested on the crimson jewel that sat atop the brass-bound chest. The Eros stone! It glowered a deep crimson under the dim flicker of the few oil lamps that graced the chamber.

Igir sat on cushions before the fire pit, now dark and dead and smelling of old embers. He examined his prizes with small beady eyes.

"Pretty boy in a cage, pretty birds with clipped wings," he crooned. "I like pretty things. There's Mizron now," he gestured idly to Skirl. "The boy's been with me for several weeks. Raided on Mistletoe's eve at the village of Voken. Cheer up, boy," he rattled on to the lad, "things can only get brighter."

Skirl's eyes turned in dismay toward the tousled-haired youth squatting in his iron bound cage. Several weeks he'd been here? The boy had tears staining his face, his knees were scuffed and his dark eyes were dull pools of lead staring into nowhere. He seemed oblivious to the words being traded.

"A pretty thing to light a middle-aged man's heart!" Igir mused. "Sometimes to sit at my side on a rainy night by the fire. Oh, lucky me, lucky me!"

Skirl cringed. The man was obviously deranged—like all these outlaw freaks whom he had overheard, drank human blood around campfires on the full moon.

Igir snuffled and yawned. "I shall return with your suppers soon enough. Have a care not to commit any mischief!"

He lifted his bulk and sidled to the door, stepped out, closing it tightly behind him.

In the silence of his cage, Skirl was left to his own devices to meditate on his turn of fortune. Who knew when the madman would be back?

* * *

It had been more than a day that they'd been confined in the dark and Vetra's gut crawled with hunger.

What seemed like hours later, he heard a key rattling in the lock. The heavy wood banged open, clapping hard against the copper-colored rock. Igir sauntered in bearing a gnawed bone and some soupy slops in a big pewter bowl. Dusky light poured in from the main cavern, stinging their eyes.

"Something for you boys to fight over." He threw a half gnawed stag bone at their feet. He set the slops in the bowl down nearby. They squinted in the half gloom to see it had a dishwater color; the chunks of meat that floated could have been cabbage as much as horseflesh.

"Wouldn't want you to get too frail before the festivities," he laughed, an evil echoey sound that intruded on the thick silence. He retreated, latching the door tight, plunging them into darkness again.

They shared the bone, eating like savages in the dark with fingers and teeth. Food was scarce...but food was food even though it tasted horrid and practically made them gag.

Nog swore. "There're going to be some heads to roll for this, Vetra."

A time came when the door burst open again and Igir stood with Jarno and two others bearing swords and knives. They snatched the two out of their lethargy and herded them back to the communal area with steel points at their backs. They prodded them down the narrow path and past the wooden portal set in the side of the leftmost hill, the one that Vetra had thought led to hell.

From there they walked them cautiously along a narrow ledge that overlooked a stone pit roughly 20 feet by 40 feet. The pit was enclosed on all sides by sheer rock. No getting in or out of the pit without assistance from above. From the ledge, natural tiers of stepped stone ran upwards on which the outlaws squatted or stood while Igir and his mates held the prisoners at the pit's edge with a knowing and conniving look on his vole-like face.

The hetman came down the narrow path with slow ceremony. He seated himself on a flat rock overlooking the pit. This perch was like a miniature throne that gave him prime view of the pit. When all were settled, he gave a brisk signal of hand.

Even though daylight still lingered in this late hour of the day, torches burned on either side of the pit and sent smoke curling down into its eerie confines. Vetra saw the stone-worn path continued on to an open vale and hills beyond: an escape corridor perhaps should the bandits' lair be compromised?

"Anything goes," the hetman intoned, "from weapons to opponents. Our boys like wild fights. With some funky surprises along the way." He gave a ratchety laugh and looked up, a devious glint in his eyes. "To honor our new guests, let's give them a big cheer, boys! We're all good sports here."

While the outlaws snorted and jeered, chugging wine from heavy incised mugs in their hands, the lieutenant Halfhan gave Vetra and Nog a strange salute. "The men who die in this pit are tied upside down at the heels, drained of their blood." He lifted an arm in a practiced ritual to bond with the rogues up in the stone seats. "Blood which we drink on nights of celebration!—" he brandished his cup and took a big swig. "We've two new recruits to raise the stakes in the games of Ranks, lads!" He pushed the cup under Vetra's nose. "Would you care for a drink, outlander, before you die? These mugs are filled with the same blood which we slug back as part of our old tradition. The corpses are tossed to the wild wolves in the hills. Blood for longevity! Blood for the men which makes them strong and keeps the clan battle-ready!"

Vetra swatted the cup away. The red liquid slopped over the man's jerkin. "It's a perverse and disgusting rite, bordering on cannibalistic."

Brule lifted his heavy bulk from the throne and strode over. "It's an evil world, mercenary! Ruled by evil people. I proudly joined their ranks decades ago." He gave a tired laugh. "Black-hearted deviltry lurks in the public markets. Behind velvet tapestries, the golden doors of the capital. In palaces, fortresses, merchant's bedrooms. In the hypocritical hearts of the priests, the greedy governors, the self-serving magicians. Who are you to lecture us about villainy? We're no more evil than any of them."

Vetra exhaled a bitter breath. The words held a note of truth in them, as his life experiences had shown. Either way, he wouldn't lower himself to reply.

On a signal from the hetman, Igir pushed Vetra into the pit. Arms pinwheeling, Nog followed. They both landed on the balls of their feet, rolling, grunting, clutching at their ankles.

Vetra staggered to his feet, peering about wild-eyed. The sand was littered with old spilt blood and refuse, from discarded boots to half gnawed bones. The rock walls were sheer and smooth, eight feet high, no handholds, grips or indentations. Forty roguish Ravenclaw-clan faces peered down at them. Vetra counted three crossbow-men in their ranks.

Muttering to himself, Igir left the prisoners to their devices and skulked on quiet feet back the way he'd come, a restless look in his eye as if he had unfinished business to attend to.

Chapter 33

Skirl examined his cage. Bands of iron framed a four foot cube with three-inch checkerboard gaps. He shook the bars. To no avail. It was quite impregnable; he sat himself down, teeth bared, head in hands. Shuttered like a caged bird, to spend the rest of his days. A pretty keepsake to a mad monster, Igir.

"It's useless," said the boy in a listless voice. "Igir keeps the door locked and our cages tight."

Skirl gripped the bars, peering out. "Where are your kinsmen? How long have you been here?"

"I don't know." The boy shrugged. "The days slip by without my counting." He did not seem to hear Skirl's other questions; only to drift off in his own fantasy world, probably a barrier he'd created to keep himself from going insane in this gloom.

Skirl slumped back on his haunches and sank into deeper misery.

After a time the door creaked open and a figure entered: a maid wearing a blue bonnet and a blue-gray dress. She had buck teeth and heavy-jowled cheeks. A woman who looked neither young nor old.

"Who are you?" Skirl croaked. He crabbed over to the bars to get a better look at her.

"I am Igir's charwoman. I come to dust and sweep while the men play at Ranks." She blushed. "To keep him company when he feels the need around the fire."

Skirl muttered wryly. "I see."

The woman was not pretty, in fact, quite an oddity. A dumpy, lank-limbed, buck-toothed maid come to dust chests and Igir's weapons.

"You are new here," she said in a bright voice. "Mizron has

been here nearly two months. Igir likes his charladies plain lest the other outlaws make eyes at her."

"I see," Skirl remarked. "But it seems as if our good friend Igir likes to collect pretty things."

"Like me!" she cried, twirling her dress, fluttering the blue fabric around her ankles with such a flair that Skirl blinked.

As she swept around the room, dusting, sweeping and humming a nonsensical tune, Skirl noticed that the maid kept making eyes at the Eros jewel posted on the chest as if she could not help herself.

A crafty thought began to brew in his mind.

"I see you like the jewel," he said.

She nodded discreetly as if ashamed of the fact.

"How pretty it would look round your neck."

"You think?" Her cheeks flamed.

"On a fine necklace inset with pearls and opals, I think," Skirl mused. He rubbed at his chin. "Bring it here and we'll see. You have a mirror over there to admire yourself in." He motioned to the aged glass on a crooked wooden frame hanging on the wall by the weaponry.

The charlady made a whimsical step toward the mirror to look at herself with shy regard: beaked nose, underslung lip, lumpy figure, moony, half-wit eyes. She shook her head almost forcefully. "I mustn't disturb master's things! I am ugly! Igir will beat me—he will do terrible things in the night if I don't—"

"Hush," soothed Skirl.

"Once when I went to sneak a bit of raven pudding from the larder, he…but I mustn't speak of that."

Beads of sweat budded on Skirl's brow. He whistled, a soothing breath between clenched teeth, "What is your name?"

"Zilda."

"Well, Zilda, Igir is gone for many moments, I daresay. An

hour, maybe more. We will see that the brute doesn't harm you. For one, I am a powerful wizard."

"You are?" Zilda's lips parted. She stood arms akimbo, peering at him askance. "Why are you in a cage then?"

For a moment Skirl's mouth hung slack. Then he licked his lips and gave a hearty laugh. "I am merely pretending to be imprisoned, dear girl! A game I play with those around me to see if they are paying attention. You, on the other hand are not so easily fooled. You have keen wits and the sense and courage to talk to me. In my estimation, these are excellent character traits, all guaranteed to win boons and favors from an Archmage of Xalgossa!"

"Boons and favors? Really?"

"Of course!"

She grew emboldened by Skirl's logic—a skewed logic which even Skirl was having a hard time keeping track of. She took five hesitant steps toward the chest on which rested the jewel. She tucked it in a palm and with a conspiratorial wink at Skirl snuck over to the mirror where she admired herself, twirling her dress, with the gem placed smartly at her throat. "It does set off my eyes!"

"Of course it does!" Skirl gave a happy laugh. He clapped. "Now fetch the key, Zilda. We will go off together and get more jewels like this one."

She blinked in startlement. "Really? How many?"

"More than you could ever imagine."

"You're teasing me!" She gave a dreamy sigh.

"We will depart today and leave Igir behind and go someplace safe where we can sit round a warm fire and eat raven pudding to our heart's content!"

She clapped her hands in delight. "Goody!" She smoothed out her bonnet. "I wish no more of Igir. He is a mean man.

Harsh and cruel. He grabs me at night with his pinching fingers. See these welts on my arm?" She pulled back her sleeve and glided over to the brassbound chest. "He keeps the key in this chest."

"I know, I have seen him stow it there. Go ahead, Zilda, retrieve the key. It is but a hop and skip away. It is yours for the taking."

She mustered the courage to pry open the heavy lid then rummage around the bottom, searching for Igir's keys. There came a rattle and jingling and finally in triumph, she held up a corroded key ring. On the feet of a somnambulist she glided over to Skirl's iron-barred cage and fiddled with the lock for several moments. The bars parted; at last Skirl was free.

Skirl wrung his wrists in glee. "You have earned your reward, Zilda! The jewel is yours. It was mine which I now freely give to you. Your master stole it from me and he means to sell it. For now, let me keep it in my safekeeping so that we—"

The door burst open with a crash and an owlish, hulking man loomed. A pair of mean eyes glared forth.

"What is the meaning of this, Zilda?" The outlaw's fists knotted. "Have you been up to mischief?"

"No, Igir, I—"

"Consorting with thieves and prisoners? I will tan your hide within an inch of your life!"

Her face flushed in terror.

Skirl snatched the jewel from the maid's fingers. He lifted it high in his left hand. "Stay back, you rascal! This gem harbors arcane powers!" He thrust it closer to the blackguard's face.

Igir drew back. "I've heard that before. You cannot gull me, ninny. I've been lenient before but my patience is wearing thin. Prepare to die!"

Zilda's eyes mooned; she fled past the outlaw, escaping his long, grasping fingers before they could grip her.

Igir's icy eyes prickled and he advanced, knife in hand, with a smiling leer and dusky menace on Skirl.

The boy heard all. He blinked, squatting in his cage, wearing a look of dull fascination.

Skirl's eyes darted about the chamber, looking for a means of escape. There was only the weaponry tacked on the wall: a mace, a knife, shield. If he could get to them…three quick steps…

He lunged, making a mad grab for the hanging knife with his right hand.

Igir reached out to snatch at the apprentice's neck. Skirl twisted aside and grabbed the first blade off the wall.

Igir's long knife flashed. In the same motion, Skirl thrust the Eros stone in his face with the speed of a viper.

The villain gazed at it and faltered. He shook his head and croaked…giving Skirl enough time to lash the blade at the exposed face and neck.

Igir teetered back, clutching at his slit throat. He gave a startled gurgle, then sagged to the ground.

Skirl's knife arm fell limp…

He panted, chest heaving. The jewel was still clasped in his nerveless fingers. This was the second man he had killed…and it felt no easier the second time round.

He stepped over the lifeless body, blood pooling around the villain's dark silhouette. Skirl swallowed the bile in his throat.

The whole scene hovered like a sordid shadow over his soul. The boy had witnessed everything. His wide-eyed gaze replaced the dull one from before.

Skirl scooted over and unbolted the boy's cage. He

scrabbled out, his doe eyes rounded with horror as if he were in some nightmare.

"Take heel, lad," Skirl whispered in his ear. "Find your way back to your village. Minutes from now this place is going to be vipers' nest. You'll wish you were nowhere near it."

Head nearly bobbing off, the youth scuttled out the door into the shadows. Skirl made a more leisurely retreat, gazing both ways when he came out into the cavern with its high-ceiling. Nobody was about. He was confident that nothing could touch him now that he possessed the Eros jewel. The warmth of the jewel spread up his palm, his arm, into his chest. His heart beat with erratic fervor. Every time he wielded the Eros Flame, he could feel its ancient power. Now he was lord! Power once stripped from his bones was returning in spurts to his veins. He felt as if his wiry frame had grown taller, stronger than before. No doubt the ancient magic at work of the priestess-sorceress Sarkala…

Now there would be a reckoning. A fierce reckoning…and a heavy blood price to be paid.

Chapter 34

Vetra looked up to see a ragged prisoner being prodded along the ledge at swordpoint. On a curt nod from the hetman, he was pushed into the pit to join him and Nog.

The man flailed and fell with a cry. He rose to his feet in a crouch not dissimilar to Vetra's, wiping his sand-flecked lips. His face was grime-streaked. A thin-boned wretch from one of the villages, Vetra surmised, with washed-out blue eyes, pale straw-colored hair and cheeks hollow as spoons. No doubt snatched on a whim for sport in the game of Ranks.

The newcomer assessed the two broad-shouldered men before him, and quavered at the sight of what he faced. He decided he was no match for their brawn and backed away on spindly legs.

Crossbow bolts thunked at his feet. The nearest archer reloaded to point steel-strung weapon at the man's chest.

The wretch cowered back.

"Fight them, damn you!" the hetman roared. He leaped up from his throne, fist clenched.

The wretch froze; his Adam's apple bobbed. A look of wide-eyed fear grew on his grimy face.

On a signal from the hetman, another bolt came whishing down. It struck him in the left foot. He screamed, a raspy wheeze from parched lips. He hopped around in anguish. With madness in his gaze he came half-shambling at Vetra.

Vetra swatted him away; the man went sprawling on his hands and knees, nose in the blood-streaked sand. Another bolt clacked at his side. He upped himself and frog-hopped toward Nog. Nog leaned in less leniently, amazed at the wretch's resilience, and hammered him down. The wretch stayed down for good.

Vetra and Nog looked up at the hetman. Brule nodded in gruff acknowledgment. "First kill goes to the outlanders. Rank goes to two!"

There were sniggers, as if Rank 2 wasn't much of an achievement.

An old boot came flying down and smacked Vetra in the chops. He rubbed his jaw, muttered and stared up, looking for the culprit. Nog was slow to move and a bucket of slop landed on his head: rotten cabbage and chicken bones. He wiped off the refuse with a sulfurous oath. The hetman slapped at his belly in mirth. Loud jeers came from the spectators, indicating they thought this funny too. Nog grabbed fistfuls of slop and flung it back at the drunken oaf who'd upended the bucket. The rodent-faced man bawled a curse of his own and drew his scimitar, a wicked curved blade. He took an exotic leap into the pit. He bobbed to his feet, his sword with hilt of scrolled brass flashing in his hand.

Vetra and Nog circled the man warily. Their arms dangled loose at their sides. Cheers and catcalls waxed from above.

Things could go badly in this arena, Vetra thought. The outlaw was armed. He and Nog weren't. A vicious sneer rolled across the man's pasty, nose-ringed face. A gaudy bangle dangled from a half-torn ear. He fingered his two-foot blade, did an acrobatic twirl, thinking to impress his mates with some bloodletting. What could the outlanders do? He laughed, and lunged.

A mistake.

Nog feinted and drew Sir Ear Bangle aside on a nod from Vetra. The vicious weapon slashed at empty air inches from his nose and Vetra slipped in and hammered the drunk with both fists in the throat.

The outlaw crumpled and Vetra stooped and snatched up

the curved blade. Now they had a weapon.

The rogue shuddered as he struggled to get up. Nog smacked him down and stomped on his throat, thus silencing him for good. Now two motionless humps lay on the blood-soaked sand.

Crossbow-man trained his weapon down at Nog's throat.

The hetman swatted the weapon aside, fouling his aim. "Hold up, you dolt!" The bolt went wide a few inches from Nog's thigh to thump into the fresh corpse near the far wall.

"They're resourceful. These rogues deserve a better challenge." The hetman rubbed his bearded chin. "Second kill goes to the outlanders. Rank is now three! So...we're having some rich entertainment tonight, aren't we, boys? Villy! Smoge! Get your hides down in there and teach these pretenders a lesson. As members of the Ravenclaw clan, you're both at Rank 6. If you win, your rank rises to 7. If the outlanders win, their rank goes to 6. Be warned! An opportunity to rise and shine and win! Show them what you're made of!"

With a rumbling cheer the two rascals hopped down in the pit. Landing cat-like on their feet, they were up, clutching weapons.

The two killers were determined not to lose this fight, their cockiness reinforced by the grim weapons at their disposal: small bossed shield and mace, and a four-foot broadsword. They approached with casual ease, if not murderous anticipation in their eyes. Coarse jests wafted on their breath. The one with the Mohawk cut twirled the spiked ball on chain and faced off against Nog. The squatter, roguish brute with the bully-boy grin, rounded on Vetra with sword extended.

Vetra smelled the grog on their breaths...an advantage they could use. Nog cast Vetra a knowing glance.

The Ravenclaw pair came at them in a sudden rush of

flashing steel. War cries were on their lips, teeth glinted in the dancing flames of the torchlight.

Vetra wielded the only weapon and he cut at the yellow-toothed weasel with the broadsword. He parried and kept moving back at an even pace, matching his attacker stroke for stroke, making him use his forward momentum to keep coming at him. When he was almost pressed to the stone wall, Vetra scooted out along the rock face, ducked a strike and flicked out his scimitar, drawing blood from the man's thigh. The man gave a grimacing cry.

There followed a vicious play of flashing steel: cut and leap, dodge and slash, as filth fell and crossbow bolts thudded at men's heels making the entertainers dance like cobras in a fakir's pipe dream. The blood-red gleam of the torches cast monstrous shadows on the walls. The reek of rotten vegetables and meat and unwashed bodies were enough to make one retch.

How many men had died in this grisly arena?

Nog ducked a spiked ball and lured the mace-wielder away from Vetra. He was not foolish enough to try to wrest the weapon from him, but rather, focused on staying out of the reach of that deadly spiked ball. He taunted Mohawk Hair and succeeded in getting him to flail away and waste energy. One strike of that globe on the head and it was game over.

The steel spike clipped the stone wall, taking chunks with it. Nog darted over to the opposite wall. He snatched up the old boot that had been hurled and chucked it in the mace-wielder's face. Like a mad bull he charged. The weapon came down at his head but Vetra caught the descending ball on his sword before it caved in Nog's skull.

In a split second reversal, Vetra launched a backhand strike that pushed his attacker back. He lashed out two quick strokes but got too close and the man's brass-knuckled fist smacked him on the forehead, a cheap shot that ripped off some flesh and sent a seashell ringing in his ears. With a snarl, he struck a volley of crosscuts that had the swordsman crabbing back. The man fell backward over the old boot. Vetra pounced. He thrust the tip of his curved blade deep in the man's throat. Reversing his forward momentum, he slashed at the mace-fighter's ribs, ripping an ugly seam across the man's waist that let out a trail of steaming guts.

The man sank in a crouch, holding his own entrails, mace slipping from his gory fingers. Nog leaped in, grabbed the hilt of the mace and sent the ball singing into the man's skull. Brains and bone flew as far as the nearby wall.

A deadly silence descended over the ragged company.

Now four corpses lay sprawled in the filth. Pools of crimson oozed on the blood-strewn sand. Nog's chest heaved. He and Vetra stood as one, their faces grim as death.

The hetman licked his lips. He held up a hand, scowling. "Outlanders rise to rank 6."

Brule twirled his mustache, perhaps wishing he hadn't sacrificed two of his cruelest scrappers for this no-win outcome. The Ravenclaw bullies didn't like it either and booed and hissed, stomping their hob-nailed boots.

The gash on Nog's cheek had reopened and now blood trailed down his grinning face. Vetra's forearm was slashed and his brow leaked blood, adding to the bright red on his surcoat emblazoned with the dragon and the eagle.

The hetman had reached a decision. On a quick signal to his crossbowman, his archer took aim.

"Wait!" Vetra cried. "Have you no other wannabes to fight us? We've won weapons so at least you'll get a fair fight." He stared up at the faces of the reavers peering down at them. "No? Are you all a bunch of chicken hearts who must hide behind the skirts of your bowman?"

The taunt raised angry sneers. The Ravenclaw bullies, perhaps pleased less by the insult than the death of their comrades, rapped the pommels of their blades on the stone terraces. Vetra's words had a ring of truth to them.

The archer was about to loose a bolt when Vetra motioned his head toward the wall to Nog. Nog moved in a lynx-like crouch to hunch underneath the ledge as Vetra tucked his blade at his belt. Vetra took a long running leap and vaulted on Nog's back and sprang up as Nog lifted him, giving him extra buoyancy. Vetra clawed his way up onto the ledge and grabbed at the archer's ankle. In his surprise, the archer fumbled his shot. Vetra pulled him down into the pit where Nog made short work of him with mace. Vetra continued his charge along the ledge and ran straight for the hetman. His scimitar was now blood-drenched and gleaming. The hetman sprang to his feet, parried the strike that would have sheared off half his skull.

At the same time, a lone figure came striding down the path onto the ledge. *Skirl.* He wielded a strange object in hand—a blazing ruby that cast a surreal, if not ominous hue over the grisly surroundings.

With an exalted gleam in his eyes, the apprentice made for the hetman, as if he'd heard whispers from the gods themselves. Now he exulted in his glory. The Eros stone, raised high like some sacred runestone, cut rays of light through the half gloom and spellbound all who peered upon it.

Vetra reached down a hand and pulled Nog up onto the ledge.

Unlike the time in the crypts under Dormoth, Skirl was not afraid. He held the Eros Flame in a steady fist. "Look into the light, knaves! Drink deep your doom!"

Nog's lips parted. His eyes glazed over.

"Don't look at it, you fool!" Vetra rasped.

Nog squinted and looked away.

The last two archers turned wicked crossbows down at Skirl. Their target was now an upstart who dared to preempt their sport. But when they took aim, they found they could not draw bolts. The mystical light stung their eyes. Their draw arms sagged. Their tongues lolled.

"Shoot, you fools!" the hetman bellowed. For the moment he alone seemed unaffected by the eerie magic.

Skirl backed away, hedging his way along the ledge. The jewel dispelled the blood-darkened carnage of the death pit. His cheeks burned with a rebellious heat, his face radiated an otherworldly glow. The full force of the Eros magic seemed to course through his blood.

While the reavers' jaws hung half open like village idiots, Vetra slit the throat of the first man, the leather-faced Jarno, thus reclaiming his trusty sword and knife. Nog snatched back one of his short swords from Halfhan, the next nearest cutthroat, and plunged it deep into his guts. With a vicious snarl, he slew the first archer he saw. He snatched up the man's crossbow and put a bolt through the last bowman higher up in the stands.

Nog aimed for the hetman's chest.

"Wait!" Vetra cried, catching the bow's stock.

The cutthroats hunched transfixed, eyes dilated like mesmerized acolytes. At any moment these dark-eyed cutthroats could break out of their grip of enchantment and massacre the lot of them. Vetra admired Skirl's concentration to hold a spell of power that kept almost forty of them in thrall. Perhaps the jewel was doing most of the work?

No, he thought not. He recalled how easily Taranis had ensorcelled him back at Dormoth while now the fledgling struggled with all his might to keep the bare minimum of the spell going. Beads of sweat had sprouted on his brow.

Skirl backed up, shielding his companions from the hetman's blade. The steel of the murderous but spellbound outlaws looked ready to erupt in a riot of slaughter.

On vengeful feet Vetra strode forth and faced Brule. "Tell me, reaver. There was a girl you took about a month ago—a fair-haired, slender maid from Tarnwold with not a mean bone in her body."

The hetman gave a swinish grunt. "I remember her. Golden hair, golden eyes, skin soft as down. What about her?"

"What did you do with her?"

"We sold her to Tork, the slave dealer who rode in from Soho or Sarnhill. Claimed to be an envoy to the Emir Jasir in Kirnland. She and three others we sold were taken off our hands. No quibbling. Silver paid at double the price."

Vetra gave a fatalistic nod. "Then it is too late."

The hetman gave his neck a rueful twist, suddenly paling and wetting his lips. "I have done bad deeds, mercenary. This ruby—" he said in an odd voice now, as if the magic were seeping into his bones "—has given me new hope." He swallowed and peered into the scarlet light. "I-It has filled my heart with a love…a love I've never known! I shall go forth and take a straighter path, mend my ways."

"That's a noble sentiment, hetman, and I laud you for it," Vetra said, "but there's still another matter."

"What's that?"

"This." With a snarl of indescribable loathing, Vetra snatched the hetman's hair and with three mighty hews, hacked the man's gibbering head off. A gush of blood slathered the stones. "Send my regards to Dal Sagoth!" he rasped.

The corpse fell and Vetra wiped the filth from his blade on

the man's jerkin. He tossed the head into the reeking pit where it bounced like a rotten melon. The staring men below glared as if half possessed.

A look of deadly earnest settled over Vetra's face. Into his smoldering eyes came a look of calm. As if vindicated, he breathed a desolate sigh, knowing that one good deed had been done for the day.

The Ravenclaws rushed at him as one. Had Skirl's magic slipped? Vetra's blade flew in cleaving arcs, a whirl of murderous thrusts and slashes. He hewed men like corn stalks under a scythe, and men died in agony, their throats ripped out or bellies torn asunder. Nog bunted others dead or alive down into the pit and did his fair share of slaying. Others crammed up on the uneven tiers above the ledge halted in their tracks. Nog swung the crossbow up on them.

Then he trained it down into the pit. "Stay where you are, you filthy pigs!" He turned to Vetra. "Shouldn't we slay the lot of these miserable scum?"

More of them were snapping out of their daze as Skirl's hand that bore the Eros Flame dropped.

"I'm sick of slaying for one day, Nog!" With a vicious grunt, Vetra snatched up the crossbow from Nog's hand. "Stay back, Raven-scum!" he cried. "The first to come creeping out of that pit or sidling after us, gets a bolt in his guts!" He loosed a warning quarrel among the wretches in the pit. By lucky chance, steel thunked into a man's thigh. He hopped about, cursing, condemning all outlanders to Dergath.

"Come!" Vetra snarled. "Let's quit this vipers' nest."

Nog and Skirl snatched up a sheave of quarrels. Vetra and Nog passed along the ledge to the oaken door that gave way to the clearing while Skirl took up the rear, hefting jewel. Vetra turned to cast the apprentice a thoughtful appraisal. "Come to pay us back for all the times we've saved your ass?"

"I heard the brutes carousing in the pit and came to see what all the fuss was about."

"Where is that ghoul, Igir?" Vetra hissed, peering past Skirl's shoulder. "Haven't seen his ugly face among these vultures since he crept away on skulking feet. Still have yet to slit that bastard's throat."

"I spared you the trouble, Vetra," said Skirl.

Vetra cast him a sharp glance. "Well, one less outlaw to send to Dergath. You've been busy I see." He kicked open the door to the communal area.

"I told you, none can stand before the Eros Flame."

No sooner had they passed through and Nog shot back the bolt when there came a thud of steel and swords on the other side of the heavy wood. The tumult echoed across the clearing. Vetra sneered. He turned in time to recognize the low growl and the pound of heavy claws on stone as the murderous mastiff leapt for his throat.

Nog's blade lanced forth. The froth-jowled killer skewered itself on the tip. While it thrashed and yelped, Vetra hacked hard at its neck, silencing its frantic leaps and whines forever.

"Is there no end to fiends?" he murmured. He gripped his hilt in rage. He wiped his bloody blade on the beast's thick fur. "Let's see to the women. Come on!"

Chapter 35

Restless, red-eyed figures shuffled and whimpered behind the pales of the stockade. Passing the fire pit, Vetra saw the charred carcasses of several deer and many broken casks of beer. A degree of feasting and ale-drinking had been enjoyed by the Ravenclaw rogues during the mercenaries' captivity.

Vetra examined the padlock and chain. Hopeful, tear-stained faces peered out between the slits, calling out, while white, trembling fingers gripped the bars.

No use blunting their swords on the chain and lock, Vetra decided. He and Nog slashed at the stakes around the lock. Those that splintered, they wrenched free and jerked the gate open. The captive women scrabbled out in a half mad rush.

"Tatla! Who among you is Tatla?" Vetra called, scanning the faces.

"I am, lord!" Vetra turned to a hollow-cheeked maid about eighteen with matted chestnut hair. In her narrow cheeks lurked a resemblance to the skinny, sloe-eyed child of eight he remembered from his youth. But he saw her features had matured nicely. She had a fine-boned, attractive face and her bedraggled look and grime did not diminish her slender, gorgeous figure. Vetra grimaced. All the better for fetching high prices at the slave auctions. He motioned briefly, "Come with us, your father awaits."

"Papa?" Glad tears sprang in her eyes. She stared, as with disbelief.

Vetra took her hand; they set off at a run to the roped off horse corral; many horses already whickered with the excitement. Some were saddled, most not.

"Take what horses you can," Nog said. He snatched at the reins of Vrigin's milky-eyed roan.

"Can any of you, ride?" Vetra peered at the huddled group.

There came ready nods.

Half could, so under Vetra's direction, they doubled up on the horses, six with saddles, while Vetra nuzzled the nose of his black mare with a grim nod.

"You ride at my side, lass." He pulled Tatla up behind him.

One of the taller, more mature women who'd been eyeing Skirl's weapon laid a hand on his arm, "Give me that crossbow. Any of those lowlifes comes near me, I'll plug iron bolts down their throat."

Vetra smiled with appreciation at her warrior spirit. He saw she was a tall, fair maid with light brown curly hair. Eyes steel blue. She raked back a rebellious lock and held his gaze without flinching. "Take it, miss. You'll not have use for it while they lie dazed and jerking each other's beards in the pit."

The woman gave a hoarse laugh. "There're always more. These brutes come at all hours of the night. Drunk sometimes, at the crack of dawn, always with more spoils."

Vetra gave a bleak nod. An uneasy thought gripped the back of his mind. "Then let's go. We don't want to be trapped in this devil's pit."

Tatla cried, "Wait."

Vetra turned and saw a tousle-haired boy scrabbling toward them. He was all knees and elbows, wide eyes. He'd been hiding behind the horse corral, in a pile of straw.

"The lad I released from one of Igir's cages," Skirl cried.

Nog reined in. He was about to scoop him up when the woman armed with the crossbow reached down a hand and pulled him up herself, settled him on the saddle behind her. The rest of the women had gained their mounts and seemed capable enough to ride, Vetra thought. Dergath help them.

Vetra swatted the rumps of the remaining dozen to get

them scattering. No sense leaving them for the outlaws. He heeled his black mare ahead. Behind him, Nog rode with Skirl clutching his talisman. Together in semi-organized fashion they trotted past the horse pen, across the grubby communal grounds, down the scrubby slope.

"You're a sight for sore eyes, sir swordsman," Tatla whispered in Vetra's ear, "or should I say Master Vetravincus?"

"You remember me?" he said incredulously.

"Yes, I remember you from my childhood. The horsemaster's son. Vetravincus of the moody tempers and the flashing sword. Always the bee in everyone's bonnet, the restless rover."

A smile crept over Vetra's lips. She clung to his back and he could feel the soft press of her breasts against him as she murmured again in his ear. "I remember when you thrashed one of those bullies harassing young Domlin's brother. That story was popular for a month!" She clung to him tighter. "When you first came to this cursed place, a hope flared in my heart, that there was justice in this world. But when I saw you all trussed up and bullied by them and taken to the cavern, my hope fled with it. Now I am on the back of a horse with you, and your friends are like gifts from the gods."

"We're not out of this yet."

"I still feel like I am caught in an evil dream," she gasped. "Still trapped in that filthy pen. Where are those other villains?"

"They lie blooded and dazed in their loathsome pit. How long they stay there, I could not say. Some had already crept out and were banging hard at the door." He left that thought unfinished. A rogue fear gnawed at him. Maybe he should have slit all their throats while he had the chance? Had he not vowed to send them all to Dergath?

Dull yellow bands of cloud hung over the hills behind

them. They rode through the screen of foliage the outlaws had erected to conceal their path. No need to restore the sheltering branches. Dusk was coming, and was but an hour away. It would bring with it a coolness to the lands and the threat of night discovery.

No sooner had they wound their way out of the foothills when specks of black shapes emerged from the dark fringe of trees to the north.

"What more foul luck to add to the day?" Vetra cursed. A stray arm of the Ravenclaw band now returning from their hunt laden with their spoils…and fast moving toward them.

They'd spotted them. Like the wrath of a blistering wind they now came galloping across the fields at a breakneck speed.

"Ride!" Vetra cried. He urged his mount to double speed. Nog dug his heels into his own roan. The women gave their horses free rein. Anxious cries spilled from their lips, drifting across the lonely countryside.

Vetra squinted ahead. The north-south track was but five hundred yards away.

It may as well have been five miles. The raiders were swift. They knew their craft. The women who lagged behind were headed off by rearing stallions. Half of them waylaid as rag-bearded men leaped off their mounts and onto the saddles of the women. The mettlesome maiden with the crossbow drew back a bolt and shot one in the face.

Vetra swore under his breath. This venture was not going well.

Already cross-bolts were raining down upon them, whistling by his ear and rattling like snakes about the horse's heels.

He could not save them all. Their only chance was to get to the road and try to escape into the protection of woods.

Nog slowed, his mare bucking with a quarrel in her rump.

Riders were all around them now. Nog hacked while Skirl spat out threats. The Eros jewel clutched in his hand seemed useless under the bucking, heaving madness.

Vetra circled back and lay steel into the first outlaw with upraised sword who was half way home to plunging a blade into Nog's throat. Tatla clung to his back. The outlaw toppled with a bellow of agony, trampled underfoot by beasts charging at the rear.

"Ride faster! Follow my lead!" Vetra called back at the panicking women. There were too many of them. "Don't try to fight them!"

The warrior-woman with the bow and boy in tow paid heed. So did one other.

The three hurtled toward the road with Nog and Skirl struggling to keep up on their wounded roan. Vetra turned his mount on the dirt track heading south, aiming for the trees around a bend in the road.

Shouts and jeers echoed behind him. Raucous wails, the thunder of hooves, desperate cries.

A startling sight lay around that bend. A massive column of riders bearing the Lvendarian flag.

Vetra huffed an explosive breath. Was it a mirage?

The column's standard-bearer bore the pennon of Lausern with the blue and yellow griffin.

So, the rumored expected invasion was real...

The soldiers heard their cheers and came at full gallop to strike terror in the black-clad riders' hearts. A strident blare of a horn announced a hundred armored swordsmen with glinting shields...and more were coming.

On sight of the mounted soldiers, the Ravenclaw riders turned their mounts and fled. Terror of the Lvendar army had them whipping their horses to a frenzy.

Vetra gave a smile of triumph. Perhaps the day had not been lost and Dergath had not deserted them completely.

Chapter 36

The rush of thunderous hooves and armored flanks of black stallions mingled with the swish of arrows and the cries of dying men. The Lvendarian guard charged forward. Men leapt off their horses and skewered four of the downed outlaws with poleaxes.

In total, Vetra estimated they were 400 mounts strong. Knights who wielded axe, sword and mace on prize destriers dressed in blue and green aprons over mailed flank and belly. The pride of Lvendar.

A stocky man in a blue-plumed morion piked his sword and kneed his horse forward. "Back to your ranks, you rascals!" he yelled at his riders. "There'll be more to kill later. We'll rout out those scum on our way back. Pressing matters loom. Let us ride!" He was a muscly jowly man with flint-gray eyes, high cheekbones, and a hard-bitten air of authority.

The courageous woman of Vetra's company with the crossbow cried out, "There are others back there, captain! We must save them." She waved her bow at the outlaws on black horses streaking off with six of the women she'd rode with. Her breath was a husky echo.

"They're going nowhere," the captain called back. "The outlaws' slavers' route is through Masern, which is where we go to break the approaching army."

"You must stop them!"

"Damn it, woman! There will be no Lvendar left if we don't halt this invasion. An insolent horde bent on splintering our borders. We must think priorities." His stony eyes flicked off her onto five of the other women his riders had brought forth. They all stared comatose, grime-streaked, cringing in the arms of the soldiers. "Take her and the boy and the others back to their people," the captain ordered.

The woman struggled in her saddle as the men-at-arms tried to escort her back to the end of the column. Vetra scowled. He reined in, but did nothing to stop them. He tried to convince himself that the maid didn't realize how lucky she was to have escaped the slavers.

But something did not sit right with him. "Hold up!" he rasped. "The woman fought valiantly. She slew at least one of those raider scum who were after us. Without her, many of us would have died."

The captain glared at him. "You giving me orders?"

"No, I merely suggest the woman deserves more than what you're giving her…to be heard and leave her her horse. I stand in her defense."

The captain rubbed his jaw. He muttered into his beard. "If you're so hell bent for leather, woman, take up a sword and fight with the men."

"That I will, and gladly," she cried.

His lips grew wide in appreciation. "Tell me then, what's your name, lass?"

"Caradwen…. Dwen for short. I come from Cairnhill, a village two leagues east of here."

"Dwen, you are hereby promoted to rank of mounted knight. Man-at-arms of the Lvendarian guard."

"Woman-at-arms, sir."

He waved his arm as if it were all one. He turned to his lieutenant. "See to it."

Caradwen was fitted in a spare hauberk, bronze helm and handed a decent sword. Vetra gave a nod of satisfaction.

The captain looked to Tatla and motioned to his lieutenant. "Go, take her home too before dusk sets in."

Tatla twisted in her saddle. "When will I see you again?"

She clutched at Vetra, blinking back her tears.

"I shall pass by Vrigin's when this is all over." His words sounded hollow even to his own ears.

"We'll make camp within the hour, before dusk—" the captain gestured. "Ahead, past that round in the trail on higher ground." His gloved hand indicated the brow of a hill. "The aspen and hemlock'll give us shelter. No fires are to be lit."

"As you wish, Lord Onas." The captain's lieutenants gave stiff nods. They rode back to give orders to the others. Nog replaced his disabled mount with one of the larger horses that the soldiers had rounded up. Skirl too rode his own horse. The company moved on sure-footed hooves up the nearby slope to spread out and make camp.

The captain took stock of Nog and Vetra. "We have known about this band of cutthroats for a while. They have lived too long…A slaver band led by a man called Brule."

Vetra grumbled. "We know. Trouble yourself no more, captain. I slew him myself."

The captain stared at him, licking his lips. "Then you've done a service to Lvendar. You're from where?"

"Tolizia."

"Tolizia? And you, sir?" He turned his piercing gaze on Nog.

"Thrakia."

The captain shook his head in wonderment, a low grumble under his breath. "Tolizia and Thrakia? Wanderers? Mercenaries?—serving justice in Lvendar? Surely this is a strange world. What next? Balborian strumpets giving lectures on chastity in the public square?"

His men-at-arms laughed.

"Five hundred yeoman infantry to be wagoned in from Alantra on the morrow! Six hundred more riders to follow from

Lausern with archers. This will swell our numbers threefold. Lord Ragnum sent us in advance to check the Mercian incursion, to slow down the march on Alantra."

A soldier slapped the captain's arm and pointed high in the sky. Onas turned and frowned up into the dying light at an odd shape.

A black speck in the west was growing larger with every passing breath. A thing of jagged wings, crusty body and sharp pointed snout. Taranis's dragon, if Vetra knew anything. Who other than the Archmagrix herself riding its back, her chin held high like some sorceress queen. The dragon was already enormous. He shuddered to think of how big it would get when it was fully grown.

"Lord, the devil rides!" croaked the man-at-arms.

"No, it is Taranis," Vetra murmured. "Sorceress from Xalgossa. She rides Drako, the dragon hatched from an egg."

"Dragon?" the captain snarled. "An egg? Are you serious? What know you of such a beast?"

"We stumbled across it under the stone stronghold of Dormoth, lord. The Hall of Mages at Xalgossa. We have fled from there these past days, evading the sorceress's wrath."

"Dergath's bane! What other imbroglios have you gotten yourself into? Outlaws, witches and now this dragon?" He shook his head violently and spat an oath. His eyes narrowed to slits as superstitious fear now crinkled his cheeks. In glided the dragon, sweeping lower over their numbers in wide circles. The batlike wings stretched wide, a duskier crimson than the burnt-umber body. Its ugly horned skull dipped and its basilisk glare swung upon the gathered horsemen. Jaws parted, revealed twin white fangs and now the puff of its smoky breath blew, as if waiting to belch a stream of fire to char them all.

"Shields up!" the captain bellowed. Horses whinnied and

four hundred knight's shields lifted in unison. "Dragons! I did not know such things existed."

"They do, captain, and you see proof with your own eyes."

"What does this sorceress want?" he demanded. His blue-gray eyes gazed up past his shield as the beast continued its arc of reconnaissance then tilted its snout to the north.

"She seeks the jewel of Eros," Skirl said, reining in closer, "the Eros Flame—" his voice pitched louder than necessary.

"Which our doughty mage guards in his robe's pocket," Vetra murmured.

Skirl held the jewel up for all to see.

The captain blinked and blocked the light from his eyes with a hand. "Put it away, you oaf! It blinds my eyes, even in this waning light."

A sea of swords piked around Skirl's neck. He quickly stuffed it back in his pocket. The swords retreated, dropping like feathers in the wind.

After a time the dragon faded in the distance as if to scout out the Mercian army to the north. For what reasons, Vetra could not guess. The sorceress, it appeared, had not spotted them among the ranks of horsemen. Or perhaps she was just toying with them.

"You say she is Umbrian?" the captain asked. "They are no friends of the Mercians. Let us hope she harries them, not us."

Vetra's thoughts were doubtful, thinking there'd be little chance of that.

"You two fight well," he said, "I may have use of you. Will you join our forces?"

Vetra shrugged. "What say you if we pass?"

The captain bared his teeth. A chill smile ran up the line of his rugged jaw. "We could also send you packing back to Alantra with the females... For a long interrogation at the bailiff's office inquiring as to why you are in Lvendar."

Vetra moistened his lips. "We'll ride with you, captain, only if you add the mage to our company."

"What, this scrawny pretty boy? Look at him, half an ear, ranting about a magic jewel and a dragon-riding sorceress. I've seen dozens of raving lunatics on the streets of Alantra. Street cats too less battered. What need have I of a jackleg magician?"

Skirl piped up in a voice of hauteur, "You have Taranis, and a dragon pitted against you. I can weave counterspells to thwart the witch and her magic spells."

"Aye, and get mixed up in a private war with the Xalgossian mages? No thanks."

"You're already entwined," Vetra intoned. "The sorceress has marked you and your army as she's marked us. You've nothing to lose. I say, take up the mage's offer." He gestured to the restless soldiers who were looking all too uneasily skyward even after the dragon's shadow had passed. "From where I'm standing, you're going to need all the help you can get."

The captain rubbed his cheek. "Perhaps you are right. But it's on your head if this goes sideways. Make sure the mage gets us in no trouble."

Vetra gave a brief nod. He didn't care about trouble, just as long as they rode in protected numbers. Nor did he care to mention that the apprentice was at best a tyro, if not an outright fraud. What the captain didn't know couldn't hurt him. Vetra's instincts told him he had to stay close to Skirl. He needed to protect him, and the mage needed to protect them, if that made any sense.

Vetra mumbled to Nog at his side. "We've got plunder-happy Mercians to the north, angry Lvendarians to the south, now a mad witch flying on a dragon out for our blood. To the west, a band of cutthroats who would ride out of the hills to slay us for fouling their nest. What more could we ask for?"

The riders settled in and made camp on the ridge as the sun sank behind brooding crags that bordered Umbria and Lvendar. Fresh loaves and cold mutton were brought out from saddlebags. The men sat in a clearing under tree cover, munching and trading stories in companionable groups. Tents were erected under the swaying aspen with their falling leaves, the horses fed and watered at a small stream running down the other side of the hill and hobbled to prevent any loss.

After they'd made camp, the captain motioned Vetra and Nog to sit by him, seeing that they sat apart. "You'll need shields, lads. Go around back of the tents to the weapons' stores and take what you need. There are daggers, mace and greaves."

Nog grinned and patted his hauberk and swords. "Got all I need right here, captain. These blades are my shield." He unsheathed the swords slung on his back and crossed them before his chest.

"Suit yourself, crusader. If dying's your wish then run with it. We move out at dawn's light. We'll meet the horde that wishes to sack Alantra and it's not going to be pretty."

"No war or battle is," Vetra muttered. He remembered his father's words long ago and missed the old man's presence more than ever.

Skirl selected and donned a steel cap, then fitted silver mail over his soiled robe. The accouterments gave his frame a bit more substance, though not much. He took a dagger from the spread which he shoved in a thigh pocket of his tattered robe. Vetra's lips curled into a wry smile. Garbed in his war gear, the mage scarecrow looked a veritable warrior but not one to strike terror in the hearts of an enemy.

Onas left to inspect the camp. He gave brief instructions to his sentries while Nog took Vetra aside. "Why do you hate these Mercians so much?"

A dark cloud came over Vetra's face. "They burned my father's gladiatorial school, raped my mother and slaughtered our finest horses."

Nog swallowed. "Who?"

"A band of Mercian raiders. As a lesson to my father who defied them. I learned of this travesty after my travels east, Nog. Those long wandering years, lost, footing it through Condoria, Mosete and elsewhere. Rumor had it, the deed was done under the orders of the mad King Aethrith of Mercia at the time, the jealous snake, as a lesson to my father, Menicus, who had trained so many good warriors to fight against Mercia. He fought against imperialism. I'll kill every one of the vermin I get my hands on."

"Understandable. But not all Mercians are evil."

"No, just the ones that matter, Nog. Crooked men working under a king who endorses crooked policies. I hate Mercian imperialism as much as my father did. They were jealous of the number of quality fighters he churned out to destroy the march on our borders. I have no doubt Minas's kidnapping had something to do with this vendetta Aethrith had against my father. Even these scum outlaws had blessings from Mercia."

Nog firmed his lip. "That's a tall accusation. This is all news to me. No matter, we will kill them all."

Even as darkness fell, Vetra glanced up into the black velvet sky through the wavering branches with a wary eye. He did not like the fact that Taranis was so near. "I can almost smell her," he said. "I feel a quiver in my bones."

Skirl drifted over to stare up beside him. "'Tis her power,

Vetra. The power she wields through the Eros Flame."

"Dergath's hell!" Vetra swore. "Am I to be forever the pawn of this she-devil?"

"If the originator of the spell is slain, the spell is broken."

"So I am to be a woman slayer then?"

Skirl lifted his shoulders. "You can conclude what you like."

Vetra bared Skirl a toothy snarl. "I rue the day I joined up with you, mage. This zany quest has caused us much grief."

Skirl tried his best at a grin. "But what fun we're having, eh Vetra?"

Vetra grabbed him by the scruff of the neck and propelled him toward the trees. He looked ready to give him a beating.

Skirl called out in protest, "Wait! Peace, brother! The only way forth is forward."

Vetra halted and patted the mage on the back. He gave a reluctant grin and shook his head. "Come on, knave! Let us see to this mutton they're dishing out. My guts ache with hunger."

CHRIS TURNER

Chapter 37

Dawn had risen far too red and early for Vetra's liking. A thin mist blanketed the camp and the shallow vale to the north. His bones ached from the abuse of the past days, not to mention the rough ground and chill dew on which he'd slept. Nog seemed spry, his black-gray mane sticking up in places like turkey feathers. He patted the spikes down and slung on his helm and stretched his long arms with a yawn. Caradwen had been given a tent of her own by Onas's tent that evening and she'd passed the night in safety.

A clatter of hooves heralded the arrival of a scout riding into the camp on a steel-gray stallion. He reined in beside Onas who was gearing up in silver-scale mail and gaudy, plumed morion. The rider dismounted and bent a knee. "Sir, I have come from the head of the Mercian march. Thousands of soldiers!" he said breathlessly. "Bearing swords, mace, axe and at least 200 archers."

Onas exhaled. "This bodes ill for us, Baldir."

"It gets worse. The Mercians have recruited a tribe of giants—from beyond the norther border of Balboria, the haunt of the Kyldrie."

"Giants?" The captain blinked in astonishment. "What in Dergath…are such things possible?"

"I have seen them with my own eyes, sir. Huge juggernauts. With steel caps like drums and wooden clubs like trunks. They take strides as men would take running hops. Perhaps fifty of them, serving as rear guard. At first I thought they were misshapen trees, or strange siege engines, but then I saw they were men of enormous size. Eldritch things brew in the haunt of the Kyldrie, sir, the place from whence the dragons came."

The captain shook his head in dismay. "I fear we are hopelessly outnumbered, Baldir. We will fight anyways! And we will die like men. Dergath help these invaders who marshal against us! The bigger they are, the harder they will fall." He rounded on Vetra and Nog who'd ridden up with Skirl on their horses. "Mercenaries, if your mage has any power, let him wield it now. We ride to war! Let us be off!"

Horns signaled the march to arms.

The company was not five minutes into their canter when two robed figures came riding up behind them. Three outriders veered off to intercept them and escort the newcomers to the captain's place at the vanguard.

Vetra recognized them immediately, inauspicious mages of the cloth of Dormoth.

"Who are you and what do you want?" the captain demanded.

"We are mages of Dormoth at Xalgossa," the first figure in white said. "I am Belgra, this is Senesch, come to secure the Eros Stone. 'Tis known as *Arkmida* in the tongues of old of the Sahirians."

"More mages?" the captain cried in exasperation. "Dergath, will I ever hear the end of this silly jewel? Is it that important?"

"It is. And scorn not our assistance," Senesch chided. He clutched his robe ever tighter about his thin frame in the chill of dawn. "Taranis, head sorceress of Xalgossa, has uprooted the garden over the crypts of Old Sagoth. She has unleashed a dragon on the world. Doubtless you have seen the foul fiend pass over at some recent time?"

"Aye, we have, old man. What of it?"

"Taranis rides it into dusky dawn and fiery sunset. She ensorcelled our fellow mages with the Eros Flame before we could intervene. I fear she has plans to enslave the entire north and become dark queen of all the lands—if she wins this battle for the stone. I fear she has learned of the location of the Dragon Lords who kept the dragons' last eggs, and will rouse them to unleash an army against the free kingdoms."

"Wizard, is there nothing but woe in your news?" Onas clutched at his beard. "All of what you speak is foul, wizard, foul!"

"Alas, captain, there's more. Our kindred mage Voydred has fallen to the Archmagrix's spells. Even now he rides behind us on a jet-black stallion. He calls himself 'The Black Mage'. No more than a few hours away. For Taranis he would wield black magic against you. You and your men will need all the sorcerous help you can get. Keren, our beastmaster, has also fallen. Once he was wise and canny, now he is under the grip of her tainted magic. He acts as her eyes and ears. A conduit some say…a scout who's taken the form of a great condor with all-seeing eye, and armed such, he can sniff out the stone bearer and its magic at a distance."

The captain rocked back in his saddle. "Is there no one who can give me favorable news?" He dragged his knuckles across his plumed morion.

Senesch shook his head. "Better to hear words of truth than false whispers, my Lord."

Onas gave a bitter nod. "You speak truthfully, old man." He scratched his head, his battle cunning at work. "Can we not devise a truce with this witch?"

Skirl made a derisive sound. "It is said she goes up to her secret observatory in the Hall of Winds on the night of the full moon…to gaze at harvest time on the blood-red moon and dream lusty dreams of Dal Sagoth. She cut off my ear on a whim." He tilted his head and its bandage. "Does this sound like one with whom you can deal truces?"

Onas shook his head.

"She will destroy anything in her path that bars way to the stone."

After a time Onas frowned. "How came you mages of Dormoth so quickly upon our company?"

"I threw the bones," said Belgra. "I asked the gods where goeth the stone, and in the pattern that fell, the shades told me that the Eros Flame would be here in this lonely corner of Lvendar on the eve of the waxing moon. And so—my divination has proven true."

"Witchcraft," the captain grumbled.

"You disapprove?"

"I don't approve or disapprove, milady. I merely dwell in the world of the living. I follow things I can see with my own eyes, not shades, spirits and heathenish magic. They are not for me or to my liking."

Senesch gave a disgruntled snort. "Then you are sorrily deluded, captain. This world is ruled by unseen forces. We are part of a whole, as wind is to air, water is to the sea. There is much mystery in this world which we will never see, or hear or understand."

"Riddles and gibberish," the captain muttered. "Which I care not to dispute with you. 'Tis time we move on. Stay back out of the way of my riders if you wish to accompany us. Wield your magic, if you must, but only if it will help us win this battle, or eliminate these fiends of whom you speak."

The four hundred riders moved on only to be met by the forces from the south, swelling their numbers three-fold as the captain had predicted. Up the dirt track they rode, many dozens of men abreast as the terrain allowed it. The terrain here, mostly open fields, pastures and scattered copses of aspen and oak turning yellow in the changing season, was pleasant country and easily navigable.

They at last mounted a hill and looked over a golden valley. The morning mist was barely clearing. The Mercians had taken up on a knoll across the valley. There the enemy armies stood separated by an open plain down which the north-south road ran. The warriors contemplated each other. Like ravenous wolves. The sun glinted off their burnished weaponry, their bronze helms and steel hauberks. Their horses finery and accouterments clinked in the distance.

"Fine day for killing," Nog remarked. He peered at the rows of mailed riders and the enemy pikemen. The standard of Mercia rose high from a polearm on a lead rider's horse—the black war wolf on a green background. A grim insignia which fluttered in the gentle breeze from the hills to the west.

"For you, every day's good for killing," Vetra said. His voice held no humor. Every time he'd had to face a wall of mailed men in a full scale battle, his stomach had churned. The notion that war is a glorious thing is a misnomer, that it brings purpose and strength to a warrior's body and soul. Pure codswallop. It may cleanse him of illusion, if there is any gain. Blood and death, the taking of lives, senseless destruction and the rape of land and women, it is a dark stain and taint on the human soul. So too the burning of crops and peoples' dreams. The whispering rush of shades of the departed is no proud thing to experience or the bristling of hairs on the back as one walks the battlefields of the dead.

Yet the poets and sages, and the pundits and scholars, would sing and scribe about it forever in many a heroic verse. They would wax on till the cows come home, in their myths and their anthologies, never lifting a blade once themselves in their valiant careers. Yet men would fight on and men would die deluded with the same thrill of battle in their breasts as the curse of war had given them since they were apes rising out of the jungle.

Both sides, the enemy nearly three thousand strong, were ready to slay each other and claim northern Lvendar for their own. In ranks of hundreds, the enemy riders poised, blue-green jupons draped over silver-scale mail, swords tipped now in a wild battle cry. Both kings were strangely absent, as if this theater were but a mere exploratory skirmish for a greater battle to come.

Vetra was puzzled. Were more troops and horses held back to pour from the heartsprings of Mercia and Lvendar at a later time? Siege engines and war machines? The puppet monarchs being content at having their ambassadors and generals do their dirty work for them seemed odd, but then again, odder things had happened in this age.

On the horizon was something that was not so puzzling—a hideous lizardish shape that come winging from the west—all burnt umber and mottled crimson. It hovered above the opposing armies out of arrow range.

Taranis's black-robed figure sat astride her pet in all her gleaming glory. And a new surprise, a gigantic hook-beaked bird, a condor half as large, but with brownish wingspan nearly as wide as the dragon's. It hovered in the dragon's shadow like some minion goliath—the ensorcelled beastmaster, Keren.

The warriors massed below. Committed thus, they heeded not the double omens. Men shuffled and roared and clacked their swords on shield. What was a freakish condor and a fabled lizard hosting a luxurious rider to them in this do-or-die moment?

The captains shouted their orders. Horns blared. Then the horses thundered forth as one as the sun lit their burnished armor aflame.

Vetra rode with Captain Onas in front of him. Nog was at his side with hundreds of mailed riders surrounding them on either flank and behind.

Behind the Mercian ranks a phalanx of foot soldiers knelt and took aim in the dewed grass with their arbalests. Volleys flew like a flock of black hornets. They arched over the Mercian ranks to find targets among the Lvendarian horsemen.

The lead riders ducked behind their wooden shields. Vetra heard a murderous thunk of bolts as they plunked on wood and some smashed through men's shields. Two score mounted riders fell, pierced through throat or breast. The rest of them thundered ahead.

Vetra and Nog spurred their mares, roaring war cries, keen to slay as many of the enemy Mercians before the next volley of arrows could punch through their numbers.

In a thunderous rush the two forces met. A clangorous clash of steel that smote the air as blades of fury met in the middle of the valley still bathed in fresh morning mist battling the golden rays. It was like the crack of divine thunderbolts sent down from the sky. Horseflesh smashed into iron. Tortured cries rang up and down the valley, curdling the men's ears.

Vetra closed with his opposing rider, his shield up. A vicious spiked ball came for his head and he blocked the blow while he jabbed and slashed at his opponent's ribs. His enemy misjudged—a bearded Mercian with glaring eyes and horned steel cap—and Vetra drove the blade forward and cut through a rent in his mail and slewed into his vitals. Blood gushed and Vetra kicked the man off his saddle. He muscled his mare in to take up the space.

No sooner had he done this than he crossed blades with another bearded foe. Nog pushed into the gap while arrows flew thick and furious. The Lvendarian archers had been slower to shoot. Smoke seared across the sky as some of these shafts bore flaming ends which set men's surcoats aflame.

Horses wheeled. Many bucked and fled in terror, free of their riders. In the maelstrom of licking blades and spurting blood there was no logic, sense or order. Any man who went down was not likely to get up beneath that roil of stamping hooves. Horses milled, jammed together. Men reached and stabbed with swords, slashing murderously at limbs and torsos. All was pandemonium.

The Mercians had not come unprepared.

Chapter 38

Skirl rode somewhere back of the confused line. As keeper of the jewel, he clutched the precious Eros Flame like a jealous maid. Belgra and Senesch flanked him, riding no less fretfully. Skirl looked to them for support, but they seemed distant, faraway, as if absorbed in their own dark ruminations. Skirl's face grew pale, his mind troubled, his eyes darting every which way. Never had he expected to be in the press of such deadly forces.

Belgra hissed, "Do you have the stone?"

Skirl gave a slow nod.

"Let me see it."

He reluctantly pulled the stone from his pocket.

Belgra gasped, as did Senesch, for the gem's starlit radiance had increased, almost stinging their eyes, degrees beyond the fake they'd remembered adorning Taranis's neck.

Belgra gulped and licked her thin lips. "Better you entrust the talisman to me."

"Why?" Skirl demanded. He withdrew the stone jealously back into his pocket.

"I garner sufficient magic to defend it. Yours was stripped, remember?"

Stonier than basalt was this Belgra who held his gaze through narrowed lids, the same who carried his child in her womb. The sorceress seemed too eager, all too grasping for this piece of magickery.

Skirl bit his tongue. A sudden swoosh and arrows came whizzing at them. He ducked, cheating again death's sting.

Belgra spoke in low murmurs, like a breeze rippling through the high treetops. The crossbow bolts seemed to shiver and warp in their flight and thud into the ground at their horses' hooves. She made a furious gesture, "We'd better hope the Lvendarians don't fall, Senesch! If the jewel passes into enemy hands—" she let the thought dangle even as Skirl's eyes traveled to two brawny figures in red surcoats hacking and slashing a stone's throw away in a knot of blue-clad enemy horsemen.

Belgra heeled her horse forward. Her intent was to stop more Mercian arrows from piercing the Lvendarian defenders.

Senesch rode in beside her. "Belgra, wait! We must counter Voydred. Look, he rides!"

Their eyes turned. Behind them, a mounted figure in black, surrounded by a dozen mage guard, galloped their way.

A wicked pike came jabbing up at Vetra's horse then through his mare's ribs. The animal gave a last painful scream and threw him. Vetra rolled and staggered to his feet, shaking the daze out of his head. His sword, blood-dripping, swiftly lifted to ward off a hive of enemy blades. In the confused fray, Nog crouched a dozen feet away unhorsed. They both gave cursing shouts and joined the foot soldiers, now a milling wheel of hacking and stabbing men hemmed in a circle of snorting horses and enemy riders.

The Mercian plan was simple…To strike hard and fast at the heart of the enemy. Kill the leader and create a rout. They had not yet killed Onas but had inflicted terrible casualties on the Lvendarian riders. The hovering dragon provided no wrinkle in their plans—yet.

Arrows flew upward but either skidded off the dragon's hide or went spinning wide. For all those who sighted on Taranis, she sent down blue globes of death to smash them to bits.

The bulk of Mercians heeded not the dragon. They at last unleashed their armored giants at the Lvendarians, who for a time thought that their scouts had exaggerated the might of these mythic beings.

They had not.

Figures of nightmare, twice as high as a man, they loped in on bare thighs the size of hemlock trunks. Their faces, grim under their horned helms, were carved like oak. They gripped massive clubs in brawny fists. Though their legs were bare, their chests were burnished with cast iron that curved around their torsos like tortoise shells. They swatted men and horses aside as wanton boys would pesky flies.

Mounted bowmen peppered the first eleven of these monsters. They began to slow, finally to sag to their knees. The raging pikemen gathered and slew them to a man, hacking their heads off and sending them to Dergath.

But other giants had broken through the clot of men and horses and now lunged forward to take down Onas and his main vanguard of defenders.

Three came roaring in, knotted clubs swinging in fists, their lips frothing with spittle. They would take down the Lvendarian commander and his horse, crush and stomp him and his lieutenants to oblivion under their iron-shod boots.

The riders formed up a shield wall.

The horses reared and neighed in terror. Mercifully, they held. One giant crashed through the wall and brought a massive club smashing down on Onas's steed's skull. In a limp heap, the horse toppled, kicking up dust and gore. Onas rolled, his sword up, cursing and frothing at the ruin of his horse. The giant's shadow bore down on him like a harbinger of death.

Vetra blinked at the sheer horror of it all. He sheathed his sword and drew his knife…he clenched it in his teeth then took a running leap to vault on the back of the attacking giant. Into the nape of his neck he stabbed the blade again and again.

CHRIS TURNER

The giant reached a ham fist back to try and get a grip on his head but Vetra jerked back in time to slash at the giant's probing fingers. He leaped off as the giant staggered forward. Uttering war cries, Onas and his bodyguard surged forth and hacked the giant to pieces.

Onas flashed Vetra a grateful, blood-dripping salute. A tribute to his good sense in recruiting Vetra from the start. But even as the token gesture was exchanged, two more giants broke through the captain's bodyguard and swarmed the hapless riders. Vetra watched in dismay as they were pushed back and Onas's head caved in to one fell swoop of a log-like club. His limp body was pulverized under the sweep of oak and mammoth feet.

The two juggernauts rose in their glory, piking clubs in the air. Their heads were tipped back in ghastly battle cries. The commander of the Lvendarian forces was slain!

Taranis watched all this with lip-curled interest, as if entertained by the gore on both sides. She gave a husky howl and urged Drako lower and lower for a better view. Arrows flew at her, but none found their mark.

She barked a harsh syllable and bade her dragon swoop down for sport. To balance the scales, she directed him toward the Mercian commander three dozen paces away amid his knot of bearded, blood-thirsty warriors who rained sword blows upon the Lvendarian defenders' shields. The dragon caught the steel-helmed commander in its jaws, lifted him high off his steed and crunched his ribs. Then it dropped one of the blood-stained halves down on the warriors' heads below. The other half it devoured, a quick morsel to nourish its growing body.

Hovering on her dragon, the sorceress bade the winged lizard breathe fire on any who aimed arrows up at her.

Witnessing this travesty, Skirl bravely spurred forward to

face the sorceress. He shook the gem in a raised fist. "Go back to your slime pit, witch! Take your dragon with you! Behold! I hold the Eros Flame. I turn it freely against you. Even its crimson light despises your sluttish hide!"

Taranis quivered in her seat, speechless with rage. Upon a furious gesture at the hulking condor at her side, she willed the hooked beak to turn her way. "Down, down, bird of faith! Seek this squawking infidel. Fetch me my gem!"

With a low guttural croak, the condor flapped mighty wings and angled its sinister beak toward the defenseless Skirl.

Skirl held the Eros jewel high, undeterred. The magical rays shone forth with a rare brilliance, straight into the descending condor's eyes...eyes that were Keren's.

Under the witch's spell, Keren was safely immune to the sway of magic while he assumed the form of this hulking bird-shape. With a flap and buffet of wings, deadly talons tore the jewel from Skirl's grasp...and unluckily, two of Skirl's fingers with it.

A spray of blood watered the grass. Skirl stared down at his missing fingers and an inarticulate cry caught in his throat. He clutched at his forked stump of hand, whimpering in grief as he slid off his horse.

The condor flapped back to where the sorceress perched on her dragon. She snatched the jewel from its upraised claws while a flurry of arrows whizzed around her. But she pressed her slim body flat to the dragon's hide. Thus clinging to its neck, the sultry witch made herself a near impossible target. "Go, good Keren!" she bawled. "Make sport of the Mercians, and the Lvendarians, I care not which." Even as she snapped the order, the brown-winged condor gave a shrill croak and dove with talons raking the helms of the fighting men below; it carved deep ruts through mail, flesh and bone.

Riders were unhorsed. Mayhem descended upon the ranks of both Mercians and Lvendarians. Vetra looked up to see chaos everywhere. Hordes of men hacking each other. Blood spraying from men and beasts.

Taranis's scintillant eyes glowed with rapture. An almost sexual heat radiated from her erotic figure as she twined her fingers about the Eros Stone. A soft moan rumbled in her throat. She caressed the gem, as if thriving on the spilling of men's blood, the blood of warriors who painted the battlefield with their life force. It was as much a thrill as the excitement of the stormy, loin-on-loin encounters with upteen men in her boudoir...under the voyeurish eye of her underworld demon, Dal Sagoth.

Arrows lanced up from all directions, but clacked harmlessly off the dragon's hard-scaled plates. Those who sighted on her were smitten by the power of the love amulet. They either sat or stood slack-mouthed, dazed in the vortex of the scintillating gem's magic.

Not all the arrows missed. One whizzed up and caught the giant winged Keren in its breast. The condor gave a mournful caw, outspread wings shredded as more bolts flew. He batted head back and forth, beak plucking at quarrels embedded in his flesh. He plummeted to the earth, crashing into mailed men, steel pikes and swords, breaking neck and crushing scores of soldiers. The beast shimmered out of existence, leaving only a naked, twisted figure of a man amid a sprawl of torn bodies.

Angered by the demise of her servant, Taranis shouted down, "Fly, Drako, fly! Let us avenge our knight!"

The dragon swooped low, and as he did, he opened wide his maw and breathed gales of fire upon horses and men alike and laid waste to hundreds in the fray.

Blackened humps lay behind her. Only a scorched ruin of

charred flesh.

The dragon bore down now on Belgra who sat alone a-saddle her gray-white mare while Senesch sat three horses away, lips compressed.

Taranis cried from the back of her steed, "You would rebel against me, oh faithless cousin? No hummingbirds or enchanted begonias to take down my dragon?"

"I cannot tolerate your megalomania, Taranis!" Belgra shrilled back. "You have brought nothing but disgrace to our Order and death to countless innocents."

Taranis clicked her tongue. The shadow of the lizard fell over the slim figure of her cousin, though she rode off like the wind, her eyes white with fright.

The servile dragon swooped, smoke puffing from its nostrils, oblivious to Belgra's shrill shrieks of terror as scaly horn and sinew hooked around her waist and lifted her off her mount.

Skirl gave a mad cry of grief. He came running after her as if he could catch up and free her from the dragon's clutch.

The dragon circled and at Taranis's whispered command, caught the apprentice too in its opposing talon.

Now the two struggling figures lay clutched in the dragon's claws and Taranis gloated vindictively. The dragon rose once more to peer down upon the host of fighting men. Many hundreds milled below in disarray, many charred.

The sorceress tilted back her head and gave another dusky laugh, which rang across the assembled warriors like an evil chime.

Dragon and rider settled above the armies. Taranis held forth the jewel, her eyes slits of blazing wrath. "You faithless curs! You would fire arrows on me, Archmagrix of Xalgossa? Look within, what do you see?"

The dragon clutched Skirl ever tighter in its right talon. Skirl cried out in anguish. Belgra, constricted in its left, squirmed desperately. Skirl's face was a mask of pure misery. He looked on the verge of weeping. He peered over at his love Belgra, in the early stages of pregnancy, clutched as tightly as himself in the dragon's foul grip. Fresh blood spurted from his wound. But this was the least of his concerns.

"Off your horses and bow now, slaves!" Taranis shrieked. "Perhaps I will spare you!"

She crouched on the dragon's back. One hand was gripped on the dragon's neck. The other hand clutched the Eros Flame. Her head was tilted back, long chestnut mane trailing behind, mouth roaring a mantra-like spell.

"Garageis Umpheunt Karwezs!"

The love jewel, twined in her fingers, burst into a flare of brilliance more vivid than ever before, its sapphire radiance blinding the eyes of all who looked from below.

The willful dragon swooped low; it breathed fire and death on the swath of those directly under his path. It swooped and rolled with the delight of a juvenile of the Kyldrie wastes allowed free reign in the sky, and carried Belgra and Skirl aloft again.

Taranis, drunk with her power, laughed, amused at the antics of her pet.

The sorceress's cruel gaze fell upon Vetra and Nog who struck and parried the swords of blood-soaked warriors below.

"Stop, you two faithless hounds!" And such was the power of her bellowing voice that their sport ended abruptly. "As punishment, you will fight to the death over me. The winner takes all! I will lie naked with the one who is still standing. Ere the rising moon this evening, I will then slit the winner's throat! Commence!" She clapped her hands and like a thunder burst, so it was done. The two began their pantomime of death. Like cobras swaying to a snake-charmer's pipe, Vetra and Nog dropped their hewing and scrambled over heaped bodies in a mad race to meet each other in mortal combat. Blood-caked swords clutched in fists, gleaming under the sallow light of the sun, with snarls on their lips, they turned on each other and steel clanked on steel. And such a fight was not to be seen on this gory battlefield that day...

Chapter 39

Even after the first clash of swords, some dim part of Vetra's brain registered that this was but a dream. A sorcerous parody of tainted magic.

But his body would not obey his reason. His muscled thews danced, like a strumpet at a bazaar; his heart beat and soared with love for this beautiful evil, black-leathered witch who hovered in the sky above him.

Nog too, caught up in his lust for the witch, possibly the chance to mate with the black widow herself, charged his closest friend and rained such a flurry of savage blows that Vetra was hard put to defend.

Vetra backpedaled, parrying, grunting. He saw an opening where Nog had overextended. The man's murderous twin blades had completed their circuit: the one clutched in his right hand was at the end of its lethal downswing, the other was drawn back ready for another strike. His left side was completely exposed. One quick thrust and he could drive cold steel into Nog's throat.

But he couldn't. Nog had saved his life on at least two occasions.

The hesitancy cost him.

Nog redoubled his fury, slashing left and right, his face beet red, lips frothing, and Vetra was pushed back to the line of enemy riders. The flickering blades of Mercians flicked out at his back to the snorting of horses.

Nog. Don't do this!

But Nog was not listening. He was beyond help, his senses completely addled by the thaumaturgy of the sorceress. He saw only red where Vetra walked, a barrier to his ultimate prize, Taranis lying naked on her satin bed.

Vetra ducked a swipe from a Mercian rider's blade. A horse's rump bunted his left shoulder and sent him sprawling forward.

Nog struck. Vetra's sword arm was slow to defend. The blade went spinning out of his grasp as Nog's weapon hit square on. Cold steel traced a dizzying arc at his head. Vetra ducked, Nog's blade sweeping hairs' breadths from his head. He scrambled sideways, snatched up a fallen shield just in time to catch Nog's raised sword as he rained blows on the Mercian wood, nearly deafening his ears.

Voydred had made better time than Senesch had estimated. On his black stallion the mage sat a stone's throw from the heart of the battle, protected by a ring of his mage guard. Three had fallen, leaving only eight to protect him, including Grindar himself, grim-faced and leering, sword dripping blood. The Black Mage cut a grim figure himself: tall, resolute, head crowned with black morion and black plume, a sightless stare on his thin pale face, eyes pits into nowhere. His was a heart of malice tainted by the Sagothian magic, without pity or remorse. With fingers outstretched, he hurled spells as fatal to the Mercians as to the Lvendarians, as if now that the jewel was in the sorceress's hand, he had no further purpose in life other than to punish all around him and unleash his dark pent-up energies.

Horses fell and men dropped from their saddles, clutching their throats as he launched incantations, sonic pulses and dark blasts of every sort. Voydred cared little who he slew, as long as they died and he could channel his destructive energies on someone.

Taranis paid little heed to this juvenile play. With the jewel in her grasp, all else was incidental. She feasted eyes on the slaughter like a drooling jackal eyes a wounded antelope, or like the old crow waits patiently for the other younger ones to fight over bits of carrion, then swoops down to peck at the spoils.

With Voydred, Keren and Belgra out of action, Senesch, eldest and last of the Xalgossian mages, stood alone against Taranis. His horse was slain and charred by dragon fire. He shook a fist up at the black-clad sorceress. "You cannot do this, Taranis!" he shouted. "The gods forbid it. They govern the scales of balance. The future of sorcery lies in peril, dangles on a thread. The balance must not be skewed toward evil."

"The balance already tips this day, old man," she crooned. "'Tis the start of a new age."

"Unleashing a dragon on the world is unthinkable! It is sacrilege! The beasts are unpredictable and dangerous. There are reasons why the Scaled Ones were entombed by our forefathers in the earth, cast to the lower realms."

At this insult, Drako, who seemed savvy to the old mage's threat, gusted a fiery breath that near singed all Senesch's hair off. He fell back with a feeble cry, tamping down the gray strands on his singed pate.

Taranis gave an unsympathetic chortle. She pushed out a hand and sent a sinister, blue-gray orb lancing down to blast the dirt at the old man's feet. He went flying face-first to land in the dirt like an old blind beggar.

"What are you but a useless geriatric?" she called in contempt. "An old bookworm groveling like a worm in the dirt. I could squash you like a bug. But you have no powers left. I can see it plain as day. I'll let you live only for my amusement, so you can scribe my glory, 'Taranis the great!', 'Wielder of the Eros Flame!'"

Upon the fall of the last mage of Xalgossa, the giants of

Balboria gripped their clubs and stared helplessly into the sky. Their brows poured sweat, their limbs dripped blood. To a half dozen their numbers had been whittled, courtesy of Drako, the fearsome dragon. They saw the inevitable, the unbeatable witch and her ruthless minion ready to pounce and unleash more fire-breathing rampage upon the battlefield. Dire warnings from their ancient myths clutched at their hearts. Four of them loped off into the grassy fields, leaving only two behind clutching their clubs to stand against the onslaught. The others had broken their vows, deserted the army and earned the curses of the Mercians.

The dragon, seeing this as a game, dove down to blitz the giants, perhaps wishing to grind their heads to pulp in his jaws.

Taranis hissed. She smote him with the edge of the stone. The dragon turned and huffed smoke of displeasure at her.

The game had become tiresome for the dragon. *Fetch the stone and puny humans and puff out fire and do as you're told.* His mistress had become a bore. Rather would he be free of his ornery black-clad albatross and fly off on his own to wreak havoc on the humans which for time immemorial the dragons had hated.

He swooped lower over the soldiers and fleeing giants and dashed and buffeted the sorceress to and fro, as if to tease her off his back. This only earned Taranis's incontestable wrath. She called strident curses and rapped the Eros stone against his horns, so that when the heavy lizardish head swung about, the lurid crimson light was again in his face to plunge him into a dream-like compliance.

Vetra scrambled to snatch up a shield, to replace the last which Nog had shattered. He stumbled, crouching, hard pressed to protect himself from Nog's incessant and ensorcelled rain of fury.

While Senesch crawled like a worm amid the mounds of bodies, he came within earshot of the Black Mage and the old man's face paled in light of Voydred's macabre incantations.

The witch had been wrong about Senesch and his powers. Like all wise men, he had kept some of them guarded. Masked like an artist's motif in a complex oil painting, they lingered in abeyance. A guiding voice in his brain had told him that one day, when it most mattered, he'd have to call up every trick he knew. Even if it killed him.

What Senesch said or did on that fateful day, even the gods do not know for the scope of his magic had been kept hidden for many decades.

An injured soldier, downed by sword thrust to his abdomen, lay moaning in the dirt and saw Senesch inch his way closer to Voydred. He caught only a brief flash of light emanating from the old man's hands, a blueish glint in his eye, as some miraculous form of star-spangled dust seemed to move from the old man's fingers and flutter about the Black Mage's head.

For a moment, Voydred teetered. Then he shook his head as some of the demonic madness seeped from his brain. The spell of the Eros Flame was splintering. Voydred saw things clearly—the slavering dragon hovering in the air, the black-robed sorceress riding its back, the crumpled and torn bodies all around. He gave a wild cry in the midst of the carnage and lifted his magisterial arms and uttered thunderous words:

"Auschkag, Vellum, Vohor!"

Voydred's lips worked and strange syllables flew like hissing snakes about the fray, sending a hollow shriek like the wind over pike and shield; men on their saddles clutched at their ears.

The dragon jerked and reeled, almost upsetting his rider,

tortured by the whistling, gale-like tumult.

The magic discord rose in pitch as Voydred's spell gathered weight and his concentration brought beads of sweat on his brow. Like the sound of an incoming tornado, the wind grew and grew.

The eerie whine broke the spell of Taranis's enchantment over the gathered hordes. Vetra and Nog shook their heads, liberated for the moment of their bewitched daze. In unison they turned their eyes to the sorceress and the enemies surrounding them.

The dragon circled over the battlefield, seeking the cause of the disturbance. Drako's keen sense pinpointed the source of his torment as the black-clad mage and he came hurtling down without Taranis's bidding, talons outstretched. He dropped his cargoes, Skirl and Belgra, then reached. Talons grappled the mage's helmed head to tear it off in one blood-wrenching sweep.

Skirl and Belgra went skidding to the soft grass amid mounds of bodies. Vetra turned his head, his senses restored, and lifted his shield to block the energy of the light from the Eros Flame that grew to a blinding, blazing ruby brilliance. The reflected glare shot back up at Taranis, straight in her eyes. For a moment she blinked, her brain stymied, smitten by her own magic.

Clutching his blood-drenched prize, the dragon swooped low.

Too low.

The last two giants lunged and swatted at his hide as he passed, even as they were fire-blackened to crisps in one huff of the dragon's foul breath.

Yet knotted clubs had clipped the left side of the dragon's hide near its tail, unseating its cocky rider. Enemy soldiers piked blades up to slash at the dragon's limbs. Drako whipped his lizard-like head back and forth.

A thousand shafts rained up at close range to pelt the dragon's scale-plated body. Most missiles merely bounced back, but some cracked through the armored hide and brought fresh blood dripping down on their heads like warm spring rain.

The dragon jerked side to side and reeled. One wing flapped wildly. It tipped dangerously earthward and dragged on the ground, slicing a score of men and riders to ribbons. Meaty flesh flew.

The sorceress who'd been thrown clear, lost grip of the Eros Flame. The gem went flying into the jumble of men and horses. Yet even her lithe body was not quick enough to escape the doom fast upon her. The dragon plummeted, and as it made one last spasm, its bulk rolled on her, crushing her from toes to hip.

Taranis died in an instant, a look of frozen horror on her white, bloodless lips.

Surprise was writ there, how fate could be so cruel to deal her such an ignominious end. It seemed her dark gods had finally deserted her.

The soldiers fell on the floundering dragon. Arrows rained from all sides like a hail of hornets, penetrating eye sockets and vulnerable areas of underbelly. A new awareness moved among the awakening hordes. Thousands had died in the senseless slaughter. The bravest warriors of both sides mustered forth, now in union rather than conflict, to slice off the beast's head, even though it was already as good as dead.

Vetra caught sight of Nog who stood blinking nearby, rubbing at his brow as if not knowing where he was. Vetra snarled and came charging at him in a fit of rage. He knocked him flying.

"What's the idea of trying to kill me, you dumb ox!"

Nog rose to his feet, shaking his head in bewilderment. "I've only a vague memory, Vetra—of hewing and slashing. You were stealing something from me. I felt like I was in a dream…having no meaning, like I was in a watery realm. My heart pounding with a passion for some prize I can't even recall."

"Well, maybe for the witch lying there crushed. I guess you were not in your right senses, Nog. I suppose I can forgive you."

Skirl and Belgra had drifted over, bleak-faced and grimed, Skirl with his mangled hand tucked under an armpit, Belgra with scratches and welts on her face.

Gruesome sights had Vetra and others grimacing with distaste. Even in death, the Sagothian witch's face was beautiful, even though her lower body was crushed under the savage weight of Drako, the dragon from the Kyldrie.

"The witch is dead," Vetra muttered. "Even her devil Dal Sagoth couldn't save her."

Senesch who had hobbled over, lay a hand on his shoulder. "This is the steep price for those who dabble in forbidden magic." His milky-gray eyes swung to the broken, twisted bodies of Voydred and Keren lying not far distant. "'Tis a foul day, Vetra. Both men and gods have forsaken each other. They've decreed it a day of death."

Vetra looked on the ghastly slaughter with unconcealed repugnance. Wincing, he wiped his chin and neck of blood with the flat of his hand.

"Dragons cannot be allowed to live," the old man continued. "They are a breed of dangerous killers, a scourge on this world that will always contrive to lay waste to kingdoms." He limped several steps away from the stench of dragon and death. "It is for this reason that the Kyldrie was purged centuries ago by fearless warriors of fable and legend. All that remains are the myths of the Dragon Lords."

Vetra was entranced, and yet only half his brain registered Senesch's words, for his eyes had turned away to stare at a point where scattered humps of bodies lay...and a familiar glint.

An object gleamed blood red amid a pile of bodies. The Eros Flame!

With a choked cry, he scrabbled for it, knocking several men out of the way.

Skirl and Belgra had seen it too and took chase.

Vetra got there first. He snatched up the mace of a dead Mercian lying nearby and brought it down hard on the jewel. The gemstone split neatly in two, to a resounding crack that echoed like the champ of dragon teeth up the valley. Both fragments showed jagged edges where they had once been joined.

Skirl gave a yelp of anguish. He leaped over to stare in horror at the two pieces. One lay near his feet, the other had skidded off to Vetra's side.

Vetra heeled the chunk behind him under an upturned helm. He stared bemused while Skirl scrabbled for the larger half that had landed near him.

Feigning a spasm from a battle wound, Vetra crouched down and snatched up the piece that he'd hid. He stuffed it in his jerkin. The bauble would come in handy when he needed it. For now its magic was dead, just the way he preferred it.

Skirl peered left and right. "Where is the other half?" he cried. With his good hand he clutched his hair in grief and scrabbled about like a frantic schoolboy who'd lost a marble. Crouching on hands and knees, he burrowed about in the rubble of bodies. "Maybe it can be resurrected?"

Senesch hobbled in closer. "Not likely, mage." He looked on with a genuine air of pity. "The Flame of Eros is not a toy that can be repaired like a broken toy sailboat. It'd be like trying to mend a piece of wood from ashes, or string a sorceress's soul together that has been sold in pieces to the nether forces."

Skirl bared his teeth. "You speak in riddles!" He shook a fist at Vetra. "Look at what you've done, you cretin! What the devil did you have to go and crack it for?"

"It's caused us nothing but pain," Vetra growled. "Look at the ruin and death around you. The thing's evil."

Skirl clawed at his hair and sank into a miserable crouch. He rocked on his heels, his words bordering on snivels. "I despise you, mercenary, I despise you! You're a bane to sorcery… And yet—" He lifted his head, grimacing with despair at his missing fingers.

Nog had wandered over to frown at Skirl and shake his head. "Stick to love, boy, like you once told us back at the market before this crapstorm came our way. It's better for one's health. Little good the magic did you." He gestured curtly at his stumps and missing ear. "Little good it did this wench either." And he kicked the hide of the dead dragon under which Taranis lay crushed.

Vetra exhaled a sickened breath. "If the legend speaks true, then this Sarkala priestess who birthed the stone would have wanted it destroyed, or at least hidden so that none could use it for nefarious purposes."

Senesch gave a slow nod. "'Tis too easy to pervert its use, Vetra. I believe you are right."

The last flicker of blue from the half fragment in Skirl's hand grew dim. For brief moments a red glare flared up, a pure scarlet burst that nearly blinded all gathered around the dragon, then it fizzled out forever.

There came a mighty gust of wind that swept down from the hills to the west and with it a gale-like roar which nearly knocked all those standing off their feet.

Senesch muttered something that it was the sorceress's last breath.

"Dergath!" murmured Vetra.

For some time Senesch spoke words that might have been protections spells against further evil...words spoken in a forgotten tongue, the last of which Vetra recognized as the name, 'Dal Sagoth'.

Chapter 40

Vetra picked his way through the battered hulks of giants and mangled horses. In his ear he was barely conscious of the clink of harness, the tramp of boots and the shift and mutter of brooding men. Carrion birds had come to circle and eye the battlefield: large noisy ravens and turkey vultures with small, black heads that vented raucous croaks. He saw Caradwen among the survivors. He was glad of that. She was picking her way among the ruins of bodies while other of the riders helped gather up Lord Onas and his fallen lieutenants to be burned. She walked with a limp and had a dent in her helm, also a cut above her right eye but otherwise looked intact.

Vetra made a slow salute and she returned it with a ghost of a grin. She was as comely as ever, in her grimed accouterments and gripping her bloody blade. In happier times he would have paused to dally with this courageous maid, but he had other business to attend to. He knew where she lived, Cairnhill, and could always return to pay her a visit.

Half of Onas's riders had been slain or lay broken amid the heaps of horses and men. Of the 5000 soldiers, Vetra estimated two-thirds lay dead from sword, sorcery or dragon fire. All the commanders were slain.

The survivors began the long trek back to their homes, with tales of grimness on their lips and of dragons and sorceresses to regale friends and family at many a hearth gathering. Whispers of an unspoken truce rustled in the air, declaring neither side a winner.

Skirl seemed to have forgotten the pain of his missing fingers temporarily, or perhaps he was in shock. He'd torn a strip of a jupon off a felled Mercian and wrapped it around his bloody stump.

Senesch groaned, suffering stolidly his many aches and pains. He lay a gentle hand on Skirl's shoulder. "As wielder of the Eros flame, I think there is a future for you at the head of the cabal, boy. I am too old. Even if Voydred were alive, he and I would be at each other's throats—" he laughed "—like dogs, squabbling for the seat." His hollow chuckle faded and a tear rolled down his grimed cheek. "I've no taste for ruling now in my hundred plus years. Keren too had his head in the clouds and would have had us all turning into birds and worshiping hawks, or carrying falcons on our arms. And Belgra? Well, you and she are good complements to each other. You'll keep the balance of power at Dormoth. I hope. What's left of it, anyways."

Skirl nodded sagely. "What remains of the Eros Stone shall hang in the Hall of Mages. Let this be a lesson to all, Senesch, how darkness corrupts. I think Vetra's right. The thing's a curse. Evil's taint will always be rooted out! I'll hang this jewel there with my own hands to stand in the Hall forever!"

Skirl's words were grandiose and Senesch, seeing Skirl reach for the half-stone in his robe, shafted him a sour look. "Are you starting to act a trifle magisterial, Skirl? Already? Careful, boy," he warned.

Skirl cupped his gored hand and winced. Belgra fluttered over to his side to bless it with healing spells and incantations. She treated his stump with salves, potions that she kept in her robe. "That was very courageous of you to come to my rescue when the dragon snatched me up," she said briefly. "Stupid, perhaps. And a death wish, but courageous all the same."

Skirl smiled. Overcome with gladness to have Belgra back in his life, he gathered her in his arms. They vowed to rebuild the shattered Order of Mages together.

"No one person shall rule the Order like Taranis did," Skirl exclaimed with an expansive sweep of arm. "It will be but two and I nominate Belgra and I!"

Nog cast Vetra a goofy look and rolled his eyes. "Double the trouble."

Vetra muttered, "Let them sort out their own affairs, Nog. I head south on the road to Alantra then Behundria. Are you coming with me?"

"I'd like to, Vetra, but no, I've had enough of these warring kingdoms. My place is by the sea. I pine for the briny coasts and the open water. It's back to the docks of Syrn for me. I feel more at ease there than here."

"Suit yourself." Vetra tipped his head. "To each his own. I shall miss you, old friend."

"And I too. You know where to find me. Ask any old sea dog there at the wharfs—if I'm still alive and not with a scimitar in my gullet." He gave a phlegm-filled laugh.

Vetra chuckled wryly. "I doubt that, Nog. You've got a few years ahead of you yet. Here's to a long life." He lifted his blade.

"To a long life, Vetra."

Nog lifted his.

Vetra's mind turned to brooding once more. There was this matter of his sister, captive to some distant lord in a seraglio. He must find her, even it was nigh impossible. The trail led south to a man called Tork, that was all he knew, a trail getting colder every day. He must not let the hope die that yet she lived.

But first he would need funds. This fragment of the Eros jewel in his pocket would be what he'd pawn first. He'd have more luck fencing it in the southern kingdoms like Galashad. Behundria? Maybe Dragonskull? The jewel's notoriety was less known there. He'd be less likely to get his throat cut by agents of the Wizard's Circle or bounty hunters.

Time would tell. The world was a fickle mistress. It was one full of changing dangers and strange dooms. Even as he flashed on the thought, his scalp prickled, for the Eros Flame, or what was left of it, still radiated a sinister warmth in his pocket where it brushed his side.

OTHER BOOKS IN THE SWORDS AND SKULLS SERIES:

DRAGON LORDS
VALLEY OF THE GODS
LAND OF MAJA

https://innersky.ca/swordsandskulls

ABOUT THE AUTHOR

Chris is a prolific author of fantasy, adventure, and science fiction. His writing spans many genres: heroic fantasy, sword and sorcery and speculative fiction.

Browse Chris's books at

https://innersky.ca/books/home

www.ingramcontent.com/pod-product-compliance
Lightning Source LLC
Chambersburg PA
CBHW020223260626
47156CB00002B/510